JOHN BURLEY

No Mercy

AVON

AVON
A division of HarperCollins*Publishers*
77–85 Fulham Palace Road,
London W6 8JB

www.harpercollins.co.uk

A Paperback Original 2014
1

A catalogue record for this book is
available from the British Library

ISBN-13: 978-0-00-755948-0

Typeset in Sabon LT Std by Palimpsest Book Production Limited,
Falkirk, Stirlingshire
Printed and bound in Great Britain by
Clays Ltd, St Ives plc

MIX
Paper from
responsible sources
FSC™ C007454

FSC™ is a non-profit international organisation established to promote
the responsible management of the world's forests. Products carrying the
FSC label are independently certified to assure consumers that they come
from forests that are managed to meet the social, economic and
ecological needs of present and future generations,
and other controlled sources.

Find out more about HarperCollins and the environment at
www.harpercollins.co.uk/green

NO MERCY

John Burley grew up in Maryland near the Chesapeake Bay. He worked as a paramedic and volunteer firefighter before attending medical school in Chicago and completing an Emergency Medicine residency program at the University of Maryland Medical Center / Shock Trauma in Baltimore. He currently serves as an Emergency Department physician in northern California, where he lives with his wife, daughter, great dane, and english bulldog. NO MERCY is his first novel.

For LG
and
MNGB

There is no real me, only an entity, something illusory, and though I can hide my cold gaze and you can shake my hand and feel flesh gripping yours and maybe you can even sense our lifestyles are probably comparable: I simply am not there.
    —Bret Easton Ellis, *American Psycho*

What is done out of love always takes place beyond good and evil.
    —Friedrich Nietzsche, *Beyond Good and Evil*

Contents

Contents

This is not the beginning.

Up ahead, a young man sporting jeans and a black T-shirt walks casually down the concrete sidewalk. He hums softly to himself as he ambles along, Nike-bound feet slapping rhythmically on the serpentine path he weaves through the late afternoon foot traffic. He is perhaps fifteen – not truly a young man yet, but certainly well on his way – and he walks with the energy and indifference of one who possesses the luxury of youth but not yet the experience to appreciate its value, or its evanescence.

The predator watches the young man turn a corner, disappearing temporarily from view behind the brick exterior of an adjacent building. Still, he maintains a respectable distance, for although he has an *instinct* for how to proceed, he now relinquishes control to something else entirely. For as long as he can remember he has sensed its presence, lurking behind the translucent curtain of the insignificant daily activities of his life. The thing waits for him to join it, to embrace it – observes him with its dark and faithful eyes. But there are times – times like this – when it waits no longer, when the curtain is drawn aside and it emerges, demanding to be dealt with.

The young man in the black T-shirt reaches the end of the street and proceeds across a small clearing. On the other side of the clearing is a modest thatch of woods through which a dirt trail, overgrown with the foliage of an early spring, meanders for about two hundred yards until it reaches the neighborhood just beyond.

The predator picks up his pace, closing the distance between them. He can feel the staccato of his heart kick into third gear, where power wrestles fleetingly with speed. The thing that lives behind the curtain is with him now – has *become* him. Its breath, wet and heavy and gritty with dirt, slides in and out of his lungs, mixing with his own quick respirations. The incessant march of its pulse thrums along eagerly behind his temples, blanching his vision slightly with each beat. Ahead of him is the boy, his slender frame swinging as he walks, almost dancing, as if his long muscles dangled delicately from a metal hanger. For a moment, watching from behind as he completes the remaining steps between them, the predator is struck by the sheer beauty of that movement, and an unconscious smile falls across his face.

The sound of his footsteps causes the boy to turn, to face him now, arms hanging limply at his sides.

As he does, the predator's left hand swings quickly upward from where it had remained hidden behind his leg a moment before. His hand is curled tightly around an object, its handle connected to a thin metal shaft, long and narrow and tapered at the end to a fine point. It reaches the pinnacle of its arcing swing and enters the boy's neck, dead center, just below the jaw. A slight jolt reverberates through the predator's arm as the tip of the rod strikes the underside of the boy's skull. He can feel the warmth of the boy's skin pressing up against the flesh of his own hand as the instrument comes to rest. The boy opens his mouth to scream, but the sound is choked off by the blood filling the back of his throat. The predator pulls his arm down and away, feeling the ease with which the instrument exits the neck.

He pauses a moment, watching the boy struggle, studying the shocked confusion in his eyes. The mouth in front of him opens and closes silently. The head shakes slowly back and forth in negation. He leans in closer now, holding the boy's gaze. The hand gripping the instrument draws back slightly in preparation for the next blow, then he pistons it upward, the long metal tip punching its way through the boy's diaphragm and into his chest. He watches the body go rigid, watches the lips form the circle of a silent scream, the eyes wide and distant.

The boy crumples to the ground and the predator goes with him, cradling a shoulder with his right hand, his eyes fixed on that bewildered, pallid face. He can see that the boy's consciousness is waning now, can feel the muscles going limp in his grasp. Still, he tries to connect with those eyes, wonders what they are seeing in these final moments. He imagines what it might feel like for the world to slide away at the end, to feel the stage go dark and to step blindly into that void between this world and the next, naked and alone, waiting for what comes after . . . if anything at all.

The cool earth shifts slightly beneath his fingers, and in the space of a second the boy is gone, leaving behind his useless, broken frame. 'No,' the predator whispers to himself, for the moment has passed too quickly. He shakes the body, looking for signs of life. But there is nothing. He is alone now in the woods. The realization sends him into a rage. The instrument in his hand rises and falls again and again, wanting to punish, to admonish, to hurt. When the instrument no longer satisfies him, he casts it aside, using his hands, nails and teeth to widen the wounds. The body yields impassively to the assault, the macerated flesh falling away without conviction, the pooling blood already a lifeless thing. Eventually, the ferocity of the attack begins to taper. He rests on his hands and knees, drawing in quick, ragged breaths.

Next time, I will do better, he promises the thing that lives behind the curtain. But when he turns to look the thing is gone, the curtain drawn closed once again.

PART ONE

The Young Man in the Black T-Shirt

Chapter 1

Although it was Friday evening, Ben Stevenson found the traffic along Sunset Boulevard heading west out of Steubenville particularly heavy during his commute home. Dr Coleman's case had finished earlier than expected, and the last specimen of Mrs Granch's partial thyroidectomy had been sent to the lab at 4:40 p.m. The surgically resected margins had been clear of cancer cells, and he'd placed a call to the OR.

'OR Three,' the circulating nurse's voice answered at the other end.

'Marsha, this is Dr Stevenson. Can I speak with Dr Coleman, please?'

'Oh, hello, Dr Stevenson,' she replied. 'One moment – I'll put you on speaker.'

There was a brief pause, then Coleman's voice, sounding slightly distant and metallic over the speakerphone. 'How does it look, Ben?'

'Margins are clear, Todd,' he replied. 'Looks good from my end.'

'All right,' the surgeon responded. 'That's all I've got for you today. I'm closing now.'

Closing. That was welcome news on any day, but particularly on a Friday when your eldest son's high school baseball team was scheduled for a game. Thomas had started the season as a center fielder, but the strength of his arm had drawn the coach's attention and Thomas had quickly proven to be an even greater asset on the mound. Tonight was his turn in the pitching rotation. The game was scheduled for a 6 p.m. start time, and Ben did not intend to miss it.

He spent the next ten minutes closing up the lab. When he was satisfied that everything was in order, Ben grabbed his jacket, locked the door behind him and headed for his car. Pulling out of Trinity Medical Center's parking lot, he flipped on the XM radio and began to hum along with the Beatles, as John Lennon proclaimed, 'Nothing's gonna change my world.'

He passed John Scott Highway, and now the traffic began to slow as he approached Wintersville. Ben had moved his family to this small town from Pittsburgh thirteen years ago. He'd met Susan during medical school at Loyola University in Chicago. They'd graduated together, and had both managed to secure residency positions at the University of Pittsburgh Medical Center. He'd trained in pathology, while Susan had pursued a program in family practice. At the end of their first year, they married – a small ceremony attended by immediate family and a few friends. They'd spent the following week hiking and kayaking through a good portion of upstate New York – Susan's idea, actually – before returning to the exhausting, gut-wrenching grind of medical residency. The week had suited their needs perfectly, providing unhurried time to spend exclusively with one another, far removed from the constant demands and commotion of residency. It had felt good to exercise their bodies, which had already started to become soft with neglect. The fresh air and vibrant green foliage had rejuvenated their senses, and they'd talked with excitement about their plans for the future. Nights had been mostly cloudless, as he recalled, and they'd made love under the stars nearly every evening before retiring to the thin, nylon shelter of their tent. Ben had finished the week with more than a few mosquito bites on compromising areas of his body. Susan had come away from the week pregnant, although they would not realize it for another six weeks. Thomas was born nine months later.

That had been a difficult time for them, so early in their marriage. Medical residency was not the ideal time to try to raise a newborn, of course, and the hospital didn't lighten the already exhausting work hours simply because there was a crying three-month-old infant at home to attend to. Neither of them had family in the area, and Susan simply couldn't bring herself to turn Thomas over to day care after her very brief maternity allowance had ended. Ultimately, she'd decided to take a year off to spend with the baby, which, in retrospect, had turned out to be the right choice for all of them.

Canton Road slipped by on his right, and Ben realized just a little too late that he probably should've turned there to detour around some of this congestion. Sunset Boulevard, which had now become Main Street, was the primary connector between the towns of Steubenville and Wintersville, small midwestern flecks on the map, lying just west of the Ohio River. Fifty miles to the east was Pittsburgh, and approximately 150 miles to the west was Columbus. Aside from a parade of small towns with equal or lesser populations, there wasn't much else in between. Certainly not enough to warrant traffic like this – one of the reasons they'd decided to leave such cities as Chicago and Pittsburgh behind them in the first place.

Must be an accident, Ben thought. *A bad one from the looks of this backup.* Inconvenient and frustrating, of course – and for one guilty moment he resented its presence in yet another way. An accident causing this much of a standstill could mean fatalities. And that often involved a coroner's investigation, which meant he might be making a trip to the Jefferson County Coroner's Office this evening or, by the latest, tomorrow morning to perform an autopsy. *Great. Absolutely perfect,* he thought to himself, and immediately felt another pang of guilt. Life as a small-town pathologist meant one-stop shopping when it came to coroner investigations. There was him, and then there was the Allegheny County Coroner's Office and Forensic Lab in Pittsburgh, fifty miles to the east. But he had known that, he reminded himself, when he'd signed on to the job here.

The Beatles had yielded to The Band, who were sailing off into the first stanza of 'The Weight' – an ominous sign, Ben thought. He switched off the radio. Traffic had slowed to a crawl and he could now see the entrance to Indian Creek High School just ahead on the right. This seemed to be the source of at least some of the congestion. He could identify two police cruisers, an ambulance and a news truck in the school's parking lot. On the right-hand shoulder, two cars had pulled off the road to exchange insurance information, apparently the result of a low-speed rear-end collision caused by a little rubbernecking. The drivers were involved in a heated discussion, and a sheriff's deputy approached to intervene before things escalated further.

Up ahead, the traffic dissipated, and Ben accelerated slowly toward home. There was still enough time to make Thomas's baseball game, although things would be a little tighter than he'd initially anticipated. He flipped back on the radio and smiled to himself. The Band was finishing the final chorus, and just like that, 'The Weight' was over.

Chapter 2

The first thing Ben noticed as he approached the house was that Susan had beaten him home, her gray Saab already parked in their driveway. He pulled in behind her, got out, and retrieved his briefcase from the trunk. Having heard him drive up, his wife had stepped out of the house and was walking down the front steps to greet him. Even after all these years she was still beautiful, Ben thought, with dark black shoulder-length hair and chestnut eyes he had difficulty looking away from. Her tall body had remained slim and agile, despite the two children she had carried. And although Ben himself was of similar athletic build, the years, he felt, had taken a harder toll on him, the responsibilities pulling steadily at the corners of his eyes, his brown hair now speckled generously with strands of gray. He smiled up at her, but the smile faded as she drew nearer.

'Tell me you've spoken with Thomas this afternoon,'

she entreated, her hands clutching at the sides of her dress.

'Why? What's wrong?' he asked, his mind automatically flipping through a list of the most catastrophic possibilities. Something was very wrong indeed, he realized as he studied her features. Susan was afraid – but she was much more than that; she was on the brink of hysteria.

'There's been a death at the school,' she blurted out. 'One of the high school kids, they think.'

Ben looked at her, dumbfounded. '*What?*'

'Someone was killed this afternoon,' she advised him. 'Initial news reports said it was one of the high school kids, but they don't know for sure.' Susan's voice shook. '*Where in the hell is Thomas?! He should've been home an hour ago!*'

'He has a baseball game at Edison,' Ben reminded her. Edison High was located in the neighboring town of Richmond. A bus was scheduled to transport the team after school. But there were other, more pressing details to be considered. He was still trying to work his mind around what Susan had just told him. 'What do you mean someone was killed? There was an accident?'

'*An accident? Don't you listen to the radio?*'

'On the ride home,' he answered. 'But they didn't say anything about—'

'Honey, it wasn't a car accident.' Susan's voice continued to waver as she spoke, as if it were riding precariously along on one of those small-time roller coasters erected at carnivals. 'One of the high school kids was murdered on the way home from school – in the woods along Talbott Drive. Ben, he was stabbed to death and just left there to die. They don't even know who he is yet.'

For a moment, Ben was too stunned to say anything. What his wife had just told him was so implausible that he felt the urge to argue with her, to tell her that she was being ridiculous. Wintersville was a quiet midwestern town of about five thousand inhabitants. The town's occupants were mostly middle-income conservative families who presumably preferred the sort of small-town life that could be enjoyed here. Golfing, fishing and hunting were popular pastimes, and in early December folks came out for the annual Christmas parade. Tax evasion, shoplifting and the occasional drag race along Kragel Road were the most hardcore criminal activities this town had seen over the past decade. After four years in Pittsburgh, it was one of the things that had initially attracted him. He had decided a long time ago that he did not wish to fall asleep to the sound of sirens. As for the murder of a high school child on his way home from school, it was simply not the type of thing that happened here. *Ever.*

'They won't release the victim's identity until after the family has been notified,' he heard himself reply numbly. 'That's how it's done.'

Susan came to him then, putting her arms around him tightly. She was trembling, Ben realized, and he hugged her back. He felt sick to his stomach, and his legs were wooden and uncertain beneath him. He

14

was thankful at that moment for someone to hold on to.

His wife looked up at him, and for a moment it seemed as if she was uncertain how to proceed, as if she was struggling with a decision that only partially involved him. Then her eyes cleared and seemed to regain their focus. 'Honey,' she said, her voice just above a whisper, 'we've got to find Thomas. I'll feel better once he's home. They would've canceled the game, don't you think? Or at least phoned the parents to let them know what was happening?'

Ben thought this was probably true. Whose number had they given the school as an emergency contact, anyway? He separated himself enough from his wife to place his briefcase on the hood of the car, fumbling with the latch. 'Where's Joel?' he asked.

'Inside,' she replied. 'I picked him up from Teresa's on the way home.'

Ben swung the case open to reveal a haphazard array of documents and medical journals. He reached inside one of the interior pockets and retrieved the phone. The digital display indicated that he had two new messages. He flipped the cell open and punched the button to access voice mail. The first message turned out to be from Susan, asking if he had heard from Thomas, and imploring him to call her as soon as possible. The second message was from Phil Stanner, Thomas's baseball coach.

'Ben, this is Coach Stanner,' the recorded voice announced, and Ben felt a wave of dread rising within him. He put the phone on speaker so that Susan could hear.

'Listen,' Phil's voice floated up to them from the phone's tiny speaker. 'You've probably already heard, but someone was killed this afternoon in the woods close to the school. The police have the whole area cordoned off, which is making it difficult to get into and out of the school parking lot. All after-school activities have obviously been canceled. Thomas is fine, and I've got the entire team here with me in the gymnasium. We're asking parents *not* to come up to the school to pick up their kids, but instead to wait at the designated bus stop where their child is usually dropped off after school. Buses will be bringing students home starting around six-thirty p.m., but kids won't be let off of the bus unless there's an adult there to meet them. Thanks for your cooperation. If you have any questions, you can contact the school, but even with four people answering phones, the lines have been pretty tied up this afternoon, so don't call unless you have to.'

The message ended and Ben closed the phone and placed it in his front pants pocket. Susan's hand was covering her mouth, and she looked up at him with a mixture of relief and sadness. Her other arm had wrapped itself protectively around her waist. It was 5:52 p.m. Ben put an arm around his wife's shoulders, pulling her body against him. He looked up at the large bay window that marked the front of their house. It offered a limited visual portal into their family room, and he could just make out the top of Joel's head, his familiar brown cowlick arching upward like an apostrophe, as he sat on their couch watching television – *hopefully not the news,* Ben thought.

He kissed the top of Susan's head, wondering if even at this very moment there was a Sheriff's Department cruiser pulling into someone's driveway. In his mind, he could see it clearly: the car rolling slowly to a stop, two uniformed officers stepping out and making that long, awful walk to the front door. He imagined them ringing the doorbell and listening to the sound of shuffling feet approaching from the foyer just beyond, a small voice calling through the closed door: '*Who is it?*'

'*Sheriff's Department, ma'am.*'

A momentary pause, followed by the sound of the voice, already afraid, calling out to someone deeper inside of the dwelling: '*They say it's the Sheriff's Department.*'

A man's voice, descending down the interior stairs: '*Well, what do they want? Jesus, Martha, open the door!*'

The sound of the dead bolt sliding back within its metallic housing. The door slowly swinging open to reveal a man and a woman, roughly the same age as Susan and himself, standing just inside the open threshold and looking out onto the cold, gray world and the unfortunate messengers standing in front of them. In this image he has conjured, the couple suddenly appear frail beyond their given years, as if this moment itself has weakened them. In a timorous glance, they take in the grave faces of the two

17

unwelcome men standing before them, who have arrived with news the parents do not want to hear, and whose expressions carry within them all of the information that really matters: *I'm terribly sorry. Your boy is gone. He was left dead in the woods, and he lies there still while we try to figure out who might have done this to him. He will never walk through this door again.*

In that moment, standing in their own driveway with familiar gravel beneath their feet, Ben offered a silent prayer of gratitude – God forgive him – that he and his wife had not been selected at random to receive that horrible message. It was a prayer of relief and thankfulness for the safety of his family, and a prayer of compassion for the ones who waited even now for the messengers to come.

'Let's go inside,' he whispered to Susan, and the two walked up the steps together.

Chapter 3

An hour later, the three of them stood on the sidewalk, impatiently awaiting the arrival of the Indian Creek High School bus. A block to the east, the sound of passing vehicles could be heard as they traveled along Canton Road on their way north toward Route 22. Beside him, Susan fidgeted restlessly. Ben shared the sentiment. A recorded message from the high school baseball coach, after all, could only go so far in placing a parent's mind at ease.

Ben glanced at his watch. It was seven o'clock. *Shouldn't the bus be here already?* he wondered. Perhaps not, considering the traffic and events of the day. Rounding everyone up and making sure that all of the kids were accounted for would take longer than expected. Some of the parents would just now be arriving home from work, and there would be no one waiting to receive the kids at certain stops. It could be another hour, he realized.

Dusk was already beginning to settle upon the neighborhood. In another forty minutes they'd be standing here in the dark. Under the circumstances, he reflected, it was probably not the best plan the school could have come up with; a bunch of families standing around outside in the dark waiting for their kids to be dropped off while somewhere out there a psychopath roamed the streets. He thought about returning home for the car, even though they lived only two blocks away. He didn't want to leave Susan and Joel standing here alone, however, and he was afraid that if they all went back together the bus would arrive during the time they were gone. Instead, they waited, watching their shadows grow long and lean as the sun continued its rapid descent toward the horizon.

Something the size of a large cicada moved against Ben's upper leg with a soft buzzing sound, startling him. He nearly cried out, but in a moment it was gone. He shuddered involuntarily, imagining its crunchy, crackling exoskeleton flitting up against him.

Suddenly, it came again, nestling up against his right thigh with a muffled burring noise. He leaped backward. '*Shit! What was that?*'

Susan looked over at him inquisitively, eyebrows raised. 'What's wrong with you?'

'*A giant bug just hit me in the leg,*' Ben advised her. '*Twice!*'

No sooner had he uttered these words than he realized two things. The first was that he had just cursed in front of his highly impressionable eight-year-old son, who would now most assuredly walk around his home, his school, and the local playground for the next week yelling '*Shit!*' at the top of his lungs. The second was that the flying cicada creature that had struck him – *twice!* – in the right thigh was nothing more than his own cell phone, which he'd left on vibrate in his front pants pocket. Feeling now like a complete idiot, he reached into his pocket and brought out the phone.

'*Shit! That's no giant bug, Dad. That's your phone,*' Joel pointed out enthusiastically.

'Thank you, Joel,' he said, looking at the phone's digital display, which simply read: 'CO.' It was his assistant calling from the Coroner's Office, which meant that the body was either on its way to the CO, or it had already arrived and would soon be ready for autopsy. In a case such as this, they would expect him to perform the autopsy tonight. Answering this call would be the beginning of a long, unpleasant evening.

'Go ahead,' Susan said with a smile as he glanced in her direction. 'You'd better answer your cicada.'

Ben flipped the phone open, and took a few steps away from his wife and son. 'Yes, hello,' he said.

'Dr S,' the voice on the other end spoke excitedly. 'It's Nat.'

'Hey. What's up?'

'You heard about that kid they found dead in the woods this afternoon, I guess. The one who was stabbed to death?'

'Yeah. We heard.'

'Well, the cops have finished with their crime scene investigation and they're releasin' the body to us. I'm about to head over there to pick him up right now.'

'Okay. Just give me a call when you get back to the office and everything's ready.'

'Sure, Dr S. No problem. *But, hey*. There's a lot of reporters settin' up outside the CO with their camera crews 'n' stuff, you know. Body's not even here yet and they're startin' to gather round like they're expecting an Elvis sighting or somethin'. I mean, this is a big case for us, don't you think?'

'Nat, listen to me.' Ben kept his voice as calm and as clear as he could. He spoke slowly, hoping that by maintaining his own composure he could exert some positive influence on his overenthusiastic assistant. He doubted that it would do much good, but at least it was worth a try.

'Yeah? What d'ya need me to do?'

Take two Valium and call me in the morning, Ben thought to himself. Instead, he said, 'You're right about this being an important case.'

'*Sure 'nough*,' Nat exclaimed. 'Murder like this – in cold blood and all – ain't somethin' you see round here every day. *That's* for sure.'

'That's right,' Ben replied. 'It's not something we see around here every day. It's big news in a small town, and those reporters are going to want some footage and a nice ten-second sound bite for the eight o'clock news.'

'Ain't *that* the truth. Things are about to get a lot

22

more interesting round here. It's gonna be a regular three-ring circus.'

'You're probably right,' Ben agreed. 'But right now we have a job to do. It's an important job. A boy was murdered today. He's lying on the ground surrounded by yellow police tape. And somewhere out there is a family whose son won't be returning home tonight. Now, our job is to gather as much information as we can about how he died, and the evidence that we have is his body. If we do our job carefully and professionally, we might find something that will help the police track down his killer.'

'*That's right,*' Nat agreed excitedly. '*Wouldn't that be somethin'*? You think they'd want me to testify in court?'

'Maybe. But I can tell you one thing for sure. If we let our emotions get the best of us – if we allow ourselves to be distracted and start thinking too much about the reporters and the police and the eight o'clock news – well, then we'll screw it up. We'll miss something, or allow a break in the chain of custody, or jump to some conclusion that we'll regret later. But by then, it will be too late.'

'Too damn late,' Nat agreed seriously. His voice was quieter now, more subdued, and although Ben could still detect a hint of the earlier excitement just beneath the surface, the boy's tone was held in check now by something of even greater significance: a sense of sobering responsibility. He could picture his young assistant standing in the lab's small office with the phone held tightly in his right hand, the adrenaline-laced muscles of his body filled with purpose and ready to act. Nathan Banks was a good kid. At twenty-two, he was a bit young for the job of pathologist's assistant. But Ben had known him for most of the boy's life, and he was also friends with Nat's father, who'd been flying for United Airlines for the past eighteen years and, as a commercial airline pilot, was away from home more often than not. Nat had taken an early fascination with the Coroner's Office. He'd started volunteering there at the age of sixteen, helping Ben mostly by preparing and cleaning instruments, attending to certain janitorial duties and the like. But Nat also enjoyed watching and eventually assisting with the autopsies Ben performed. His mother, Karen, had given her hesitant permission, although she'd expressed some reservations to Ben about the interest her son had taken in the field. One afternoon she'd shown up at the office and had asked Ben with a worried look if he thought it was normal or healthy for a sixteen-year-old boy to want to spend his days working around dead people. Ben, who had entered medical school at the age of twenty-six, but who had volunteered both in his local hospital's emergency department as well as at the Allegheny County Coroner's Office since the age of eighteen, explained to Karen that her son's interest in the work was probably nothing to worry about. It might even serve as a potential career someday, he'd suggested, and over the next two years Nat had slowly been allowed to assume a more hands-on role in the autopsies Ben performed. Eventually, he became skilled enough to be a real asset in the lab, and when Nat graduated from high school Ben had offered to turn his volunteer position into a paid one. Nat had enthusiastically accepted, and he had been working there ever since.

'What you and I have to decide,' Ben now said into the phone, 'is whether we want to be part of the three-ring circus, or whether we want to act like professionals and focus on the job in front of us. You can do either one, Nat, but you can't do both. What I need to know from you now is how you want to handle it.'

'Well, let's do our J-O-B,' his assistant replied. 'Don't sweat it, Dr S – I've got your back.'

'That's what I needed to hear.' Ben glanced back at Susan and Joel, who were standing on the sidewalk in the gathering darkness. 'Listen, I've got something I need to do before heading over there. You think you can go pick up the body and give me a call on my cell once you get back to the CO?'

'No problem.'

'And if the reporters want a few words from you for the evening news, what are you going to tell them?'

'I'll tell them, "*No muthafuckin' comment!*" Excuse my French. We've got a job to do.'

'That's right.' Ben smiled, feeling a modicum of levity for the first time since arriving home that afternoon. 'I'll see you in a little while.'

'Over and out,' Nat saluted, and terminated the connection.

'Over and out,' Ben sighed to himself as he returned the phone to his pocket and turned back to his wife and son. A moment later, he heard the sound of an approaching diesel engine, and as it rounded the corner they were silhouetted in the headlight beams of the approaching bus.

Chapter 4

Fifty minutes later, Ben found himself sitting in the darkened interior of the Honda as he headed east toward the Coroner's Office. A tentative drizzle had begun to fall from the sky as his family had walked home together from the bus stop, and by now it had progressed to a steady drumming that pattered the car's rooftop insistently with its heavy, hollow fingers. A light fog clung to the ground, and Ben was forced to negotiate the dark, rain-slickened streets slowly and with exceptional caution. He'd habitually turned on the radio as he started the car, but most of the local stations were running news of the murder, and the more distant ones that he could sometimes pick up on clear days were reduced to static in the mounting storm. He flipped the knob to the off position and decided to simply concentrate on driving.

Thomas had stepped off the bus that evening to

the warm embrace of his relieved and grateful parents, and to the boundless questions of his spellbound younger brother. As it turned out, Thomas didn't have much more information on the identity of the victim or the details of the crime than his parents had already received from Phil Stanner. This stood to reason, since the police were remaining tight-lipped until after they'd had a chance to notify the victim's family.

What was clear from the moment Thomas stepped off the bus to join them was that he regarded the day's events with a certain quiet thoughtfulness that Ben had not anticipated. He spoke very little during the walk home, and let his family's questions wash over him without much comment. Ben wondered whether his son might be in a mild state of shock, or simply trying to wrap his mind around the idea of a violent attack so close to home and school. Ben felt that children of Joel's age tended to regard death as an obscure and distant entity, far removed from their own daily lives and therefore relatively inconsequential. This view seemed to change as children entered their teenage years and began to explore and sometimes even to court this previously intangible eventuality. Popular movies often romanticized the notion with blazing shoot-outs among beautiful people against an urban backdrop at sunset, or titanic ships that slowly sank in the freezing Atlantic while lovers shared their final fleeting moments together aboard a makeshift life raft only buoyant enough for one. This was not the type of death that Ben encountered as a physician. He supposed it could be described as many things, but mostly his experience with death was that it was impersonal, and seldom graceful.

During his intern year as a medical resident, Ben had been working his third shift in the emergency department when paramedics brought in a fifty-eight-year-old man with crushing substernal chest pain radiating to his left arm and neck. Ben had examined the patient quickly in the limited time available, and after reviewing the EKG he'd decided that the man was having a heart attack. Emergency treatment for heart attack patients with certain specific EKG changes called for the administration of thrombolytic agents, powerful clot-busting drugs designed to open up the clogged blood vessel and restore adequate blood flow to the heart. The supervising physician was not immediately available and the patient's clinical condition seemed tenuous, so Ben had given the order for the nursing staff to administer the thrombolytic drug to his patient. The results had been almost immediate. Within five minutes, the patient was complaining of *worsening* pain, which was now also radiating to his back. Eight minutes later the patient's blood pressure plummeted, his heart rate increased to 130 beats per minute and he vomited all over himself and the freshly pressed sleeve of Ben's previously impeccably clean white coat. Several moments later the patient lost consciousness, and Ben could no longer palpate a pulse. He attempted to place a breathing tube into the patient's trachea but couldn't see past a mouthful of emesis. Instead, the tube slipped into the patient's esophagus, and each squeeze of the resuscitation bag aerated the patient's stomach instead of his lungs. Ben began CPR, and the first several compressions were accompanied by the sickening feel of cracking ribs beneath his interlaced hands. '*Call Dr Gardner!*' he shouted to the charge nurse standing in the doorway, and he soon heard the overhead paging system bellowing: '*Dr Gardner to the ER, stat! Dr Gardner to the ER, stat!*'

For eight minutes Ben pumped up and down on his patient's chest, attempting to circulate enough blood to generate some sort of blood pressure. Every so often, he paused long enough to look up at the patient's heart rhythm on the monitor. '*Shock him, two hundred joules!*' he ordered the nurse, who would charge the paddles, place them on the patient's chest, yell '*CLEAR!*' and press the two buttons that sent a surge of electricity slamming through the patient's body like an electric sledgehammer. '*No response, Doctor,*' the nurse reported each time, and Ben would order another round of electricity to be delivered like a mule kick into the patient's chest before resuming chest compressions over splintering ribs. Somewhere during the nightmare of that resuscitation – Ben's *first* resuscitation as a physician – the patient's bladder sphincter relaxed and about a liter of urine came rushing out of the man's body and onto the bedsheets. A small rivulet of urine began trickling steadily onto the floor. Ben continued his compressions on the patient's mottled chest, which was now tattooed with burn marks from the defibrillator paddles, as the nurse had failed to place enough conductive gel on the paddles before delivering each shock. The room stank of burnt flesh and a repugnant potpourri of human sweat, urine and the vomited remains of a tuna fish sandwich that the patient had apparently eaten shortly prior to his arrival. The endotracheal tube, temporarily forgotten, slipped out of the patient's esophagus and fell onto the floor with a resounding splat.

'*What in the* hell *is going on here, Dr Stevenson?!*' Dr Jason Gardner, Ben's supervising physician, stood in the doorway, gaping in disbelief at the scene. He appeared to be moderately out of breath from having run across the hospital from the cafeteria on the other side of the building. Ben noticed a small bit of pasta clinging like a frightened animal to his yellow necktie.

'Heart attack.' Ben's voice was hollow and uncertain, small and desperately apologetic, and his words fell from his mouth in a rush as he tried to explain. 'He came in with chest pain radiating to his arm, neck, and back. Only history was hypertension. He had EKG changes – an ST-elevation MI, I thought. I gave him thrombolytics. I was going to call you, but I didn't think there was enough time. He coded shortly after I gave the 'lytics. I tried CPR and defibrillation, but I couldn't get him back. I don't understand it. I had the nurse call for you as soon as he lost his pulses, but—'

'What did his chest X-ray look like?'

'His chest X-ray?' Ben thought for a moment. Had he ordered one? 'I . . . I don't know. I think they got one when he first came in, but I didn't get a chance to look at it.'

'What do you *mean* you didn't get a chance to look at it?'

'I just . . . he started crashing, and there wasn't enough time . . .'

'For God's sake, Stevenson! Stop doing compressions and go get me the goddamn chest X-ray!'

Ben looked down at his hands, surprised to see that they were still pressing up and down on the patient's chest. He forced them to stop. 'Maybe if we tried another shock . . .' he suggested hopefully.

'The patient's dead,' Gardner growled. 'You can shock him all you want, and he's still going to be just as dead. Now, go get that X-ray. Let's see what you missed.'

Ben left the room and walked across the hallway to the viewing box. A wooden repository hung on the wall containing several manila sleeves of radiographic images. He shuffled through them, found the appropriate one and returned with it to the resuscitation room. Dr Gardner stood next to the cooling body, leafing through the patient's chart. Ben noticed that the dead man's eyes remained open, staring lifelessly at the door through which he'd recently entered. Throughout the course of his career, Ben would never forget the look of those eyes, which were not accusatory or vengeful, but simply, unabashedly dead. For some reason, that was the worst of it – the detached finality of that look. It was the first thing he learned that day; when things go bad in this line of work and someone dies, there is always plenty of blame to go around, but there is only one soul who truly no longer cares.

'Let's see that film,' Gardner grunted, and Ben handed him the envelope. He watched the man remove the X-ray from its sleeve and slap it onto the resuscitation room's viewing box. The seasoned physician studied it for a minute, then queried, 'Well, what do you make of it, Dr Stevenson?'

Ben cleared his throat hesitantly. 'The lung fields are somewhat hyperinflated. Cardiac silhouette appears slightly enlarged, although that can be an artifact of a single AP view. Costophrenic margins are well visualized. No evidence of an infiltrate or pneumothorax.'

'Uh-huh. And how would you describe the mediastinum?'

'Widened. The aortic knob is poorly visualized.'

'Exactly. What comes to mind, Dr Stevenson, in a fifty-eight-year-old gentleman with a history of hypertension, who presents with chest pain radiating to his arm and back and has a widened mediastinum on chest X-ray?'

'Aortic dissection?' Ben ventured. 'But what about the ST elevation on the patient's EKG?'

Gardner snatched up the EKG, glanced at it perfunctorily, then handed it to Ben. 'Inferior ST elevation consistent with a Stanford type A aortic tear dissecting into the right coronary artery. Pushing thrombolytics on this man was a death sentence. He bled into his chest and pericardial sac within minutes. He would've stood a better chance if you'd just walked up to him and shot him in the head with a .38.'

Those last words – Dr Gardner's final commentary on the case – hung in the air, defying objection. Ben stood in the room between his boss and the dead man, unable to conjure any sort of meaningful response. His face burned with anguish and humiliation. In the corner of the room, a nurse pretended to scribble notes on the patient's resuscitation sheet. She glanced up briefly in Ben's direction, her face cautiously guarded.

'Notify the medical examiner, and submit this case to the M&M conference on Friday,' Dr Gardner instructed him. 'Get back to work. You've got three patients in the rack still waiting to be seen. Oh, and Stevenson?'

'Yes?' Ben looked up, needing to hear *some* token of consolation from his mentor, this man he respected.

'Try your best not to kill the rest of them,' Gardner advised him blandly, and left the room without looking back.

One of the hardest things about being a physician, Ben now thought as he recollected this horrendous experience in the ER as a young intern, was forcing yourself to continue along in the wake of such catastrophic events as if nothing had happened. The three patients still waiting to be seen had turned out to be a child with a common cold, a drunk teenager who was brought to the emergency department by her friends and a forty-two-year-old man with a wrist fracture. Routine, mundane cases, in other words. Ben had attempted to clear his head as best he could, and he interviewed and examined them all carefully and professionally. But while looking into the child's ears with an otoscope, he thought to himself, *I just killed a man.* While ordering an anti-emetic for the teenager now puking through the slots between the side rails of her gurney, he thought, *There's a man in Resuscitation Room 2 covered by a white sheet because I was in too much of a hurry to look at a simple chest X-ray.* In the middle of examining the man's broken wrist, he recalled holding the wrist of the dead man in his hands as he searched for a pulse that was no longer there. During these moments, his patients were aware of none of this. Two more people arrived in the department during the time he had taken to examine and treat the previous three patients. After that, an ambulance had shown up with a moderately severe asthmatic, and four more people checked in to triage.

In most jobs, when something horrible and traumatic happens to an employee, they are instructed to take the rest of the day off and are possibly sent for counseling. There is time to process what has happened, to remove oneself from the environment. There is time to take a breath, to discuss the incident with your spouse, or to simply get wasted at the local pub. In medical training, you are instructed to notify the medical examiner and to get back to work. You are given the helpful advice '*Try not to kill the next one,*' and you are desperately afraid that you will.

Recovery from such events occurs on your own time, in private, once you've fulfilled all of your other duties and obligations. And in medicine, those duties are never truly fulfilled. There is always another patient, another conference, another presentation, another emergency in the middle of the night, another fire to be put out. *Always*.

The night's precipitation continued to fall on the darkened street ahead. Xenon headlights cast their artificial glare on a hundred tiny rivers of water racing desperately toward the town's sewers, and wherever they might lead beyond that. Four miles from here, Nat was preparing the body of a young boy for his final medical examination. It was going to be a long and exhausting night, and Ben was pretty sure there would be more to follow. Things would get worse before they got better. Things like this always did. He didn't want to be here, driving away from his family on a night like this. It didn't feel like the right thing to do, and he wondered to himself, not for the first time, exactly where his allegiances were. He could feel the storm tugging at the hole inside of him, another chunk of earth pulled loose by the water's greedy fingers. He imagined himself being swept away into the sewers, one nearly imperceptible piece at a time. *What will it feel like when there's nothing left?* he asked himself. *And will I even know when that moment comes?* Within the car there was only silence, except for the steady thrum of the rain falling all around him.

Chapter 5

Nat had been right about one thing. The press was going to have a field day with this one – a regular three-ring circus. Ben could make out the congregation near the front entrance to the Coroner's Office from a quarter mile away. The usually dimly illuminated front steps of the CO were now bathed in bright artificial light as at least three different television crews jostled for position. Two patrol cars were parked just across the street, and a third one blocked the left lane of traffic to allow room for the news crews to set up their equipment without running the risk of being plowed over by a distracted motorist. Ben quickly decided that there was no way he'd attempt to enter through the CO's front entrance; instead, he turned left on Broadway and right on Oregon Avenue, hoping to sneak in through the building's rear delivery access.

He parked the car on Oregon and hopped out. Shielding himself from the downpour with his jacket as much as possible, he trotted the half block through the gathering puddles toward Brady Circle. The rear of the CO stood mostly in darkness. The parking lot behind the building was vacant except for two vehicles. One was the coroner's van that Nat had used to transport the body. Beside it, a second van, which Ben didn't recognize, sat idling, a white plume of exhaust rising up in a dissipating cloud from its tailpipe. As he approached, the side door of the vehicle slid open and two men stepped out, making their way toward him across the parking lot.

'Dr Stevenson?' one of them asked from the darkness.

'Yes?' he replied cautiously.

Ben was suddenly bathed in the bright light of a television camera.

'Dr Stevenson, is it true the victim was stabbed forty-seven times? Has a positive identification been made yet?' asked the reporter, thrusting a microphone in his face.

'I haven't examined the victim yet. That's what I'm here to do now.'

The man with the microphone didn't seem to appreciate the finer points of Ben's statement, for he continued to fire off questions one after the other. 'Is the victim a resident of the town, Dr Stevenson? Someone you happen to know? Was there any weapon found at the scene?'

'How am I supposed to know *that*? You should be talking to the police.' Ben fumbled for the keys in his pocket.

'What was the last homicide of this nature that you investigated, Doctor? Have you spoken with the County Coroner's Office or the state police?'

'I haven't spoken to anyone except my assistant.' Ben turned the key in the dead bolt and swung the door open just wide enough to step inside. 'Now if you'll excuse me . . .'

'Dr Stevenson, you have a son of your own that attends Indian Creek High School. How did he take the news of a murder only a few blocks away from the school?'

'He seems to be handling it much better than you are,' Ben replied, then closed the door against the deluge of questions from the overzealous reporter. He flipped on the light in the back hallway. It was blessedly quiet inside the building. He could hear the faint sounds of Nat moving around in the autopsy room beyond the door at the end of the hall. His assistant had the habit of humming softly to himself as he went about the task of laying out the equipment and preparing the body for examination. It was mildly endearing, although Ben could never recognize the melodies, which belonged to a musical generation that was not his own. Ben hung up his jacket on the coat rack to his left and proceeded down the hallway.

'Hi, Nat,' he said as he entered the room.

'What's up?' Nat responded cheerfully. 'Did you get hit by the reporter brigade on your way in?'

'Of course,' Ben replied. 'I thought that I might outsmart them by coming in the back way, but they had their sentries waiting for me.'

'No doubt, no doubt. They were on me like flies on sh – , like flies at a picnic, you know, as soon as I pulled the wagon into the back parkin' lot. "*Tell us this! Tell us that!*" Those guys are pretty damn . . .'

'Importunate? Unremitting?' Ben offered.

'Pretty damn *annoying,* if you ask me. Hell, I don' know the answers to any of those questions. Might as well be askin' me who's gonna win the Kentucky Derby. And if I *did* know, I wouldn't be tellin' 'em nothin' anyway. Just like you said, Dr S: "*No muth-afuckin' comment!*" Right?'

'I think that was actually *you* who said that.' Ben glanced at the shape on the examination table, still zipped up inside of the black cadaver bag. 'How are we doing?'

'I just got back about ten minutes ago. Fog's gettin' thick out there, and the wagon's front windshield defroster ain't workin' so hot. Rainy days – and rainy nights especially – you've got to drive slow, or else you might find yourself joinin' the gentleman in back, if you catch my meaning.'

His assistant continued to move about the room as he spoke, laying out instruments and checking connections. He was a study in controlled chaos: his light blond hair eternally tussled as if he had just recently climbed out of bed, the tail of his shirt tucked into his pants in some places but left free to fend for itself in others, one shoelace frequently loose and on the brink of coming untied – and yet within the autopsy room he was highly organized and efficient, as if the manner with which he conducted his personal life did not apply here.

'I'll ask Jim Ducket to take a look at it,' Ben told him. 'If you're having trouble with the wagon, maybe we can get a replacement from the county until we get it fixed.'

'Aw, the wagon ain't no trouble. Just needs a little kick in the nuts every now and then. If you want Jimmy Ducket to take a look at anything, have him check out the radio. Hell, half the stations were set to classic rock when I climbed in it tonight. I take one five-day vacation and the whole place has gone to hell.'

Ben smiled. Nat had gone on a ski trip to Utah with his father last week, and Ben had been left making the pickups himself, just as he'd done before his assistant had come on board with him full-time several years ago. A few radio station adjustments had been the first order of business on his way out to pick up Kendra Fields, who'd died in her home last week of a ruptured cerebral aneurysm. When Ben arrived at the residence, Kendra's husband, John, had been waiting for him at the front door. '*Guess she's gone and done it this time, Doc,*' the old man had said matter-of-factly. John was eighty-nine and belonged to the congregation at Ben's church. Kendra had been three years his elder, and during the course of her life had survived two heart attacks, a serious stroke, breast cancer and a small plane crash. All things considered, it was time for her to pack up and head for home. Ben had chatted with John for half an hour. Then he'd loaded Kendra's body into the back of the wagon and had treated her to some Creedence Clearwater Revival on the short ride back to the CO, cranking the volume up enough to turn people's heads as he drove past. Hell, on top of everything else, Kendra Fields had also been a touch deaf during her final ten years on this earth.

'Well, that's what you get when you skip town and leave us old farts to drive the wagon,' he advised his young colleague.

'Yeah? Well, never again,' Nat assured him. 'Next time I leave town I'm takin' the keys to the wagon with me. You can use that old beat-up jalopy of yours to pick up folks if you have to. Stuff 'em in the trunk, for all I care.'

Ben crossed the room and pulled a plastic apron down from the hook on the wall where it hung. He donned an eye shield, head cap, shoe covers and latex gloves, and approached the awaiting corpse. He was glad that Nat was here to assist him and to keep him company with his incessant, irreverent chatter. Ben filled his lungs with a deep breath, and let it out slowly through his nose. With his right hand he grasped the bag's zipper and pulled it down.

The first thing he noticed was that the subject was young, perhaps fourteen or fifteen years old. His skin was smooth and slightly freckled around the face. His eyes, still open, were dark brown, interlaced with a touch of mahogany. His hair was also brown, but several shades lighter than his eyes. A long lock hung partially across his forehead, tapering to a point and ending just shy of his left cheek, above the first of several obvious facial wounds. The flesh in this area had been torn completely away, leaving a jagged vacancy.

'Jeeeesus,' Nat commented. 'That's one hell of a chunk gone from his face, Dr S. What do you think he hit him with?'

Ben studied the gaping wound for a moment, peering closely at its serrated edges. 'That's a bite wound,' he said quietly. 'Hand me the camera.'

Nat walked across the room, opened a cabinet, and returned with the lab's digital camera. 'Bit him,' he repeated softly to himself, mulling it over. 'Now, *that's* messed up.'

Ben snapped off several pictures of the facial wound. 'In multiple places.' He pointed to the right side of the boy's lower neck. 'See here?'

A second, wider piece of flesh was missing at the spot Ben was indicating. The boy was still dressed in the clothes he had died in, and the collar of his black, loosely fitting T-shirt was torn in this area and caked with dried blood. Ben inspected the wound carefully, using forceps to pull back a flap of skin that hung limply across the opening, partially obscuring it. A voice-activated recorder hung around Ben's neck, and he spoke into it in a neutral, practiced tone as he worked: 'Dr Ben Stevenson; March 29th, 2013; case number—' He looked at the large dry erase board hanging on the wall. 'Case number 127: John Doe. Received directly from the crime scene, custody transferred from Jefferson County Sheriff's

Department.' He took a breath. 'Subject is a Caucasian male, approximately fourteen years of age, dressed in a T-shirt and blue jeans. Inspection of the face and cranium demonstrates a 3.6-by-4.1-centimeter soft tissue avulsion injury beginning superficial to the left zygomatic arch and extending inferiorly to involve the lateral portion of the orbicularis oris. Avulsions of the zygomaticus major and minor are noted, with wound depth extending through the masseteric fascia.' He lifted the boy's chin slightly with one gloved finger, using a thin metal instrument to probe a penetrating wound noted there. 'Inspection of the submental region demonstrates a puncture wound measuring 0.75 by 0.9 centimeters, which extends through the mylohyoid and hyoglossus muscles, continuing superiorly and dorsally through the body of the tongue, soft palate and nasopharynx. There are seven – correction, eight – similar puncture wounds to the cranium that extend through the scalp, underlying musculature and galea aponeurotica. Two of the eight wounds penetrate the skull and enter the cranial vault. A second avulsion injury is noted at the right inferolateral aspect of the neck 5.3 centimeters medial to the acromioclavicular junction and involving the inferior platysma, lateral trapezius and sternocleido-mastoid muscles, as well as the right external jugular vein.'

This part of the examination – the initial inspection and description of the body – was the portion of the necropsy Ben always found most interesting. Every corpse, he found, had a tale to tell, and the details of one's life were often prominently revealed by the compilation of physical marks collected along the way, like scrapes and gouges on the underside of a boat. Prior scars (both surgical and traumatic), tattoos, track marks from a lifetime of IV drug abuse, burns, calluses, fat and muscle mass distribution, exaggerated spinal curvature from decades of stooped physical labor, tan lines, nicotine-stained fingertips, chewed fingernails and even the state of a person's teeth often spoke volumes about the course of their life. In Ben's opinion, these were not only the most interesting details of the examination, but also the most aesthetically beautiful – strange words to describe the physical blemishes of a corpse, perhaps, but he was a pathologist, after all. These marks and imperfections represented more than simple anatomy. They had been born from action, behavior and life experiences, and were therefore the most human, the most in touch with the life they had left behind.

In the case of traumatic deaths, however, it was different. One's eye is inexorably drawn to the fatal injury – that which has extinguished the flame of life so abruptly. Especially in the case of young people, the autopsy ceases to be about discovering the marks left behind from a life richly experienced, and rather is about bearing witness to the end of a life barely begun. Such was the case here, as Ben moved from one disfiguring injury to the other, each one denoting a blatant disrespect for the life of this young man, and for human life in general. It was a tragedy to behold. He wanted simply to stop, to cover the form in front of him with cloth, to save it from this last final disgrace. Instead, he continued, using practiced and precise descriptive terminology like a shield to defend himself from what was real.

'Inspection of the thorax demonstrates puncture wounds to the right fourth and sixth intercostal spaces anteriorly, and to the right fifth, seventh and eighth intercostal spaces along the midaxillary line. There is a 4.1-by-3.8-centimeter serrated avulsion of the left areola and underlying pectoralis muscle, similar in appearance to those of the face and neck, described above. There is a displaced fracture of the xiphoid process. Inspection of the abdomen demonstrates a 0.8-by-0.9-centimeter puncture wound to the right upper quadrant, and two similar puncture wounds to the right flank. There is a 35-centimeter diagonal incision extending from the right upper quadrant of the abdomen to the suprapubic region, penetrating the rectus abdominus and peritoneal fascia. There is evisceration of the small bowel. The genitalia are . . . missing.'

He paused for a moment, looking up at Nat, who was positioned across the table on the other side of the body. Most of the color had run out of his round, boyish face as he stood bolt upright and unmoving, eyes transfixed upon the body. Ben was suddenly embarrassed. He should've had enough sense to send Nat home as soon as he'd unzipped the bag. This was not something a twenty-two-year-old needed to watch, regardless of his chosen occupation. When Karen Banks had agreed to allow Nat to volunteer at the CO, she had done so with an implicit under-standing that Ben would watch out for her son's physical and psychological welfare, and he regarded the trust and deference Nat's parents had extended to him seriously. During his time at the CO, Nat had taken part in scores of autopsies, in cases ranging from the ravages of metastatic cancer, to self-inflicted gunshot wounds, to the death of young adults involved in motor vehicle accidents. He had even assisted during pediatric autopsies – cases of SIDS and child abuse. The boy was no novice at witnessing some of the trauma and unpleasantness that could descend upon the human body. But this . . . well, this was a different matter altogether.

'Listen, Nat. Why don't you let me finish up here,' he said. 'It's late, and I'm going to need you in the office early tomorrow to help Tanya man the phones. From the look of Brady Circle out there, I don't think the press is going to give up that easily, and I imagine that Sam Garston from the Sheriff's Department will be stopping by bright and early looking for the coroner's report. The rest of this stuff I can just take care of by—'

'Umm . . . Dr S?'

'What is it, Nat?'

'This case here is the most interesting, most important thing we've had come through these doors over the six years I've been workin' here.'

'I know. It's pretty—'

'And if you think . . . if you think I'm goin' home in the middle of the autopsy just because some nutjob

47

lopped off the guy's wiener and chucked it into the woods, well . . . you can forget it.'

'I wasn't trying to—'

'You wanna weigh all them organs by yourself, type the report and spend another forty minutes cleanin' up afterward?'

'I think I can handle—'

'How many hours you wanna be here tonight anyway, Dr S?'

'It's not about—'

'*No way*. Discussion over. *I'm stayin'*. Or . . . or you can find yourself another assistant.'

Nat stood across the table, arms crossed, glaring defiantly back at Ben. The two considered each other in silence, neither flinching, for perhaps twenty seconds. Apparently, Ben realized, his assistant was quite serious. He considered his short list of options: send Nat home and risk losing him as an assistant, or allow him to stay, thereby rendering himself at least partially responsible for the possible long-term effects the experience could have on the boy's psychological well-being.

'How do *you* know?' Ben asked. He was buying time while he tried to make up his mind.

'How do I know *what*?'

'How do you know the assailant chucked his wiener, as you like to put it, into the woods?'

'Oh. Cops found it at the scene. Fifty yards away from the body. Police canine actually tracked it down. It's in a Ziploc bag taped to his right ankle.'

'I . . . see,' Ben said.

The two men stood there for a while longer, neither speaking, as they surveyed the mutilated body.

'Well, what's it gonna be?' Nat challenged, impatient for a decision.

'I don't know,' Ben sighed, tapping his fingers on the table. 'I'm trying to decide whether I want to be responsible for further corrupting your already quite tenuous psychological stability.'

'*Too late, Dr S!* I hang out in a Coroner's Office. My psychological stability is already all blown to hell. Now gimme that scalpel. I'm gonna slice-an'-dice this turkey like a Thanksgiving dinner.'

Ben looked at him incredulously, shaking his head. 'That's so inappropriate I don't even know where to begin.'

'How 'bout you begin by pluggin' in that Stryker saw for me, will ya?'

'*Riiigghht.*'

'Okay. I'll do it myself.' Nat bent over and plugged the instrument's umbilical cord into the outlet on the floor. 'You want the chest opened, right? The usual?'

Ben said nothing.

'Great.' Nat nodded, as if he'd been given the green light to proceed. 'Now step back, boss. I don't wanna get shrapnel on your pretty white apron there. You jus' leave this part to me.'

He picked up the bone saw and went to work.

Chapter 6

It was nearly 2 a.m. by the time Ben pulled the Honda back into his driveway and set the parking brake. The rain had tapered to a thin drizzle, and the town seemed to have finally resigned itself to sleep. The interior lights of most of the houses Ben passed on the way home had been extinguished, and a fitful state of quietude had settled upon the neighborhood like a fine layer of fresh snow. Ben's own house sat mostly in darkness, except for the exterior motion-sensor light near the front door, which snapped dutifully on as he approached the dwelling. He turned his key in the door lock, hearing the reassuring click of the dead bolt sliding back within its housing. Placing his hand upon the cold brass knob to which the evening's precipitation still clung, he opened the door and stepped inside.

The front foyer sat mostly in shadows, and he snapped on a small lamp that rested atop a wooden cabinet to his right. The Stevensons' massive harlequin Great Dane, Alex ('Alexander the Great,' as Joel lovingly referred to him with reverent, exaggerated bows), ever present at the front door to greet new arrivals, nuzzled Ben's hand for affection, tail whipping ardently back and forth. True to his typical style, Alex stepped heavily and obliviously onto Ben's left foot and, as the dog leaned into him, Ben was forced backward against the front door. At 180 pounds, the domesticated Goliath didn't find it necessary to wait to be petted – he simply stood next to the closest person and leaned. The affection lavished upon him was merely an act of self-defense.

Ben ruffled the side of the big dog's head as Alex buried his face in Ben's leg. Ben placed his keys on the wall rack and took off his coat, listening to the subtle sounds of the house. The kitchen refrigerator hummed softly, warm air blew steadily from the wall vent to his left and the grandfather clock in the living room down the hall ticked quietly to itself, keeping its own perpetual rhythm. But it was more than these simple, mechanical sounds that he heard. On a deeper level, the house seemed to breathe of its own accord, shifting slightly as it continued to settle, growing more comfortable and more secure upon the foundation on which it rested. Both practically and figuratively, it held within it the very core of the family that lived here, providing warmth, refuge and an irrefutable sense of home. In doing so, it seemed infinitely stronger than the material from which it had been constructed. No matter what transpired during the course of the day, coming home to this place filled him with gladness, and helped to put the day's events in better context. Alexander the Great wagged his tail contentedly from side to side in complete agreement.

Ben trod quietly down the hall and across the living room, Alex padding not so softly behind him. He crossed the family room and ascended the stairs. At the top of the staircase he paused for a moment, then turned right and walked down the short hallway leading to the bedrooms of his two sons. He stood outside their rooms in the darkness for the span of about thirty seconds, simply listening, needing to be close to them for a moment. Then he turned and headed back down the hallway in the opposite direction toward the bedroom he shared with Susan. Having successfully escorted his owner to the appropriate sleeping quarters, Alex turned and descended the stairs to his own bed beside the living room's front-facing bay window. Ben pushed open the bedroom door and entered quietly, trying not to wake his wife.

For Susan, sleep was often restless and difficult to initiate. She'd suffered from some degree of insomnia for as long as Ben had known her, and had experimented with a multitude of unsuccessful remedies throughout those years. Contrary to the experience of many women, however, she'd managed to sleep well during both of her pregnancies. Even during her third trimester, sleep had come easily to Susan, and she was often breathing slowly and softly within ten minutes of turning out the light. Ironically, it was Ben who seemed to have difficulty initiating and maintaining sleep during that time. He would lie in bed and watch the shadows cast from the swaying branches of the oak tree in their front yard play deftly across their vaulted ceiling. He would listen to the steady respirations of his wife lying blissfully in bed next to him, and he would consider the day's events – the slow but perpetual ascent of gasoline prices that summer, the upcoming gubernatorial election, the positive gram stain of Mr Flescher's cerebrospinal fluid last Thursday. The hours of potential sleep would slip away from him like water over a steep ledge, leaving him befuddled and sluggish the following day, a dull heaviness clinging to his head like a massive barnacle. He would blunder through the day in this hebetudinous state until the sun finally descended once more beyond the horizon. Dinner that evening would be absently eaten and barely tasted, and although he tried to be interested in conversations with his wife, he always seemed to fall behind, finding himself at a break in the dialogue and wondering whether she had just asked him a question or whether it was simply his turn to speak. Excusing himself apologetically, he would head off to bed early in search of the nocturnal respite that had eluded him the previous night. Sometimes sleep would come, mercifully falling upon him like a summer storm. When it did, his dreams would be strange and wild, and he would often awaken in the night, sweating lightly and wondering whether he had cried out and, stupidly, whether he and Susan were alone in the room.

He'd continued in this tormented state for most of Susan's pregnancy, watching her with growing jealousy as she slipped effortlessly into sleep every evening and awoke refreshed and good-spirited the following morning as brilliant sunlight flooded their bedroom. It was as if Ben had somehow taken upon himself all of Susan's familiar struggles with insomnia and had shouldered them through the course of her pregnancies so that the children could develop unfettered within her. If that were the case, it was a noble yet arduous deed, and he was relieved when – oddly, but almost predictably – the balance returned to its original state within a month of the birth of each of their sons. Suddenly, Ben found himself having to set the alarm clock in order to awaken for the infant's nightly feedings. On many of these occasions, he would find Susan's side of the bed empty, and he would get up to investigate only to find her already tending to the baby despite the fact that it was his turn at the helm. '*Honey, I can do that,*' he would say to her sweetly in a tired voice. '*It's okay,*' she'd reply. '*I was already up.*'

'Tough day at the office, hon?' Susan greeted him from the darkness, startling Ben as he unbuttoned his shirt.

'*Jesus,* babe. You scared me.'

'Sorry,' she said. 'How was the autopsy?'

Ben unlaced his shoes and slipped them off, then pulled off his slacks and placed them in the closet hamper. His eyes had adjusted to the darkness and he could now make out the figure of his wife, propping herself up on one elbow as she surveyed him from their bed.

'Pretty horrible,' he answered. He exhaled deeply and stretched, trying to release as much of the day's stress from his body as possible. He felt old and tired, and more than a little unnerved by the evening's events.

'Want to talk about it?'

'Not really,' he said, climbing into bed. He felt utterly exhausted, emotionally as well as physically.

Susan wrapped her arms around him and squeezed tightly, spooning his body with her own. She was warm beneath the covers, her soft breasts pressing up against his skin. 'I love you,' she said.

'I love you, too,' Ben replied in a voice that was just above a whisper in the silence of the room. And he did. After seventeen years of marriage, he realized that he loved her more now than in all the days and nights that had come before. It was a love that had grown within him steadily throughout the intimate partnership of their lives, and continued to evolve in ways that surprised and amazed him. He turned to her now and kissed her softly in the darkness. Her hand found his own, and their fingers interlaced with the familiarity of the years between them. Then she was guiding his hand to the bare skin of her left hip. Her body rose to meet him, and this time her kiss was more passionate, more insistent than before.

'I'm glad you're home,' she whispered, and Ben decided that sleep could wait just a little while longer.

Chapter 7

That night he dreamed of Thomas, and a trip he and Susan had taken with their oldest son to the circus twelve years before. It had just been the three of them then – Susan's pregnancy with Joel still three and a half years down the road.

The smell of hot dogs and candy apples hung thickly in the air, intermixed with the less pleasant aroma of animals pacing restlessly in their cages. Hay and broken peanut shells crunched underfoot as they exited the colossal tent. Thomas was four years old, and Ben had stopped to buy him an orange helium-filled balloon from one of the countless vendors. The transaction had taken less than thirty seconds, and he'd assumed that Susan had been holding on to their son's hand during the process, but by the time he turned around Thomas had vanished into the crowd filing out into the massive parking lot in a great swarm.

Suddenly, everything changed. The music being

piped out to small speakers high above them took on a taunting, grating, fun-house air. The faces of the strangers shuffling by seemed to smirk at Ben nastily, their eyes darting to the side to watch him as they passed. A man in a purple vest and lime-green bow tie hawking peanuts ('*Fresh peanuts! Get your fresh peanuts here!*') to the exiting patrons turned in Ben's direction and, covering his mouth halfheartedly, spat something onto the ground that looked like a mixture of mucus and dark blood. His eyes caught Ben's incredulous gaze, and he grinned up at him through a rotten, toothless mouth. '*What about it, mista? Wanna peanut?*' he asked, and then burst into a cackling laugh that caused Ben's skin to break out in gooseflesh.

For twenty endless minutes they looked for Thomas, with Susan anchoring the spot where they'd first lost sight of their son and Ben setting out through the crowd in expanding circles around her, calling out Thomas's name into an ocean of passing strangers, trying to make his voice heard above the blaring music emanating from the speakers above him. In that short time, his mind discovered the ability to think of every possible evil thing in the world that might have beset his son.

Then, through a small opening momentarily created between the bodies of the shifting crowd, Ben spotted his boy – or at least thought he did.

'Thomas,' he called, pushing his way roughly past a large man clutching an enormous bouquet of cotton candy.

'*Hey!*' the man protested indignantly, but Ben barely heard. For on that warm August night, with the first tendrils of fall still three weeks away and the trees holding steadfastly to their summer foliage, it *had* been Thomas, the familiar brown cowlick of hair rising like a question mark from the top of his head as he stood looking up at the unfamiliar faces all around him.

Ben dropped to his knees and swept his startled son into his arms. '*Jesus Christ, you scared me!*' he scolded him, hugging the boy tightly. The man in the purple vest and lime-green bow tie ('*Fresh peanuts! Get your fresh peanuts here!*') glanced over at them suspiciously.

Ben muttered a prayer of gratitude, then stood up, holding Thomas in his arms as he began to make his way toward Susan through the thinning horde.

'*They git away from ya, those little ones.*'

Ben turned in the direction of the voice, and found himself facing the peanut hawker, whose yellowed eyes stared back at him accusingly.

'Pardon?'

The man considered him for a moment. The olive shirt beneath his purple vest was dark with sweat stains and his black boots were caked with mud and flecks of trodden hay. He sneered at Ben with a rotten, toothless mouth. '*Ya oughta watch ya kid more closely nex' time,*' he admonished Ben, and spat another wad of maroon phlegm onto the ground, where it seemed to twist and hiss like a pat of butter on the scorched brown earth before it finally lay quiet and dead. He leered at Ben contemptuously, his buckled jaw listing to the right at an impossible angle as if it were dislocated from his skull. Still, his mandible moved up and down as he chewed, and bits of mashed peanut shells spilled out from between his twisted lips like dead insects and came to rest at his feet. '*Kid like that needs ta be watched.*'

Ben, not knowing what to say, simply stood there, transfixed, staring back at the man.

'*Yaah,*' the peanut hawker said to himself after a moment's consideration, as if suddenly coming to some irrefutable conclusion. He spat again on the ground, then wiped his mouth absently with the back of his hand. '*Kid like that'll jus' slip away from ya, if ya not careful wit' 'im.*' He paused for a moment, reflectively. Then he unfurled a gnarled, accusatory index finger and held it out in Thomas's direction. Ben pulled the boy closer against himself, turning slightly so that his own body was between his son and the figure in the purple vest.

'*Ya nevah know what a boy gonna do when he git out 'n the world,*' the man said, observing Thomas with a predatory gaze. The volume of his voice began to rise now, high above the crowd like a Bible-thumping preacher before a spellbound congregation. 'Ya think 'e's safe, mistah. *But 'e ain't!* Ya think ya gotcha boy back now. *But ya don't!* You don' know whe'ah 'e's been, who 'e's been consortin' wit'. Jus' lookit 'im. *'E'S BEEN EATIN' PEANUTS! AN' THE'AH ROTTEN! EV'RY LAS' ONE!!*'

And with that, Ben turned to look at his son, whom

he held protectively in his arms. Thomas turned his face upward, glancing at Ben with a doomed expression of guilt and horror. It was obvious now that the boy was sick. 'I'm sorry, Daddy,' he said. 'I didn't know.' Then his small body convulsed sharply, and he vomited an enormous torrent of bloody, macerated peanuts onto the ground at Ben's feet.

PART TWO

To Witness the Dead

Chapter 8

Sam Garston was the sort of man who made it seem as if the job of county sheriff had been established not so much because there was a need for it, but because the Jefferson County legislature realized that they needed to come up with some way to make use of the man's talent and steadfast dedication to public service. Having moved his family to the area thirteen years ago, Ben had not known Sam for as long as some of the true locals. Nevertheless, his position as medical examiner brought him into contact with Sam frequently enough that he felt he knew the man fairly well. He was not surprised, therefore, to find a Jefferson County patrol car parked in front of the Coroner's Office at nine o'clock on this bright Saturday morning and the six-foot-five, 260-pound chief of police leaning casually against the wall of the building, waiting for Ben to arrive.

'Good morning, Chief,' Ben greeted him as he ascended the six steps to the building's front door.

'It's a nice one,' Garston agreed amicably, squinting slightly as he surveyed the blue sky above. His left thumb was tucked casually into his gun belt, and the large man seemed to lean against the building with enough purpose to make one wonder whether he perhaps moonlighted as a structural support beam for the CO's front exterior façade. As Sam pushed away from the building's wall with his right foot Ben could almost feel the CO shift slightly as it resumed responsibility for the entire weight of its frame.

'Thought I might actually beat you here this morning, Sam,' Ben commented as he unlocked the front door and stepped inside. A fine mist of dust floated within the identical sunbeams cast through the lobby's two large front windows. The CO was old, erected at least eighty years ago, and had served as county post office for many distinguished decades before its eventual reassignment. The floors were swept and mopped five days a week by a janitor who took pride in his work and did his job well. Nevertheless, the dust inhabiting the old building had apparently decided long ago that it had a right to be there, and returned every evening after the lights went out and the place was locked up tight. It provided a familiar welcome on mornings like this when Ben was the first to arrive and startle it up from its resting place on the wooden floorboards.

'You won't be beating me anywhere showing up at nine a.m.,' the big man countered. 'Far as I see it, day's almost half over. Been up since five-thirty, and waiting here for you since eight. Hell, I'm almost ready for lunch.'

Ben unlocked the door to his small office, and the two men entered. Ben walked behind his desk and sat down in a swivel chair on plastic rollers that tilted slightly to the left. Garston stood next to the only other chair in the room, his head nearly brushing against the low tile ceiling. His massive frame eclipsed the token ray of light emanating from the hallway just outside, and Ben switched on the desk lamp.

'Have a seat, Sam,' he said, indicating the vacant chair. The chief descended upon the hapless piece of furniture, which groaned in modest protest. The look of guarded anticipation that darted across Sam's face suggested to Ben that more than a few chairs had failed him unexpectedly during his tenure on this earth. Ben was grateful when this one did not. He liked Sam, who was sharp as a tack and conducted his job with surprising kindness and decency.

'Looks like this one's gonna hold,' Sam observed, optimistically glancing down at the chair beneath him.

Ben smiled. 'If it don't, we'll take it out back and shoot it.'

'Won't be the first time,' the chief commented. He interlocked his fingers and cracked the knuckles loudly, the noise reverberating off the walls of the small office. It was a bad habit he'd abandoned twenty years ago at the request of his wife, but it occasionally resurfaced during times of stress. He looked up guiltily. 'Sorry about that.'

'No problem.'

Sam took a deep breath and let it out. 'So, what've you got?'

Ben opened the left drawer of his desk and pulled out a dark green file. It contained multiple photographs and his typed dictation from the night before. 'Young kid, as you know,' he began. 'I'd say about fourteen.'

'We think we have an ID on the victim,' Garston said. 'Kevin Tanner – a fifteen-year-old high school student from a neighborhood adjacent to the spot where the victim was found. Apparently, he didn't come home last night. Wasn't reported missing until this morning, about two and a half hours ago. Kid's mother and younger brother are out of town visiting relatives, and the father works nights at a shipping company in Steubenville. Father came home this morning to an empty house and became concerned. Contacted us at six thirty a.m.'

'This Tanner kid might have just gone over to a friend's house overnight, or left early this morning before his old man got home from work.'

'Not likely,' Sam replied. 'Father says his son wouldn't spend the night at a friend's house without checking with him first. He also says he got home a little before six this morning, so it would've been pretty early for the boy to be up and out of the house. Also, the family has a dog. The animal urinated on the carpet overnight. Father says he's never done that before. Probably hadn't been let out since Mr Tanner left for work at five p.m. yesterday afternoon.'

'Long shift,' Ben commented.

'He works twelve-hour shifts a couple of days a week. The father's description of the boy matches that of the victim. He's down at the station right now filing a report. They'll keep him for some brief questioning, but we'd like to get him over here to ID the body after that.'

'That'll be ugly,' Ben said. 'The body's in pretty bad shape. Someone did a number on this poor kid.'

'Uh-huh.' Sam cracked the knuckle of his right index finger. *Pop!* It sounded like a firecracker within the tight confines of the office, and Ben jumped slightly in his seat. 'Why don't you tell me about it?'

The pathologist looked down at the report in front of him. 'Well, there were multiple stab wounds from an unknown instrument,' he began. 'I don't think it was a knife. The entrance wounds measure about 0.75 by 0.9 centimeters, and all appear to be made using the same weapon.'

'Screwdriver?'

'Maybe. There's a wound entering the neck and extending to the skull base. That would mean the instrument was at least six to eight inches long. There were eight stab wounds to the head itself. Two of them pierced the skull.' He was sliding pictures across the desk as he spoke.

'Interesting.'

'Yeah, that takes some force – or at least determination.'

'Or rage,' Sam commented, studying the pictures.

'The attack *was* extraordinarily violent,' Ben

continued. 'The victim was bitten by the assailant several times. In fact, he wasn't simply bitten – he was ravaged. There are several large avulsion injuries to the soft tissues of the face, neck and chest where the skin has been partially torn away.'

'Consistent with bite wounds?'

'It appears so.'

'Could the bite wounds have come from an animal, perhaps one that came across the body after the boy had been murdered?'

'Unlikely.' Ben shook his head. 'Most animals have much sharper canines than humans, and a different dental structure. These serrations along the wound edge' – he pointed to a picture lying in front of them on the desk – 'are consistent with a human dentition pattern.'

Sam studied the picture for a moment. 'I see what you mean,' he said, and when he looked up at Ben his face was slightly ashen. 'It just seems so . . . savage. I don't understand it.'

'I haven't gotten to the best part yet,' Ben replied.

'You mean the fact that the victim's genitals were discovered in the woods fifty yards from the site of the body?'

'Yeah. That won't be easy for the father to hear about.'

'Then I suggest,' Sam said, eyeing Ben from across the table, 'that you don't tell him.'

'I wasn't planning on it,' Ben said. He swiveled around in his chair so that he could look out through the open office door while Sam shuffled through the photographs sprawled like fallen soldiers across the desk. It was Saturday, but the Coroner's Office was beginning to come to life. Tanya Palson, who tended to most of the clerical responsibilities of the office, had arrived and could be heard at the front desk answering the phone.

'There's one other thing you might find of interest,' he commented as Chief Garston continued to study the photographs in front of him.

'What's that?' Sam asked, eyebrows raised slightly.

'I think the perpetrator was left-handed.'

'Yes, I was just noticing that,' Sam observed. 'The puncture wounds to the body are clustered along the right chest and flank. Assuming the assailant was facing the victim, he must've been holding the weapon in his left hand.'

'Exactly,' Ben concurred. 'Also, the two head wounds puncturing the cranium follow a trajectory through the brain that angles slightly to the victim's left. They enter through the coronal and sagittal sutures.'

'The what?'

'The skull is actually made up of several different bones which merge together during early childhood along what are called suture lines. They're weak points in the skull.'

'Fault lines,' Sam suggested.

'Yes,' Ben agreed, 'in a manner of speaking.'

'So he got lucky, then?'

'Perhaps. But there were eight wounds to the skull, and *all* of them were clustered around the suture lines. I think,' Ben said thoughtfully, 'that maybe he knew what he was doing.'

'What are you saying?'

'My overwhelming impression' – Ben looked somberly across the table at the Jefferson County Sheriff – 'is that he's done this before.'

Pop! Pop-pop! Sam's knuckles sounded off beneath the table.

'Yeah.' Ben nodded.

In the front room, the phone was ringing. 'Coroner's Office,' Tanya answered. 'How can I help you?'

Ben gathered the photos and returned them to the olive file marked simply 'John Doe'. 'Do you want to see the body?' he offered.

'Not really,' Sam replied. 'But they tell me it's part of my job.'

'I thought you had detectives to take care of this stuff.'

'Oh, he'll be by soon enough,' Sam answered. 'Carl Schroeder. Good man. Fifteen years on the force. He's questioning the boy's father right now. It's his case.'

'Okay. Then, if you don't mind me asking, what are *you* doing here?'

Sam stood up slowly. He was such a pleasant man that you forgot how physically intimidating his size could be until he was standing directly in front of you. 'I'm the chief,' he said. 'I have an overriding responsibility to protect the citizens of this county that goes well beyond any single investigation. What happened yesterday . . .' He seemed to mull it over in his mind, searching for the right sentiment. 'What happened yesterday *offends me*, Ben – and I aim to take a special interest.'

At that moment, Ben was very glad to be on the right side of the law. 'I see.' He nodded seriously, then gestured toward the open door and the autopsy room just beyond. 'Well, . . . this way, Chief.'

The two men filed out of the tiny office and made their way toward a lonely shape lying patiently on a steel table in the next room.

Chapter 9

Eleven a.m., Coroner's Office. Ben sat in his small office and waited. Chief Garston had received a call from Detective Schroeder that he was on his way to the CO with the boy's father. That had been ten minutes ago. It was not a long drive.

Sam had gone out to stand on the front steps of the building. Reporters had been gathering since 9:30 a.m., and they were expecting a statement from the chief regarding the results of the autopsy and the early progress of the investigation. Sam hoped his appearance would draw their attention while Detective Schroeder ushered Mr Tanner into the CO through the back door. It wasn't a flawless plan, but it was the best one they had.

Ben could hear Tanya fielding calls at the front desk. The phone had not stopped ringing since Ben's arrival, and he simply wished it would stop. Then again, he considered, the silence might be worse. He sat at his desk and tried to focus on something – *anything* – except for the covered figure in the next room.

Sam Garston, he considered, was an interesting man. His formidable physical characteristics and dogged devotion to his job suggested a no-nonsense approach to life. It was undoubtedly one of the reasons for his continued success throughout the course of his career. But there was also a different side to him, one that Ben had come to witness on at least one occasion previously.

Two years ago Ben had had the unfortunate responsibility of performing an autopsy on a four-month-old infant from Pleasant Hill. The child had come from a nice, hardworking middle-class family from a suburban neighborhood just north of Steubenville. The father wrote for the sports section of the local newspaper, and the mother took care of their daughter during the day while simultaneously managing to run a small online resale business from their home. One Friday evening they'd hired a babysitter so they could catch a movie at the local cineplex and dinner at a popular Italian restaurant afterward. When they'd come home that evening, the babysitter was watching television in the family room and the child was asleep in the upstairs bedroom. They'd popped in to check on her, paid the sitter, and the father had driven the teenager home. When he returned, he'd found his wife waiting patiently for him in their bed, naked under the covers. They had made love, and had fallen to sleep amid a discussion about their plans for the upcoming weekend. All of this had been documented in their statement to investigators the following day. When they went into the little girl's room the following morning, the child was dead.

On the surface, it sounded like a case of SIDS – sudden infant death syndrome, a term used to describe an unexplained infant death (what used to be called a 'crib death') during the first year of life. The autopsy, however, had identified retinal hemorrhages – small areas of bleeding in the back of the eyes. The postmortem had also discovered multiple subdural hematomas, a type of brain injury commonly seen with shaken baby syndrome. Ben had contacted the investigating detective with these preliminary findings, and both the parents and the babysitter had been brought to the police station for further questioning. Most of the focus had been on the teenager, who adamantly denied shaking the infant the night before. The child, she reported, had been sleeping when she arrived. An hour later, she'd gotten her up for a feed and to change her diaper. The infant slept through most of it, showing little interest in the bottle. The detectives interrogated the girl for several hours at the station. They had reasoned and bargained with her. They'd lied to her about factitious evidence proving the case against her, eventually scaring her into tears. Throughout everything, however, she had stuck to her story.

Sam had stopped by Ben's house that night with the investigating detectives. The girl's story was convincingly consistent, they informed him. She was either innocent or an exceptionally good liar – which left one or both of the parents as the only remaining suspects. The detectives wanted to know how hard they should press the parents, and whether the evidence from the autopsy suggested one more than the other as a likely culprit. The mother and father were already traumatized, Sam noted, and they didn't want to go after them unnecessarily. It was a fragile situation.

Of the two detectives accompanying Sam that evening, one of them – a small, wiry man named Harvey Nickelback – had not exactly been in agreement with the cautious approach Sam had asked them to take.

'I don't see why we have to pussyfoot around this,' he'd objected vociferously, tracing the outline of his thin mustache between his right thumb and index finger. 'This kid had retinal hemorrhages and a head full of blood. That's pretty convincing evidence for child abuse, as far as I'm concerned.'

'That's why the case is under investigation,' Sam had replied. 'If this death was due to shaken baby syndrome, then whoever did it will go to prison.'

'All right, then,' Nickelback agreed ardently.

'But we have to be careful,' Sam continued. 'I don't want to go after these parents with everything we've got until we're fairly certain that we're going after the right people. Keep in mind that they've just lost their only child. They're in a world of pain right now.'

'Or guilt,' the detective countered.

'Probably both. But we only have one chance to do this right.'

That was the thing that had impressed Ben the most about Sam: the delicacy with which he had handled the situation. He'd never mentioned it, but Ben thought that perhaps Sam had had an instinct about the case – somehow sensing that things didn't quite fit together in the way that they should, although he probably would've been hard-pressed to explain why. In the face of nearly overwhelming evidence, he had asked the detectives to wait, to suspend their judgment a bit longer. In the end, it had been the right thing to do. The forensic chemist's report that had landed on Ben's desk the following week had identified high levels of glutaric acid in the infant's organs, particularly in the brain and muscles. The abnormal levels raised suspicion for the possibility of a rare metabolic disorder, glutaric acidemia type 1, in which the body has difficulty breaking down various amino acids. The accumulation of the metabolic by-products, the report went on to explain, often results in multiple clinical manifestations, including mental retardation, alterations in muscle strength and tone, and hemorrhages in the brain and eyes that can be mistaken for child abuse. That explained the retinal hemorrhages and subdural hematomas Ben had discovered on autopsy. The forensic chemist's findings had changed everything, for it became clear that the infant had not been the victim of child abuse, after all, but rather had died from complications of a rare genetic disorder. Sam's instinct to wait, therefore, had been correct.

'—evenson?'

It had been a remarkable thing, that intuition, and –

'Excuse me. Dr Stevenson?'

Ben looked up from his desk, his eyes clearing. The CO's secretary stood in the doorway of his small office, looking in on him.

'What is it, Tanya?' he asked.

'That was Detective Schroeder on the phone,' she said. 'He's here with the boy's father. They're pulling into the parking lot now.'

Chapter 10

Phil Tanner was a tall, lanky man with a weathered face and a darkened, sun-battered complexion. He still wore his work clothes from the night before – faded dungarees and an old navy blue button-down shirt that bore the unmistakable bulge of a pack of cigarettes (Marlboros, if Ben had to guess) in the front pocket. Detective Carl Schroeder stood beside him, wearing a dark suit with a maroon tie. His black gelled-back hair matched the color of his shoes perfectly. He was shorter than both Ben and Phil Tanner by several inches, but his build was lithe and wiry, his eyes cool and watchful, and Ben imagined that in a physical altercation the detective was a force to be reckoned with. Schroeder introduced the two men in a brisk, practiced manner.

'Mr Tanner.' Ben greeted the boy's father, shaking the large, calloused hand extended in his direction.

The man nodded slightly, saying nothing. He stood tense and rigid in the hallway.

'Sir, I know this must be an extremely difficult time for you,' Ben continued. 'You are welcome to come sit in my office for a moment until you feel that you're—'

'Where's my boy?' Tanner responded, looking over Ben's shoulder into the next room. His voice was deep and gruff, the product of too many years spent smoking too many cigarettes.

'Well, we were hoping you could identify—'

'Let me see 'im then.'

'Yes, of course,' Ben agreed. He led the two men into the next room. He had taken as much care as possible to prepare the boy's body – his face, anyway – for viewing. His injuries had been severe and disfiguring, and Ben was no plastic surgeon. Suddenly he wanted more time to work on the boy, especially that gaping bite wound across his left cheek. He'd been able to pull the wound edges together using a series of horizontal mattress sutures, but now it didn't seem nearly sufficient to withstand the eyes of the boy's father.

'The wounds were fairly extensive,' he explained to them, somewhat apologetically. 'There's been some significant disfigurement to the face.' Ben carefully folded down the edge of a cloth blanket he'd placed over the body prior to their arrival. He tried to brace himself for the father's response.

Phil Tanner was quiet for a long moment, studying the boy's marred but placid appearance. He looked upon him with a surreal and uncertain fascination. In the front room the phone rang, and Ben heard Tanya answering it. 'Coroner's Office,' she said, and

Ben silently kicked himself for forgetting to have her put the phones on hold during the visit. The sound seemed to break Phil Tanner's trance, and he looked up at them with confusion.

'That ain't my boy,' he said, and Ben exchanged a surprised look with Detective Schroeder.

'That's not your son, sir?' Schroeder asked.

'No,' the man answered. He shook his head as if to clear it. 'Wait. That's not exactly right. What I mean to say is that, yes, it *is* my son, but it . . . it's just that he don't *look* like my son.' He searched the faces of the two men standing before him, attempting to make himself understood.

'He's sustained some injuries that alter his appearance,' Ben explained again.

'I can see *that* for myself, Doctor.' Phil Tanner's eyes flashed at Ben, who took an involuntary half step backward. 'I'm not an idiot.'

'Take it easy, Mr Tanner,' Detective Schroeder interjected in a calm and level voice. 'Something like this always comes as a great shock. I can assure you that Dr Stevenson was not implying—'

If Phil Tanner heard him, he didn't seem to notice. His left hand groped beneath the blanket, finding the boy's cold, insensate hand. He grasped it tightly.

'Kevin?' he asked, puzzled and unbelieving. 'Kevin? *Kevin?*' His voice rose steadily in pitch and urgency each time he spoke the boy's name. The words echoed slightly off the room's concrete walls. They had a hollow, lonely sound, like a knock at a door that will never be answered.

At last Tanner looked up at Ben, his eyes pleading. 'That ain't my boy, is it, Doctor? I mean . . . *Jesus . . . Tell me this ain't my son lyin' here on this table with his face torn to pieces! Tell me that, won't you, Doctor?!*'

'Mr Tanner, please,' someone said without much conviction. Ben wasn't certain if it had been Detective Schroeder or himself.

'*Kevin?*' the boy's father went on, his voice continuing to escalate. 'Kevin? *Son?! Kevin?? Tell me this ain't you!! Kevin, are you dead?! ARE YOU DEAD, BOY?!!*'

There was no answer from the form beneath the blanket.

'*What did they* do *to you?!*' he asked the dead boy lying pale and mute before him. '*WHAT . . . DID THEY DO TO YOU?!!*'

At that last tortured utterance, Phil Tanner's feverish eyes leapt up at Ben and fixed themselves upon him as if Ben, himself, had been responsible for the boy's death.

'*I WANT TO KNOW WHAT THEY DID TO MY BOY!!*' he said again, only this time it wasn't a question but an accusation. Ben took another step backward. His left hip bumped into a small metal table supporting an electronic scale. The scale skittered to the edge of the table, hung on precariously for a brief moment, then went crashing to the tiled floor below. The sound was thunderous in the small room, and Ben could hear Tanya's voice calling from the front desk, 'Dr Stevenson? Is everything okay?'

'That's *enough*, Mr Tanner.' Carl Schroeder took the man by the arm and tried to lead him away.

'*FUCK YOU!! I WANT TO BE WITH MY SON!!*' Tanner protested wildly, trying to shake off the detective's grasp.

'You will spend the night in jail if you don't get a hold of yourself,' Schroeder said quietly but sternly. '*That's enough!*'

Phil Tanner looked from the detective, to Ben, to the body lying on the table before him. His eyes were wide and uncomprehending. The muscles of his neck and forearms bunched and jerked beneath his blue shirt, and Ben thought to himself in a strangely detached way that if Tanner leapt for him across the table, he would break to his right and make for his office. If he could get the office door closed, he'd be out of harm's way long enough for Detective Schroeder to subdue the man. *Fight or flight,* Ben thought randomly. Let Schroeder do the fighting; he was trained for it. Ben would opt for the latter.

Suddenly, as quickly as it had come, all of the struggle within Phil Tanner was gone. His eyes appeared to clear a little, but the inner strength he had brought with him when he arrived was gone. His shoulders slumped forward, his body bending at the waist as if he'd been sucker-punched low in the gut. A calloused hand touched the table where his son lay supine beneath the sheet, but Tanner would not look at him. For a long time he said nothing, staring at the broken remnants of the tattered scale splayed out across the floor. When he finally spoke, his voice was barely more than a whisper.

'I'm sorry. I shouldn't have reacted like that.'

Schroeder placed a hand on the man's shoulder. 'You're under a great strain, sir,' he observed. 'Under similar circumstances, I don't know if I would've behaved any differently.'

'Well, I'm sorry anyway. It's just . . .' For a moment his face struggled for control. 'It's just that I . . . well . . . I don't *want* him to be dead.' This last part came out so softly that, if there had been any other noise in the room, Ben would not have heard it. Phil Tanner's eyes filled with tears. 'When I got home this morning and he wasn't there . . . and then they told me that a boy had been found in the woods . . . I just . . .'

'It's okay,' Schroeder said. His voice was calm and empathic. Ben stood in silence, studying a thin strip of grout between the floor's tiles as if it were the most interesting thing he'd ever seen in his entire life.

Tanner looked up at the detective. 'I just didn't want it to be *him*. I thought . . . you know . . . I thought maybe I'd come here and it wouldn't be him. I wanted it to be someone else's son. Not Kevin. Not *my* boy. That's what I was hoping for. I wanted it to be someone else's goddamn son. Can you . . . can you believe that?'

'Yes, I can,' he answered.

Phil Tanner stood next to the table, head low, as if waiting for someone to tell him what to do next. He stood like that for a minute or two, and none of them spoke. Then, suddenly, he looked up as another realization occurred to him. 'Oh my God,' he said. His eyes revealed a sickening dread. 'What will I say to his mother? *She doesn't know. How am I going to tell my wife that our boy is dead?*'

The intrusive ringing of the phone at the front desk had finally stopped, and the CO was quiet and still, at least for the time being. The only sound in the room was the shushing cadence of breath that slid slowly in and out of each chest but one.

There was nothing else.

Chapter 11

'You're not going out tonight, Thomas. End of discussion.' Ben was tired of arguing, and he was through being reasonable.

'*Fine, Dad!*' his son yelled back, throwing up his hands in frustration. '*Whatever you say!*' He stormed out of the kitchen and up the stairs toward his bedroom. Six seconds later came the sound, and the subsequent reverberation, of Thomas's bedroom door being slammed shut hard enough to make the pictures in the downstairs hallway rattle.

Joel sat quietly at the kitchen table, pushing string beans around the perimeter of his plate with his fork. He'd wisely decided to stay out of the fray. His father looked down at the remaining vegetables. 'You planning on eating those?'

'No,' Joel replied honestly.

Ben continued to look at him, eyebrows raised. Joel stared back, mentally preparing himself for the stand-off. *Nobody told the Punisher* – his favorite comic book hero – *to eat his vegetables,* he thought crossly. You'd get so far as 'Pardon me, sir, but are you planning on eating—' Then, *blam*! You'd be staring down the barrel of a .45 long-slide.

'I guess you're prepared to sleep in the kitchen tonight then?' Ben asked. 'You want your pillow?'

Joel sighed, rolling his eyes. Alex looked up at him from where he lay on the floor next to Joel's chair. Two abandoned string beans also lay on the floor next to the dog, Joel's failed attempt to feed the beans to his canine companion. Apparently, Alex didn't care much for string beans, either.

'Dad, I'm full. This is my second helping.'

'That's your *first* helping,' his father responded. 'And don't think I didn't notice those two beans on the floor next to Alex, too.'

'I dropped them. Honest. It was an accident.' He looked over at his mother for support.

Ben shook his head. 'Give me at least *some* credit, son.'

'How about if I eat three beans?' Joel suggested.

'How about if you eat *all* of them?' his father responded.

'Okay, I'll eat half,' Joel agreed, and shoveled the appropriate number of beans into his mouth, chewed them up, and swallowed them in one giant gulp followed by a milk chaser. 'Now, may I be excused?'

'Yes, you may,' Susan said. 'The rest of those beans will be waiting for you at breakfast.'

'Thanks, Mom.' He jumped out of his chair and

darted from the room. Alexander the Great immediately got up and followed him, the boy's 180-pound shadow. Joel's parents watched him go. For a moment they sat in silence at the table, enjoying the sudden tranquillity that their son's departure had left in its wake.

'I'm going to go talk to Thomas,' Ben announced.

Susan placed a hand on his sleeve. 'I don't think that's such a good idea.'

'He needs to check his attitude,' Ben said. 'I'm not going to have him yelling at his parents and slamming the bedroom door just because he can't go out with his friends.'

'Let him be,' Susan advised him. 'He's sixteen. You remember what that was like? He's got so many emotions churning around inside him that he can barely see straight.'

'I still don't like the yelling. We've never tolerated that before. I don't see any reason to change course now.'

'That's true. But he's right, Ben. What are we doing telling him he can't go out with his friends on a Saturday night?'

'We're trying to keep him safe, that's what we're doing. A young boy Thomas's age was just murdered in our own neighborhood. I don't think it's unreasonable to ask him not to go out at night for a while.'

'That was eight weeks ago, and it happened in broad daylight,' Susan reminded him. 'Should we be keeping him home during the day, as well?'

'It's a parent's responsibility to act in their child's

best interest. The first priority is keeping our boys safe.'

'But we can't always do that,' she pointed out.

'We can try,' he told her. He stood up, filled a kettle with water and placed it on the range to boil. 'Maybe we should think about getting out of town for a while.'

'We have responsibilities – obligations, Ben.'

'A few weeks is all I'm suggesting.'

Susan shook her head. 'I have a private practice to run – a full schedule of patient appointments. You have a job. The kids have school. We can't just pick up and leave.'

'You might think differently if you'd seen the body of that boy, Susan. He'd been ravaged – his features mutilated. The person who did that to him is still out there somewhere. Do you *get* that?'

Susan looked at him from across the room. Her face was a mask: set, composed and completely unreadable. Ben didn't care. Right now all he could think about was the safety of his children.

'It won't make any difference,' she said at last.

'*What?*'

'You want them to run like cowards? Is that what you want to teach them?'

'I don't care about teaching them *anything* right now,' he said. 'I want them *safe*.'

'But you can't *make* them safe, Ben.'

'I can try,' he replied. He could feel the emotions warring inside of him: anger, fear and frustration. He almost didn't say the words that came next. If he hadn't – if he'd taken a moment to think before speaking – things might have turned out differently for them.

'Someone has to,' he said.

The room was very quiet for a moment.

'What is *that* supposed to mean?' she asked finally, her voice low but rock steady. 'You think I don't care about the well-being of our boys?'

'That's not what I said.' He was backtracking now, a little too late.

'You think that you actually understand what love and protection are? *Do you?*'

'I . . .'

'You have *no idea* about the measures I am prepared to take – *that I have already taken* – to safeguard the lives of those children. You have no idea, Ben.' She shook her head in exasperation. 'I would do anything – *anything* – for them. Do you really mean to stand here and tell me that I wouldn't?'

'I didn't mean to imply . . .' He trailed off, not really knowing *what* he'd meant to imply.

She stood there, regarding him with a look of defiance and contempt. 'I believe that we *both* would do whatever we could to protect our children, at whatever cost is necessary.'

Ben sat down in a chair, or rather collapsed into it. His fingers kneaded his right temple where a dull headache had begun to blossom. 'And how do you plan on fighting this?' he asked.

'As a family,' she replied. 'We have to take care of each other. Just as we always have.' She studied him from across the table for a moment. 'They're safer here with us than they would be anywhere else without us.'

'Are you sure?' he asked.

'I'm certain.'

She took his hand in her own and held it. 'You know I love you.'

'Yes, I know th—' he began, but she held up her hand, indicating for him to be quiet.

'You know I love you,' she said again. 'And I would never break up this family.' Her eyes continued to watch him, and Ben knew enough this time to be silent. 'I *will* fight for them. I will do whatever it takes to protect them. And I would fight for you. Do you know that?'

'Yes.'

'Good.' She glanced down at their hands, folded together on the kitchen table, then looked up at him again. 'And Benjamin?'

'Yes?'

'Don't you *ever* think or imply otherwise. I won't tolerate that form of betrayal from you.'

She watched him for a moment to make certain he understood, then slid her hands away from him, stood up, and left the room.

Chapter 12

That night Ben went to bed early, feeling broken and exhausted from his arguments, first with his son, and subsequently with his wife. His interactions with Joel at the dinner table hadn't been particularly stellar, either, now that he thought about it. Susan had told him that they didn't take sides, that they were a family. That was all well and good if you weren't the one on the outside looking in, if you weren't the odd man out. But that was exactly how he had felt lately, with all of them. The problem was, none of them had seen that boy's body that night. None of them had tried in vain to sew up the boy's face so it didn't look like someone had taken a huge bite out of it – which, in fact, they had. His wife and children had the luxury of thinking about that violence in an abstract way. He did not.

Despite his best efforts to keep the lines of communication with his family open, things had been strained between them over these past two months. How could they not be? To make matters worse, Ben hadn't been sleeping well, and he felt perpetually fatigued and irritable. Last Wednesday, he caught himself dozing off at work right in the middle of reviewing a pathology slide of a needle biopsy from a breast mass. He was looking at the specimen under the microscope and started to hear the sound of snoring. When he glanced up, he realized that he was the only one in the room and that the snoring had been his own. The slide had fallen off the microscope's stage and onto the counter, cracking the cover slip. *What in the hell was I doing catching a few winks in the middle of a cytology exam?* he'd flogged himself. *Sorry about your invasive Stage IV breast cancer, ma'am. It probably could've been properly diagnosed and treated five years earlier if I hadn't been taking an afternoon siesta while examining your biopsy.* That had been completely unacceptable.

The thing of it was, he kept going over the kid's autopsy in his mind: driving to work, walking up and down the aisles of the local supermarket, having dinner with his family and certainly lying awake at night, staring for alternating periods at the ceiling and the bedroom clock. He kept picturing the post-mortem examination – his mind running over the details repeatedly in the same way that his gloved fingertips had traced a line from puncture wound to puncture wound that day. It seemed to him that there was something he'd seen but not quite noticed, some detail he had overlooked. The consequence was that the small frame of a young boy now lay still and muted beneath the ground without, at the very least, the justice his death demanded.

Ben turned onto his left side and stared at the empty space in the bed next to him. It was still early, but Susan would be coming to bed soon. They didn't play that one-of-us-sleeps-on-the-couch-after-an-argument game. She would come to bed and, when she did, he would apologize for being such a jerk. Tomorrow morning he would apologize to Thomas, as well. Susan was right. He couldn't lock his boys away in a vault for the rest of their lives just because he was afraid for their safety. Thomas was a sophomore in high school. By next spring he'd be driving, and in a year and a half they'd be poring over undergraduate catalogs together, planning visits to college campuses and filling out admission forms. Ben only had a short period of time left with his oldest son before Thomas headed out into the broader world for good. Now was the time to be bolstering his son's confidence and encouraging his independence, not stomping all over it. *Things could be better again,* he reminded himself. *We just have to stick together as a family, that's all.*

He lay there for another half hour, listening to the sounds of the house. He could hear music coming from Thomas's room down the hall. Susan was on the phone downstairs, giving admission orders to a nurse for one of her patients who required hospitalization tonight. Joel was giggling as he played with Alex in the living room. The big dog's thudding tread echoed through the house as he chased down whatever object Joel was throwing for him.

Twenty minutes later, Ben heard the sounds of Joel preparing for bed. Water ran in the upstairs sink as his son brushed his teeth, and a few minutes later he could hear his wife tucking Joel into bed. The sound of music coming from Thomas's room continued at reduced volume after Susan asked him to turn it down just a bit. No protest there. Thomas responded differently to her than he did to Ben. The two seemed to have a special connection, and for a moment Ben felt a surge of jealousy and resentment. It seemed like it had been that way for as long as he could remember.

The bedroom door opened, and Susan's silhouette appeared in the entrance. 'You still awake?' she whispered.

'Yeah,' Ben spoke up. 'Still here.'

She crossed the room and sat on the edge of the bed. 'I thought you'd be asleep by now.'

'Me, too.'

She brushed back his hair and planted a kiss on his forehead.

'I'm sorry about tonight,' he told her.

'You don't need to be sorry,' she replied. 'You're worried about the kids. That's your job as a parent.'

'No, but lately I've been afraid to even let them out of my sight. That's not good for them, it's not good for me and it's not good for our relationship as a family. I can change that. I'm going to try to loosen up a little.'

'Okay.' She nodded. 'I'm going to get ready for bed.'

He watched her proceed to the doorway leading to their bathroom, watched her pass through, shutting the door behind her.

Somewhere in the midst of the next few minutes, while he waited for her to return to their bed, thinking that perhaps they would make love, the stress and exhaustion that had been chasing him over the past eight weeks finally caught up with him, and at last he slept. In his dream, he was standing with his family on the platform of a vast subway station. A flurry of passengers scurried around them, making their way toward a massive steam locomotive, which waited silently on tracks that passed into the tumescent mouth of the subway tunnels at either end of the platform. Fastened to a wall high above the platform was a large clock whose minute hand emitted an audible clunk with each sixty-second progression, and the train's conductor watched it from his position with strained intensity.

Although they stood together, Ben and his family, the crowd seemed to pull at them with the momentum of a brisk stream. Already he could see Joel wandering off a few paces to his right. An old man in ratty clothes sat on one of the platform's few benches, holding a small piece of glass – a specimen slide with a transparent cover slip on top – pinched between his thumb and forefinger. A small biopsy of tissue was trapped beneath the slip, and it appeared to writhe and struggle as Joel reached a cautious hand in its direction.

'*Joel, don't touch that!*' Ben called out, moving quickly toward his son. '*It's dirty!*'

But already Joel had grasped the slide in his small, delicate hand and was examining it with fascination as the thing beneath the slip – pink and vascular and pulsating slightly – continued to squirm.

'*No! Put it down!*' Ben yelled as Joel began to lift the cover with his careful fingers. Free of the slip, the specimen shot up the slide toward the boy's hand with horrible, blurring speed. His son dropped the slide, but not before the thing disappeared beneath the sleeve of his jacket. A moment later, he began to scream.

Ben lurched forward and spun the child around to face him. Staring back at him was the tattered face of Kevin Tanner. The sutures Ben had placed in the autopsy room had sprung loose, and the gaping bite wound hung half open once again, seeping some yellow, putrid fluid from its recesses. '*Joel!*' he called into the boy's face, but Joel was gone and all that remained in Ben's arms was the corpse he had examined in the CO two months before.

He lifted the dead child into his arms, unable to leave him lying crumpled and deserted on the subway station's floor. Ben turned back to what remained of his family, but the spot where they'd previously stood was now empty.

'*Aalll abawwwed!*' the conductor called into the crowd, and the pace of the foot traffic quickened. People began running toward the waiting cars, jostling with one another on the steps for purchase.

An old woman was knocked to her knees by the surge of would-be passengers, and Ben watched helplessly as she was trampled underfoot in the mounting stampede.

'*Aaaalll abawwwwed!*' the conductor called out again, and this time the remaining crowd on the station's platform erupted in panic. The stairs leading into the passenger cars were hopelessly clogged, and people began climbing on top of one another in an effort to squeeze through the cars' open windows. A middle-aged man with a developing paunch grabbed a lady of perhaps seventy by the hair and yanked her from the steps in order to make room for himself. She went flying backward and landed gracelessly on the platform, the back of her head striking the tile with a sickening crack.

Ben continued to scan what was left of the crowd for his wife and son. *Did they make it onto the train?* He began walking along its length, looking into the cars as he went. The body of the boy grew heavy in his arms. A piercing whistle filled the station and steam spewed upward from the locomotive's smokestack. The coupling rods began to move, driving the massive steel wheels that propelled the train forward.

Finally, at the second-to-last car, Ben spied a familiar face hanging out through one of the open windows.

'*Sam!*' he yelled, craning his neck backward. '*Sam, it's Ben!*'

Chief Garston looked down at him casually. 'Oh. Hi, Ben.'

'*Sam, I can't find Thomas or Susan. Have you seen them?*'

'No, I haven't seen them,' he responded. Then, with more urgency: 'Hey, you'd better get on the train.'

'*I can't find my family,*' Ben repeated. The train was starting to pick up speed, and he had to walk quickly along the edge of the platform – stepping over several bodies as he went – in order to keep pace with the car Sam was in.

'Oh, I wouldn't worry about them,' Sam chuckled reassuringly. 'I'm sure they'll be fine. But – *say!* – you'd better worry about yourself. You don't want to be left standing here when *this* train leaves the station. That wouldn't be good at all.'

With growing unease, Ben realized that Sam was right. He didn't want to be left behind – but now the train was moving too fast for him to climb aboard. If he tried, he would be swept neatly beneath the wheels and crushed in an instant.

Ben's feet slowed, and he came to a shuffling halt. The last car was past him, heading into the tunnel. He stood alone on the platform, except for the dead boy in his arms and the few scattered bodies lying motionless around him. As the train began to disappear, he saw Sam Garston's receding face looking back at him, hanging half out of the open window. His friend looked a little sad.

'So long, Ben,' Sam called out to him, his voice small against the background of the rumbling machine. 'Take care of that boy of yours.'

The last passenger car vanished into the darkness.

For a few seconds Ben could still hear the sound of the wheels moving along the tracks. Then all was still. He stood holding the dead boy and wondering what was next for him, until a tentative voice floated up to his ears. It was little more than a croak, and it came from the lifeless thing that he held in his arms.

'Father?' it said. But Ben was too afraid to look down.

PART THREE

The Girl

Chapter 13

Thomas lay in bed listening to music. He kept the volume low so he could also hear the sounds of footsteps in the hall, should they approach. He didn't think they would, though. Now that his parents had gone to bed, it was unlikely they would get back up to check on him. Still, he'd locked the door just in case. Saturday night. Sixteen years old. And here he was, trapped in his own bedroom. Which was total bullshit, by the way. He'd been going out on his own for three years now. He'd never wound up drunk in the bushes, and he didn't use drugs. He hadn't knocked up a girl yet, either, which was more than he could say for at least one of his friends. And he knew how to protect himself. So what was the big deal about going out all of a sudden?

He knew one thing; his dad had been totally freaked out about the corpse they'd found in the woods two months ago. He supposed his old man had gotten a good first-hand look, since he'd been in charge of the autopsy and everything. It was probably good for him – rattled him up a little bit. That was the problem with getting old; you let yourself get comfortable. Complacent. It was up at seven with a cup of coffee, off to work all day, come home and maybe crack a beer in the evening before falling asleep in front of the tube. And even *that* was livin' large. It was pathetic, really.

Then again, he imagined his dad probably felt the same way when *he* was sixteen – just never thought he'd turn out like this: old and scared and worried about getting enough fiber in his diet so he wouldn't get constipated. It wasn't really his fault. He'd played by all the rules and had gotten predictably screwed over just the same. What'd he expect, really? People live their whole lives for someday down-the-road, and eventually there is no down-the-road left.

They'd been asleep for forty minutes now, his parents. He'd been keeping an eye on the clock. It still wasn't too late to catch a little action, which was exactly what he planned to do. He'd snuck out before – hell, he'd been practically *forced to* in this house. In the old days he'd sometimes tiptoed down the stairs and right out the front door. These days, however, Alex made it impossible to keep quiet; wagging his tail and whacking it on railing posts, shaking his head, sniffing and sneezing, clomping around behind him with those big, clumsy paws. It was ridiculous.

Two summers ago he'd taken a rock climbing course, and *that* had changed his whole approach to the home-escape business. He'd learned how to use a rope and carabiner, how to make a quick harness with webbing, how to set up anchors and how to rappel. He'd learned about ascending, as well – using a set of Prusik hitches to scamper back up a rope into one's bedroom at the end of the night, for example. No more sneaking down the stairs. No more Alex, the Amazing Blunder Dog, to get him busted. It was truly a beautiful thing, and had worked like a charm on countless occasions.

Thomas went to his closet and retrieved a navy blue backpack. Inside was a fifty-foot climbing rope, a single carabiner, a nine-foot piece of one-inch webbing, a pair of leather gloves and two short thin ropes that he'd tied into Prusiks, one slightly longer than the other. He tied one end of the climbing rope to his bed frame using a figure-of-eight follow-through, opened his bedroom window and lowered the rest of the rope to the yard below. With the webbing, he fashioned himself a basic harness, and he clipped the carabiner in at the waist. He fastened the longer Prusik to the rope and clipped it into the carabiner for self-belay, then wrapped the rope itself three times around the 'biner and locked the device. He shoved the remaining unused Prusik into his jacket pocket to be used later for the ascent, put on his gloves and turned out the bedroom light. He took a moment to glance out through the front window at the street, ensuring that it was quiet and empty. Then he went to the side window and slid it open. Taking the rope in his right hand and placing it against his hip to serve as a break, and using his left hand to mind the self-belay Prusik, he stepped through the opening and quietly lowered himself to the yard two stories below, pausing for a moment at the top to slide the window closed as much as possible. Once he was on the ground, he unclipped himself from the rope and left his equipment in the grass for when he returned.

The street was quiet and empty as he walked down the sidewalk, but two and a half miles away Devon Coleman was throwing a party to kick off his parents' recent departure for their week-long vacation in Cancún. The night was cool, and a light mist of rain had begun to fall. But Thomas felt good. After all, he was young, smart and, as far as he could tell, pretty much invincible. His gait was brisk, and he hummed softly to himself as he walked along. In no time at all he was turning onto Overlook Drive and could hear the pumping rhythm of music coming from the well-lit house down the street.

Chapter 14

As far as high school parties went, this one appeared to be a huge success, if the throng of teenagers already swarming the place when he arrived was any indication. Devon's parents might have a different perspective when they returned home next week, but tonight that was probably the furthest thing from anyone's mind. Devon's family lived in one of those big brick Neocolonial-style homes that had become so popular with the upper middle class these days. The place was 5,600 square feet, Devon had once told him – a monster – and as the street name implied, it was perched atop a hill along with another twenty-some similar-looking dwellings, all with a commanding view of Main Street and most of western Steubenville. Tonight the place was pretty well packed.

Last week Devon had mentioned that since he had the house to himself, he wanted to have a few people over this weekend. Thomas had told him he would come, not realizing his dad was going to impose a mandatory lockdown for the rest of the year. He'd expected maybe twenty or thirty people, but as was the case with most high school parties, over the remainder of the week word traveled with the speed and dissemination of a brushfire in high wind. Judging from the masses assembled on the front lawn alone, Thomas guessed that at least half of the entire damn high school had decided to turn up. He shook his head. *Just a few of Devon's closest friends, my ass.* Then again, with the combination of an adult-free party and plenty of free booze, what'd he expect?

He saw Bret Graham standing near the front door, plastic beer cup in hand, talking with Cynthia Castleberry. Bret, who wrestled in the 152-pound weight class just above Thomas during the winter season, had asked the attractive but somewhat standoffish varsity soccer starter out twice that year, and had been turned down both times – mostly because she'd been going steady with the same guy since freshman year. If nothing else, though, Bret could be pretty damn determined when he set his sights on something.

'Tommy boy, you finally decided to show up,' Bret greeted him as Thomas ascended the stairs leading to the front door.

'Nobody told me *you* were gonna be here, Graham,' he replied. 'You bothering the ladies already?'

Bret feigned offense. 'Take no notice of this one,' he told Cynthia. 'He's just upset because I remind him of what a substandard athlete he really is.'

'That's right,' Thomas countered. 'If beer bong ever makes it to the Olympics, you're all set.' He turned to Cynthia. 'You planning on driving this guy home, or should I call his grandmother to come pick him up again?'

She laughed. Her right hand, which had self-consciously abandoned its subtle but strategic caress of Bret's upper arm when Thomas arrived, now returned to its previous position. 'I'll keep an eye on him, Thomas.'

'Then he's in good hands and I'll tell the grandmother she can stand down for the evening.'

'Screw you, Stevenson,' Bret said with an exaggerated bow, holding his arm out to gesture Thomas through the open front door.

Thomas smiled and squeezed past a small congregation of six or seven freshmen standing in the front hall. Dave Kendricks spotted his entrance and motioned to him from across the living room, where he stood with Eileen Dickenson, Monica Dressler, Lynn Montague and Kent Savage.

'The man of the hour has arrived,' Dave announced, handing Thomas a beer. 'Ladies, please wait for him to remove his jacket before ravaging him in your usual manner.'

All three of the females in the group colored slightly and glanced away. At six foot one and 145 pounds, Thomas was lean but well muscled, the confident, agile movements of his body an amalgamation of power and grace. His brown hair, cropped short in anticipation of summer, was just a few shades lighter than the deep tan of his skin, and his green eyes had a calming, almost mesmerizing effect that made them hard to look away from once they'd set themselves upon you. In a way, he was almost too good-looking, and he actually dated far less than some of his physically flawed counterparts, as if prospective girlfriends judged themselves more harshly in his presence, and had not yet developed the self-confidence to push on nonetheless.

'Eileen here was just telling me that she didn't think you'd make it,' Dave advised him. 'Seems the general consensus is that you're too good for the rest of us lowly peasants.'

'I didn't say that,' Eileen protested. She dared a quick glance up at Thomas, then looked away, fiddling with the cup in her hand. 'I didn't say that,' she repeated.

'Well, it was something of the sort.' Dave frowned, his brow wrinkling in concentration. 'I mean, I don't remember your exact words . . .'

'I do,' Kent Savage piped in. 'She said, "You think Thomas'll show up? I can't wait to get him drunk and jump his bones."'

Eileen blushed a deep crimson. 'I *definitely* didn't say that.' She shook her head in irritation and embarrassment. 'I'm out of here,' she told them, and walked off toward the kitchen.

Lynn Montague headed after her, turning back quickly to admonish the two boys. 'You two are such assholes. Do you know that? Like, grow up.'

'*What? What did I say?*' Dave asked, pursuing the

110

girls with a slightly unsteady gait. Kent looked at the two remaining individuals, considering them seriously for a moment. Then his face brightened into a broad smile, the decision made. 'More drinks!' he announced, arms raised triumphantly to either side, and he marched off through the crowd like a man on a mission.

Thomas and Monica watched him go. They were quiet for a moment within their own corner of the room as the din from the party continued unabated.

'I don't think more drinks are the answer,' Thomas commented, placing his own beverage on the fireplace mantel.

Monica stared down into the recesses of her plastic cup. 'She didn't say any of that,' she told him quietly. 'Just so you know.'

'Oh, I make it a practice never to believe anything either one of those intellectual midgets tells me,' Thomas assured her.

Monica nodded, her eyes still focused on her drink.

'So, how's it going in Tulley's class?' Thomas asked. 'Is AP Chemistry as hard as people say?'

'It's not that bad. Mostly balancing equations and knowing how things react with one another.'

'Sounds intimidating to me. My dad wants me to take it next year, but I don't know.'

She looked up at him. 'You're smart. You could do it, no problem.'

'I'm smart enough to get by,' he said, 'but I have to work at my classes. You're brilliant in a way that I'll never be. There's a big difference.'

He smiled down at her, and she reflexively smiled back, then shifted her stance as she tried to think of something self-deprecating to say. Such compliments often made her uncomfortable – especially coming from one of her classmates. Since the first grade, she'd never gotten anything less than an A in her classes. The mere fact that she was now studying college-level material as a sophomore in high school was unlikely to put a dent in that perfect record. She was destined to become valedictorian without even breaking a sweat. But instead of being proud of her abilities, she often imagined them as an algae-covered chain around her neck, holding her at the bottom of the ocean while on the surface her peers enjoyed the ease and social camaraderie of normality. She wondered whether Thomas, with his natural athleticism and broad popularity, ever felt the same. Somehow, she doubted it.

'I'm a good test taker,' she finally replied. 'It's no big deal.'

'No, you're smart. Very smart,' he told her. 'There's nothing wrong with that.'

When she shook her head he placed a hand on her shoulder to emphasize his point. The touch made her feel a little dizzy, and she had to make a deliberate effort to steady her breathing.

'Don't shake your head like what I'm telling you isn't true, Dressler,' he said. 'And never apologize for what you are. The only sane choice is to embrace it.'

She looked up at him, thinking that perhaps he was just making fun of her, but his face was solemn and earnest. 'Is that what *you* do?' she asked.

He studied her for a moment. 'I don't have what you have. But if I did – *hell yes,* I'd embrace it. I mean' – he turned his head to either side to indicate the people milling around them – 'look at these morons. We *all* envy you.'

'Hmmm,' she responded, grinning.

Thomas removed his hand from her shoulder, and she did her best not to ask him to put it back. 'Listen,' he said, 'I've got to go find the man of the house, lest he think I didn't show up to his lame-ass party.'

She nodded, raising the cup to her lips.

'I'll catch you later,' Thomas told her. He turned and maneuvered his way slowly through the crowd in the direction of the kitchen, figuring he'd probably find Devon tending bar or replenishing supplies of ice, beverages and plastic cups for the masses. But when he got there and scanned the room there was no sign of him – although there should've been. People were making an absolute mess of the place. Someone had decided, in fact, to start cooking fajitas. The house reeked of booze, Tabasco sauce and freshly chopped onions.

Thomas moved down the hall and checked Devon's room. The bed was mounded with jackets, but the room was otherwise empty. The door to the adjacent bathroom was shut, and he rapped lightly with his knuckles. 'Yo, Devon. You in there, dude?'

'Room's occupied!' a female voice called back. In a quieter, more soothing tone the same voice was telling someone, 'It's okay, honey. I've got your hair. Go ahead and throw up if you need to.'

Oh, man, Thomas thought, turning around and heading for the kitchen once again. In the hallway, he saw Ernie Samper.

'Hey, Ernie,' he said. 'You seen Devon?'

'What?' Ernie looked a little stoned.

'Devon. You seen him?'

'No, I don' know, man. *You* seen him?'

'If I'd seen him, I wouldn't be asking you now, would I?'

'Oh, that's a good point, man.' It was a small miracle the guy was still standing. Thomas started to move past him down the hall, but Ernie called after him. 'Hey, Thomas. You know, I think he might be out back. I saw him smacking some golf balls or something out there.'

'Finally, some information I can use,' Thomas called back, and proceeded toward the rear of the house.

'Hey, bro!' Ernie hollered after him. 'Grab me a drink while you're back there, would ya?'

Thomas reached the door leading out onto the back porch and stepped outside. In slightly more hospitable conditions, the porch would've been considered prime real estate at a party like this, and therefore full of people. Tonight it had been drizzling intermittently, however, and the uncovered deck was vacant. He looked around briefly and had turned to head back inside when he heard a noise – a cracking sound, like a hammer striking plastic – coming from the backyard below. He walked to the railing and looked down into the yard. Devon was standing in the grass with

114

a golf driver in his hands, the shaft of the club resting against his right shoulder. Scattered at his feet were several balls. Two metal buckets stood half empty beside him. At the sound of Thomas's footsteps on the porch above him, he looked up. 'Tommy boy, is that you?'

'Yeah, it's me. What are you doing?'

'What's it look like?' Devon smiled up at him, shielding his eyes against the glare of the porch light. 'I'm practicing. Grab yourself a club out of the bag there and come hit a few.'

Thomas walked down the short set of steps and joined him on the lawn. His friend's hair was soaked and dripping, and Devon raked it back from his face absently as Thomas selected a driver from the bag, set one of the balls on a tee and lined up his club. The house, prestigiously situated atop the very hill that provided the residents of Overlook Drive that much-coveted overlook experience, gave way to a backyard that sloped sharply down and away. About two hundred yards to the south, the open grass ended where a thick patch of woods began. Thomas pulled the driver up and back, locked his eyes on his target and swung hard. He was much more used to swinging a baseball bat than a golf club, and although his stroke connected soundly, the small white orb sliced wickedly to the left and landed out of sight deep in the spread of trees below them.

'Nice slice, T,' Devon remarked. He removed a tee from his right pocket, planted it into the soft earth, squared his shoulders and swung with the practiced form of someone who may well have spent more than a few nights in this very spot pounding balls deep into his own backyard and the forest beyond. Thomas watched the ball sail through the night sky. It seemed to hang in the darkness for longer than simple physics and the gravitational pull of the earth should allow, and then disappeared into the canopy of foliage, whooshing through leaves and cracking into a few branches along the way. About a half mile south of them, a stretch of Main Street was illuminated in the pale yellow cast of streetlights. The distant buzz of passing motorists ascended the hill and reached their ears like excited children returning from play.

'You ever pound one all the way out to Main Street?' he asked.

'Nah,' Devon said. 'That sucker's about a thousand yards from here. Tiger Woods couldn't hit one out to Main Street from this place. But I do try.'

To illustrate, he set up another ball and smashed it deep into the woods. Thomas hit another one himself, although this time he got on top of the ball a little too much and punched it straight and low along the ground. It hit a tree trunk at the far end of the yard and bounced halfway back to them.

'You need some practice, my friend,' Devon observed.

'Indeed.'

The two of them spent the next fifteen minutes hitting balls into the woods. The rain had stopped, at least for the time being, and the only sounds were the thumping music and laughter coming from the house behind them and the crack of the club heads striking dimpled plastic.

'You know your house is getting totally trashed right now, don't you?' Thomas asked after a while.

Devon only shrugged. 'Wouldn't be a good party unless it did.'

'You ever worry about your neighbors ratting you out to your folks when they return?'

'Hey, it's one of the costs of them going on vacation,' he said. 'My folks know there's gonna be a party while they're gone. Besides, this year I've got a new arrangement with the neighbors.'

'What's that?' Thomas teed up another ball and sliced it deep into the canopy below them. He was getting better at it already – just had to straighten out his swing a little, that was all.

'It's understood that nobody here drives home drunk, and the neighbors pretty much leave us alone – maybe turn the volume on their TV up a little bit tonight if the music gets too loud.'

'Oh yeah? And how do you manage to hold up your end of the bargain?'

'Everyone comes and leaves either on foot or by cab. No exceptions. I presume, by the way, that your cheap ass traveled by foot.'

'I like to walk.'

'Right. Anyway, you know Frank Dashel, who lives four houses down from me?'

'No.'

'Well, he operates a tow truck company. He's got

one of his rigs sitting in his driveway tonight, all set to haul off any miscellaneous parked vehicles within a half-mile radius. Either you park in your own driveway or you get towed tonight. All the neighbors have been duly notified.' He dug into his pocket for another tee. 'Actually, they love the idea.'

'So, you've got your own hired gun.'

'I didn't have to hire him. Towing teenagers' cars is a lucrative endeavor. Nobody wants to get the parents involved, everyone wants their ride back, and best of all, they almost always pay cash.'

'Any guilt about having your friends' cars towed?' Thomas asked.

'Very few people actually get towed,' he said. 'They know the rules. No one drives home drunk, and that way everyone makes it home alive. If they do end up getting towed, it's the direct consequence of a personal choice. I really have nothing to do with it.'

'Your conscience is clean then.'

'It's the only way to go.'

'Any visits from the cops?' he asked.

'Mike Stoddard lives in that ugly blue house across the street. Sheriff's deputy. We also have an understanding.'

'Sounds like you've got it all figured out.' Thomas pegged another grounder across the grass.

'Nice shot, Jack Nicklaus.'

'*Who?*'

Devon shook his head. 'Dude, you're embarrassing yourself.'

'I'm just misunderstood, that's all. Most geniuses are.'

'And a few morons, as well, I've noticed.'

Thomas shook his head. For a while longer, they continued to take turns driving golf balls into the darkness.

'So your parents are pretty cool about you throwing a party like this while they're away?' Thomas asked. He was thinking about his own rather uptight father and how he'd probably have a massive coronary if his son ever invited half of the high school student body to their house for booze and fajitas, the evening culminating in a line of kids puking into the toilet.

'Of course not,' Devon said. 'But honestly, T, what are they gonna do?'

'I don't know. Ground you? Beat you to within an inch of your life?'

Devon shook his head. 'Corporal punishment came to a screeching halt last year when I finally became big enough to fight back – and did.'

'I was only kidding,' Thomas remarked.

'Well, I'm not.' *Thwack!* Devon punched another shot into the evening sky and marked its progress until it disappeared into the vegetation.

'You don't care much for your parents, do you?' Thomas asked.

'No, I don't,' Devon replied.

'Why is that?'

Devon raked his hand through his hair, exhaling slowly. 'The simplest reason, I suppose,' he began, 'is that I no longer respect them.'

Thomas rested his club against one of the porch's support beams and sat down on the steps. 'What do you mean?'

'What I mean,' Devon said, sitting next to him and looking out into the yard, 'is that they have *lost* my respect. Especially my dad. I used to really look up to him, you know? Until I was about thirteen I used to think he was the total bomb. Smart guy, surgeon, hell of a golfer. I used to practically worship the ground he walked on.'

'So, what happened?'

'I guess I just started thinking for myself more. Questioning things. Challenging their point of view – and my own.'

'Yeah, that tends to happen.'

'Right. But you expect the people you admire to listen to you, to entertain the possibility that perhaps there's more than one way to look at the world.'

Thomas shook his head. 'You even discuss this stuff with your parents? Man, I gave up on mine a long time ago.'

'But that's not the way it should be, T,' he said. 'I mean, look at it this way: they've lived a lot longer than we have, right? They know the world is a complex place. So why shouldn't they listen to us when we come to them for guidance, instead of telling us how we *should* be thinking, what we *should* be doing. It seems like the longer they live, the more closed-minded they become. They're *de-evolving*, for Christ's sake, and they want to take us along for the ride.' He used his club to tap mud from the sole of his left shoe. 'We're not looking for an instruction manual on the steps we should be taking to become just like them – that's exactly what we're afraid of. I mean, *don't they get that?*'

'I guess not,' Thomas replied. He was thinking about his own battle with his father earlier that evening – how their relationship had turned into less of a collaborative bond over the years and more of an enforcement of rules and regulations, his father's decree being: *These are the things I am afraid of, and therefore the following restrictions on your life will apply.* 'My mother understands me to some degree, but I don't think my father has any idea who I really am.'

'And once you realize that your parents aren't in a position to help you because they've stopped questioning things a long time ago, then you're pretty much on your own,' Devon continued. 'It's intellectual abandonment. Are you telling me I shouldn't be pissed-off about that?'

Thomas held up a hand. 'Hey, I'm not telling you anything. Except that you sound like you're in serious need of a beer.'

'Nah, I stopped drinking,' Devon said. 'It was making me stupid. There comes a point when it's easier to get drunk than to get mad. That's a dangerous place, T. When it's all you have, it's important to hang on to your anger.'

'Oh yeah? Then why the big party?' Thomas pointed a thumb in the direction of the house full of drunken teenagers directly behind them.

'Oh, that.' Devon cast a dispassionate glance up the steps toward the back door. 'It'll provide a topic of conversation for when my folks get home. I have a responsibility to wake them up if I can. Lord knows I keep trying.'

They sat in silence at the foot of the steps, listening to Axl Rose belting out 'Paradise City' – an oldy-but-goody – from the living room speakers just inside. Devon returned the clubs to the golf bag, clapped his friend on the back, and started up the steps toward the back door. 'Plus,' he said, 'I have to admit I enjoy the background noise.'

Thomas rose from his own seated position and ascended the steps behind him.

Chapter 15

The party started breaking up around 1:30 a.m. Twenty minutes after Devon placed a call to the cab company, a line of checkered taxis were assembled in front of the house. A number of people called their parents for rides home, and the kids who were only *mildly* intoxicated set out on foot. A few people lingered – they always do – but by 2 a.m. most of the crowd had dispersed. Thomas, himself, had set out on foot around 1:45. He had a long walk and needed to save some of his energy for shimmying back up the rope into his bedroom.

Bret Graham bid good night to Cynthia Castleberry. Her hand touched his arm one last time, and he placed a delicate kiss on her right cheek. 'Call me,' he said, placing a slip of paper with his phone number into her soft palm, and he thought this time she would.

Devon, who was ready for the place to clear out,

began cleaning up the kitchen. That was enough to make even the die-hard partiers realize the time had come for them to go. The art of attending a good party, of course, was to linger right up until the cleanup begins, and then to get the hell out of there before you wound up with a garbage bag in your hands. There was a fine line between being part of the problem and being part of the solution, and it was important to determine which side of the line you wanted to end up on at 2 a.m. Most people picked the former.

Brian Fowler and Monica Dressler were among the last people to set out on foot for home. They exited the community, turned right and continued along Powells Lane to the north, talking and joking about the party. Ernie Samper had been totally shit-faced by the end of the evening and wound up giving a fairly decent reenactment of Jim Carrey's karaoke performance of 'Somebody to Love' from *The Cable Guy*. Toward the end of the song, Ernie had been pelted in the side of the head with a spinach-dip-laden cracker, which had started a brief but rather messy food fight. Around that time, Devon had started calling for the cabs.

'*Don't yoou want somebody to loovvve?*' Monica now sang, as Brian gesticulated spastically to the imaginary music.

'Yeah, baby. Summer of luuuvvvv!' he proclaimed into the night. Somewhere nearby, a dog began to howl, which sent them both pealing off into laughter.

'Watch out for that spinach dip,' Monica warned.

'Incoming!' Brian yelled. He ducked his head and ran forward along the street, crouched at the waist. Monica laughed. The sound came out as a powerful snort, and she covered her mouth with her hands.

'Captain Pig at six o'clock, Commander!' Brian snapped to attention, saluting an imaginary officer.

'Shut up,' Monica admonished him, trying to sound stern. She couldn't hold it together, though, and another snort escaped her.

'The swine approaches, Commander!' Brian said. 'Shall we deploy the slop-guns?'

'You'd better shut up, Fowler,' she said, and this time he did. One shouldn't call a girl a pig more than twice, even in jest. At sixteen, he didn't know much about women, but he did know that. He waited for her to catch up.

To change the subject, he said: 'Hey, have you gotten started on your paper for Ms Bradford's class, yet?' They shared English together and had a book report due next Thursday. Brian hadn't begun yet, and if his usual and customary strategy was to be followed, he probably wouldn't begin the project until late Wednesday evening. *An Incredibly Insightful and Comprehensively Developed Book Report on J. D. Salinger's Catcher in the Rye,* he planned to call it – or something of the sort. He paused for a moment: *Catcher in the Rye?* Or was it *The Catcher in the Rye?* He couldn't remember, but a small detail like that might sink him if he wasn't careful. He'd make that his first research question.

'. . . tomorrow.'

'What was that?' he asked.

'I said I've already put together an outline. I'm planning on working on the report tomorrow.'

Brian was impressed. 'You made an outline?'

'Yes, of course,' she said. 'It's part of the process. It helps me organize my thoughts. How do *you* write a paper?'

Wow, he thought. *Girls are so weird.* Nevertheless, he considered her question carefully for a moment. Develop a process? Organize your thoughts? That sounded like a lot of work. It might even take more than one night to complete. Maybe even *several*! No, no – that wasn't for him. 'How do *you* write a paper?' she'd asked. The answer had always seemed so obvious to him.

'I just fuel up on Mountain Dew and Reese's Peanut Butter Cups,' he responded seriously, to which Monica smiled, shaking her head.

They crossed the bridge over Route 22 on foot and followed the road to the left onto Ross Ridge Road. Here the lane cut through heavy foliage, and trees hugged the pavement closely on both sides. Three hundred yards ahead, a black mailbox stood sentry at the entrance to a dirt driveway leading to Brian's house. They stopped here for a few more minutes to talk, then Brian proceeded down the driveway and Monica continued on along Ross Ridge. Her family lived in a cluster of homes off Bluck Drive, less than a half mile ahead.

She walked along, listening to the soft sound of her tennis shoes slapping and scuffing themselves across the wet asphalt. She thought of the party, of the swarm of teenagers spilling out onto the front lawn at the end of the night, of the sense of isolation she sometimes experienced even while among her friends, of the feel of Thomas's hand on her shoulder and the way her heartbeat had accelerated at his touch. The rain had stopped falling at least an hour ago, and the sky had cleared, revealing the depth of space above her. She looked up into the heavens, realizing that what she was seeing were not the stars themselves exactly, but merely the arrival of light from those celestial bodies after a long journey through time and space. The vastness of that distance made the light of her own brief existence seem almost inconsequential.

She stopped walking in order to push herself up onto her tiptoes and stretch her arms out toward the sky, watching the shimmer of starlight as it played through her fingers like tiny grains of sand. That was when she heard a step. One single step, and then nothing.

She listened.

Silence played out as if it had something to hide.

A single step that had not been her own. It had been faint, but she'd heard it. She stood there quietly, listening now more intently to the night sounds all around her.

She was cautious now, holding her emotions at bay. She did not run. She did not look around. She pretended that she hadn't heard, and began to walk again – just a little faster. Up ahead, she could see light cresting the hill, and she knew that on the far side of that hill was the community in which she lived. It lay maybe two hundred yards ahead. It was a tangible thing.

She stopped again, quickly. This time there were two steps before the silence. She heard them distinctly. *Step-step*. Silence.

She stood there in the middle of the street and tried to think. She told herself to remain calm. But all she could think about was the sound of those stealthy footsteps – *step-step*, silence – and what it meant. Someone was following her. Stalking her. They didn't want to be heard, but they were taking two steps for her one, trying to close the distance.

Should I run?

She could feel the adrenaline pumping through her, but her legs felt wobbly and she didn't trust them to do what needed to be done.

Should I scream?

It was almost 3 a.m., and the night was very quiet. Her scream would be heard. But how much time would pass before help arrived? Five, maybe ten minutes? That would be too late. And if she screamed now, she thought that whoever was following her would waste no time in trying to overtake her. In a way, she would be beckoning him to either cut loose or finish the job. Some primitive instinct told her that he would not cut loose. Not now. He was too close. She could feel it.

Step-step, silence.

There it was again. But where was it coming from?

She glanced behind herself into the darkness, along the route she had just traveled. The road seemed to disappear into the forest on either side, as if it were being swallowed whole. She could see perhaps sixty feet in that direction. Beyond that was blackness. She looked at the trees to her left and right – tried to look past them into the shadows – but the foliage was thick here and it was impossible to see beyond the edge of the woods. Besides, the footsteps were not coming from the woods; she was certain of that. The sound they had made was flat and crisp, like the sound of her own footsteps on the asphalt. Whoever accompanied her tonight was either lurking in the shadows of the road behind her, or . . .

Step-step-step. Again, silence.

Her follower seemed less concerned now about being heard, which meant it wasn't crucial for him to close the distance unnoticed. Because he had her now. He was close enough. And even if she ran, he must feel certain that he could overtake her. But the crest of the hill was so close now: a hundred yards, if that. Maybe he was underestimating her. She could run fast if she needed to. She knew she could. Her legs no longer felt wobbly and untrustworthy; they felt strong and prepared for whatever was to come next. But it was either now or never. She had a choice to make. If she faltered, it might be too late. She paused only long enough to draw in a deep breath and set her sights on the horizon the road ahead of her made as it topped the small hill. If she could reach that, she would stand a good chance of making it the rest of the way. She could hear the drum of her heartbeat strong and steady as it coursed through the frame of her young body. *I am strong. I can do this,* she thought to herself. Then she ran.

She ran with a dogged intensity of purpose – her legs pumping up and down, propelling her forward with all the force she could muster. She covered half of the remaining distance between her initial position and the top of the hill in perhaps eight seconds. She listened as she ran, anticipating the sound of pursuit, but behind her there was only silence. She had time to think that perhaps there was no one there at all, that the footsteps she'd heard had been nothing more than the product of an overactive imagination combined with a touch of alcohol. The image of her hauling ass up the hill at top speed, running only from her own imagination, made her feel stupid and more than a little embarrassed. She allowed herself to slow slightly, listening more intently for any more footsteps except her own. There were none. She stopped and looked back. Most of the road was still shrouded in shadows. Nothing moved or uttered a sound. Even the insects had been startled into silence by her unexpected fifty-yard dash. She placed her hands on her hips, breathing heavily, and she let out an uneasy laugh. *I'm such a moron,* she thought.

Then she heard it again: footsteps, coming quickly – running this time! They grew distinctly louder, and still she could detect no movement along the roadway behind her. *Doesn't matter,* she told herself. *Get the hell out of here!* She once again turned to run.

That was when he crested the hill ahead of her, blocking off her only route of escape – her only plan. The distance between them was only fifty yards, and he closed it quickly. To her credit, she wasted no time, for there was really none to waste. She followed the only course of action that occurred to her, as she turned left and barreled into the woods like a panicked animal. The branches slashed at her face and the bramble tore through the legs of her pants, leaving thin red marks on her ankles. She cut a jagged path through the scrub, trying desperately to lose him.

For a moment, the tactic seemed to be working, for she could hear him floundering behind her as he tried to push his way through the thorny undergrowth. A single thought raced around in circles inside her head as if it were a dog on a track: *If I can put some distance between us, I can find a place to hide! I can lie low and quiet in the darkness! Cover myself with leaves! He'll run right by me! If I can put some distance between us, I can find a place to hide – lie low and quiet in the darkness! Cover myself with leaves! He'll run right by me! Low and quiet . . . cover myself with leaves . . . distance between us . . . run right by me . . .*

As she ran, her breath slid in and out of her chest in terrified, ragged waves. Her legs shot out into the night, feet scrambling for purchase on the wet leaves and uneven terrain.

(. . . a place to hide . . . low and quiet in the darkness . . . run right by me . . .)

And she could make it! She could!! Just a little more distance was all she needed. *But where was he?!*

She might have made it if she hadn't looked back – if she'd concentrated only on what was ahead of her. But she simply couldn't help it. Not knowing whether he was gaining on her or whether she had lost him already was more than her panicked mind could cope with. And so she turned her head quickly to look, saw that he was still behind her – *much closer than she'd hoped!* – and the vision of him barreling through the woods after her sent a jolt of extra adrenaline into her bloodstream like a white-hot bullet. She spun her head around and shot forward, propelling herself over a fallen log, her sneakered feet barely touching the ground. But the act of glancing behind her had momentarily taken her eyes off what was in front of her and, as her left foot touched the earth, she ran directly into a stiff, leafless branch that jutted out at her at neck level.

She took the limb in the throat – its broken, slightly blunted end catching her directly in the windpipe. She heard the sound of her own teeth clicking neatly shut, as if she'd just chomped into a crisp stick of celery, and for a full second the world became completely hushed around her. The muffled slug of her heart beat twice in her ears, and she had time to wonder – *even then* – whether he was still there, tearing through the brush directly behind her. Then the pain in her throat rose up to meet her like magma erupting from the earth. She tried to draw in a breath but found that she was incapable even of that, and she fell gracelessly to her knees as if her lower legs had disintegrated in mid-stride. Her outstretched hands met the soft earth as she pitched forward, and a moment later she was crawling along a floor of muck and leaves and thorny brush that clawed at her face, arms and legs. All at once, her breath returned. She greedily sucked in air through her bruised windpipe, emitting a high-pitched whooping noise that sounded to her like a scream in reverse. She drew in another breath and another, each accompanied by that same eerie shriek. She was no longer able to control the ragged, terrified sobs that poured forth from her body like heavily bleeding wounds. She refused to look back this time, and when the pressure of his foot pressed down on her left ankle, she kicked out blindly with her right leg, striking him high in the thigh – but not quite high enough. She tried to scream, but the sound that escaped her was small and without hope.

'Shhh,' he whispered. 'It'll be over soon.'

And then he was upon her.

Chapter 16

Sam Garston was polishing off a second helping of Carla's blueberry pancakes when the phone rang, disturbing them from their usual Sunday breakfast. He looked up at the clock, which read 8:14 a.m. His wife, who was seated closer to the phone, rose from her chair to answer it.

'Hello?' she said. Sam watched her closely from where he sat. Sunday morning phone calls were typically either one of Carla's friends or the Jefferson County Sheriff's Department dispatcher contacting him regarding some matter that required his immediate attention. He always hoped for the former, but frequently ended up with the latter.

'Oh. Hi, Carl,' she greeted the caller. 'How are you? . . . Yes, we're just finishing up breakfast. You're welcome to stop over if you'd like . . . Oh, I see . . . No, that's quite all right. He's right here. Hold on just a moment.' She cupped her hand over the mouthpiece and turned to him. 'It's Carl Schroeder.'

Sam had already gotten up from his chair and was making his way across the kitchen. He planted a kiss on Carla's cheek, took the receiver and walked around the corner into the living room. He drew back the curtain to improve the light in the room, but the day outside was overcast and rainy, and the change was modest at best. 'Yeah, Carl. What's up?'

'There's been another attack, Sam,' Schroeder's voice advised him over the slight static of a cell phone. 'Sixteen-year-old female this time.'

Sam's body stiffened and he placed his large left hand on the window ledge. '*Damn it,*' he said. 'Where?'

'North of town, along Ross Ridge Road.'

'You have the area cordoned off?'

'Of course.'

'Fine. I'll be there in twenty minutes. Go ahead and contact the medical examiner.'

'Well, that's the thing,' Carl replied. 'We may not need him just yet.'

Sam had already moved to the bedroom, and was pulling his uniform shirt off a hanger. 'What do you mean?' he asked.

'The victim,' Carl said, and this time there was no static over the line to garble the connection. 'Sam, she's alive.'

Chapter 17

Martin Vance shifted in his chair, turning his head briefly to eye some of the other patients in Trinity Medical Center's psychiatric unit. He glanced again at the metal sprinkler head projecting from a small hole in the ceiling directly above him. He didn't like the looks of it. No, sir, Scooby-Doo-in-a-half-shoe – he didn't like the looks of it at all. This was a real amateur job, of course. He could tell *that* right from the start. Could see the actual flip-floppin' microphone up there – see it plain as day. He knew what they were doing, too. He'd been through it all before. When you knew the sort of things that he knew, when you had connections right out of Liberia and the Far East on a mainline receiver into your geranium cranium at 538 bits per second – well then, everyone had their ear to the grand ol' wall, Paul. Not that it mattered. Not in the least. If they thought he was just gonna spill his guts for a little Geodon, a little Haldol truth serum in the form of one big hummer of a syringe . . . well, they had no idea who they were actually dealing with, did they? He'd seen this type of action before – in a thousand other disease-infested rat pits far worse than this mojo dime-bag. And he hadn't talked then. Hadn't told them a *damn thing*.

'Mr Vance?'

Tight as a clam, he was – *never* get the pearl!

'Martin?'

He glanced over at the woman sitting across from him. Ms Queen Mojo Dime-Bag, herself. Little Miss Harley-Davidson on the Seroquel Express.

'Martin, I see that you've been looking at the overhead sprinkler quite a bit during our session today. Does it bother you?'

He said nothing. It was best to just keep your mouth shut during the interrogations. He'd learned that much. Learned it the hard way. Let 'em play out their own string until they hung themselves with it, for all he cared.

He checked the corners of the room for traps, but didn't see any. That was the worst kind, anyway – the ones you couldn't see until it was too late. You step into one of those zombies and you'll be cleanin' up your own body shrapnel till next Easter.

'Would you prefer to sit somewhere else, Martin?'

Stupid sling-blade witch doctor talkin' at him again. Which doctor? Witch doctor. *Ha!* That was a good one. Funny but it ain't, as people like to say. Chief Interrogator Numero Uno. She'd been on his case since they'd dragged him in here yesterday afternoon.

Black as night in the heart of darkness, that one. She'd cut him down to pieces in a second if she had any idea the sort of technical intel he was carryin' around in his long-term memory. Enough to topple the balance of power, that was for sure.

'Yeah, any electric chair will do, right, doc?' he said. Let her chew that over for a while.

'I assure you that you're in a safe place,' she replied. 'Nothing in this room is designed to hurt you.'

He scoffed at the remark. Check the traps, baby. Check the traps.

'You don't believe me?'

'It's not what it's *designed* to do – it's what it *can* do. Isn't that what they teach you in that military boot camp of yours? What if Mother Goose never came home? That's the thick of it. Funny but it ain't.' He glanced up at the microphone above him. It was capturin' every flip-floppin' word. *Man,* he had to be more careful with what he said. He couldn't chance a slip-up. They'd be all over him. 'You get those sektars off my back and maybe we can talk.'

'You've used that word before: *sektars.* I'm not familiar with that term.'

'Well, you should *get* familiar with it, tipsy-top. You and the goon squad, both.'

'Can you explain what it means?'

'Not if I wanna stay alive in this rat pit. Place is crawlin' with 'em. Flip-floppin' sektar parade last night. Couldn't sleep a wink if I wanted to.'

'We can talk about strategies to improve your sleep,

138

or I can ask the nurse to give you something in the evening to help you rest at night.'

'I'll bet you could. You'd like that, wouldn't you?'

'I'd like for you to feel better, yes. I think that the medications will help. Maybe we could start with just one.'

'And I'll be up to eight H-bombs by the end of the week, with my brains oozin' outta my ears. No thanks, Dr Frankenstein.' He checked the corners again – thought he saw one. Just a glint of metal razor that was gone by the time the eyes focused completely.

'I respect your concerns, Martin. But I really am here to help you. Many of the thoughts you're having are symptoms of a disease called bipolar disorder with psychotic features. The medications I'm recommending are designed to help improve those symptoms. That's the goal.'

'Yeah? Well, you can kiss the bird with those word turds, you psychological nerd. *This meeting's over!*' Martin Vance leapt up from his chair, which toppled backward, striking the floor with a reverberating bang. Dr Subina Edusei was on her feet almost as quickly, positioning her own chair between herself and the patient. Two of the psychiatric unit's techs exited the nurses' station in a hurry and were three-quarters of the way across the room before Subina held up her hand for them to stand by a moment.

'Settle down, Martin. This is a safe place for you.'

Martin frowned. 'No-no-no-no-no-no-no.'

'I'd like you to walk over to the other side of the room now. We can talk more later if you want.'

'I don't *want* none of your magic beans,' he advised her, shoving his fallen chair with his foot and storming off toward the far wall. The few patients who'd briefly turned their heads to watch the standoff quickly lost interest as Subina left the common area through the locked doors leading to the nurses' station.

'You okay?' Tania Renkin – one of her favorite nurses – asked, meeting her at the door.

'I'm fine,' Subina said. She sat down at the desk and began entering a note in the chart. 'Martin's a little riled up this morning.'

'You want him to receive anything else?' Tania asked. 'He got ten milligrams of Zyprexa IM early this morning. I don't think it's touched him.'

'See if you can get him to take a Zydis ODT.'

'If he refuses?'

Subina shrugged. 'Show him the needle, and tell him that's his next option. See if that changes his mind about taking the oral medication.'

'It often does,' Tania agreed. She looked out through the thick glass partition into the common area. Martin was pacing at the far end of the room, muttering to himself. 'Martin doesn't scare me. I've taken care of him before.'

'So have I,' Subina replied. 'About four months ago, in fact.'

'When he's taking his medication, he's actually quite pleasant.'

'Yeah. He'd definitely pass the bus stop test.'

Tania smiled. 'The bus stop test; if you encounter

140

a person at a bus stop and don't think to yourself, *Hey, this guy's crazy . . .*'

'. . . then they pass,' Subina finished.

'It's amazing how many mentally ill people can pass the bus stop test. I wonder,' she mused, 'out of all the people we come in contact with in our daily lives, what percentage do you think are psychologically unstable?'

'If you knew the answer to that question,' Subina said, returning the patient's file to the rack, 'you'd probably never leave your house.'

'Right.' The two of them watched Martin as he continued to pace the room. 'By the way' – Tania pointed a thumb toward the security monitor behind them – 'have you had a chance to see the guy in Seclusion Room Two yet?'

'I looked in on him this morning when I got here. What's his story?'

'Don't know.' Tania shook her head. 'He presented to the ER last night, ranting and raving, covered in scratches, obviously psychotic, unable to provide any useful information. The ER doc gave him five of Haldol and two of Ativan, and he got medicated with Geodon and Vistaril before we brought him over.'

'How did he respond?'

'Not well. It still took four security guards to get him into that room. He almost bit one of them.'

Subina studied the monitor. The man inside the seclusion room looked like a human wrecking ball: probably six foot four and pushing 250 pounds, most of it muscle. He'd removed his hospital clothing, revealing a crisscross of superficial scratches that covered the dark black skin of much of his torso and extremities. As she watched, he walked to the padded door and punched it hard. The muffled sound of the impact reached their ears a moment later.

'Do we have a name?'

'Not yet. He's not someone we've seen here before.'

'Well, he's going to need more medication – but right now I think the safest course of action is to just let him be.' Subina opened the door to the hallway leading back to her office. 'I need to make a phone call before rounds. I'll see you in the conference room in a few minutes.'

'Okay,' Tania replied as she entered her ID number into the automated medication delivery unit in the corner. 'Let's see if Martin will take his Zydis. We've got to get him looking good. In a couple of days, he might have a bus to catch.'

Chapter 18

The usually vacant stretch of asphalt along Ross Ridge Road just north of Route 22 was presently flanked with vehicles positioned closely together along both shoulders of the roadway. Police cruisers composed the majority of parked cars, but an Action 7 News truck was also already on-site and two men were unloading camera equipment from the rear of the vehicle. *Perfect,* Sam thought, pulling over onto the soft shoulder. He killed the ignition, popped the trunk, and stepped out of the car. Down the street near the parked news van, he could see Diane Sellars making her way quickly toward him, camera crew in tow. Sam whistled to Tony Linwood, who stood nearby directing the occasional passing vehicle. 'Tony,' he called over, 'I do not wish to be interviewed by Ms Sellars right now.'

'Okay, Chief,' the young deputy said with a nod, then headed off to intercept them.

Sam walked around to the back of his car. He retrieved a rain jacket from the trunk and donned it against the midday drizzle, which would steadily work its way to a respectable downpour before the afternoon was through. He crossed the street to join a small cluster of officers standing in a loose-knit circle in the wet grass. 'Hey, Chief,' one of them said in greeting as he approached. The others turned.

Sam nodded. 'Hello, Mike.' He regarded the yellow DO NOT CROSS police tape stretched along the edge of the woods for about a hundred yards. At the far ends, it turned a right angle perpendicular to the roadway and headed straight back into the forest. 'Where's Detective Schroeder?' he asked.

'Right here, Chief,' Carl announced from thirty yards away, walking toward them. He'd been canvassing the road slightly to the north, covering the area from where the police tape ended to a small cluster of houses just over the rise of the next hill. As he approached, he held up a Ziploc bag containing the tattered remains of a few small white cylinders. 'Cigarettes,' he said. 'Four of them, lying in the grass just on the other side of the hill. Pretty soggy and mashed to hell from the rain last night, but definitely worth a look.'

'Good,' Sam commented. He nodded at one of the officers. 'I want that area cordoned off as well – and have the forensic guys examine the ground for shoe prints and anything else they can come up with.'

'Sure thing,' the deputy said, grabbing the police

tape and a few stakes from the back of his car and heading off in that direction.

Sam turned to Carl. 'What've you got so far?'

Carl pointed to a spot where the road's asphalt met the shoulder. 'She was discovered here.'

The grass in this area was matted down, and in a few places tufts had been pulled from the wet earth. The rain was doing its best to wash the area clean, but Sam could see what he presumed to be bloodstains in several areas. It didn't take much of an imagination for him to picture the girl lying there weak and exhausted, having pulled herself hand over hand from the dark recesses of the woods. 'Where was she attacked?' he asked.

'It looks like most of the struggle occurred at a spot about two hundred and fifty yards in,' Carl said. 'Lots of broken branches and a fair amount of blood.'

'We need to get a canopy up in that area,' Sam said. 'And one here, too. Get these areas protected from the rain as much as possible while there's still any evidence left worth collecting.'

Carl motioned to one of the deputies standing behind them, who nodded and went to his vehicle.

'Who found her?' Sam asked, studying the woods.

'A motorist on her way to work came across the victim at 6:45 a.m. We got the 911 call at 6:48.'

'You've interviewed her?'

'Yeah. The lady's a nurse at Trinity Medical Center, and was heading in for a 7 a.m. shift. She says she assessed the victim's injuries and rendered what aid she could before placing the call to 911. Said the girl was unconscious, and that her breathing was so slow and shallow that at first the nurse thought she was dead. Fortunately, she checked for a pulse.'

Sam nodded. 'Where's the victim now?'

'They took her to Children's Hospital of Pittsburgh.'

'Why not take her to Trinity? It can't be more than a ten-minute drive from here.'

Carl shook his head. 'Trinity's not a trauma center. The girl's injuries were . . . severe.'

Sam's eyes met the detective's. 'How severe?'

At first, Carl didn't answer. The precipitation falling from the sky was really beginning to pick up now, and large drops of water congregated on the edge of his hood before cascading the remaining several feet toward the pavement. He looked down at the grass in front them, imagining what it must've been like for the girl as she crawled all that distance through these woods after the attack, as she lay here in the darkness staring up at the rain. 'I don't know,' he said finally. 'She might not survive.'

The chief considered this for a moment. Behind him, the forensics van arrived and pulled to a stop on the opposite side of the street. Sam glanced over his shoulder as the two technicians emerged from the vehicle, then he turned back to Detective Schroeder. 'Let them know what we've found so far,' he ordered. 'Then come with me.'

'Where are we going?' the detective asked.

'Pittsburgh,' Sam called back, making his way toward the car. 'I want to go see her.'

Chapter 19

Pittsburgh's Lawrenceville neighborhood lies along the southeast bank of the Allegheny River. When approached from the Fortieth Street Bridge in the late afternoon, the sun, low in the west, deepens the redbrick exterior of the neighborhood's buildings to the color of bloodred clay, as if the river's soil were giving birth to the edifices themselves. Behind them rises the massive structure of Children's Hospital of Pittsburgh, serving the area's youngest, most vulnerable citizens.

'Wow. It's huge, Dad,' Joel Stevenson exclaimed from the front passenger seat, his freckled face squinting upward as the Honda turned left on Forty-Fourth Street and came to a momentary halt in front of the hospital.

Ben smiled at his son's awed exuberance. *It doesn't take much to impress an eight-year-old,* he thought. Joel had complained of being bored for most of the hour-long ride from Wintersville, and Ben had been second-guessing his decision to bring him along. Now he was glad to have him here. He'd needed the company, and the boy's incessant chatter had kept Ben's mind from lingering on the horridness of what he'd been summoned here to witness.

He turned right at the next intersection and entered the mid-campus garage. They wound their way up several tiers and Ben nosed the Honda into an available spot. He'd received the call from Sam Garston at about 3:30 p.m. this afternoon. The girl had been in surgery for most of the morning and early afternoon. She'd sustained multiple life-threatening injuries and had briefly gone into cardiac arrest twice in the OR, but had managed to make it out of the operating room alive and was now listed in critical condition in the hospital's pediatric ICU. *Could Ben come up and speak with the trauma surgeons?* Sam had asked. *Maybe take a look at some of the wounds to compare them with those from the first victim?*

Ben and Joel descended the garage's stairwell, then took the enclosed walkway to the hospital's first-floor information desk. After a brief consultation with the volunteer at the desk, they received visitor ID badges and were directed to the pediatric ICU waiting room, where they found Chief Garston and two detectives conversing quietly with a man and woman whom Sam introduced as the girl's parents.

'This is Paul and Vera Dressler,' he informed Ben. He turned to the couple. 'Dr Stevenson has been assisting us with the investigation.'

Ben recognized Paul Dressler from a golf tournament they'd played in together a few years back. The man's arm was wrapped protectively around the shoulder of his wife, who stood among them but looked at no one. Her right hand was clapped tightly across her mouth, as if ready to stifle a scream that threatened to erupt at any moment. Her gaze fixed itself on the front of Ben's jacket as he stepped forward, offering his hand. 'I'm so sorry this happened,' Ben heard himself saying. 'If there's anything I can do . . .'

The woman made a small, indecipherable sound. Her husband nodded his head slightly in appreciation of Ben's condolences.

Sam gestured toward the man standing to his left. 'You know Detective Schroeder.'

'Yes,' Ben said, shaking hands.

'And I don't believe you've met Detective Danny Hunt,' Sam continued. 'I've assigned him to assist us on the case.'

Ben shook the young man's outstretched hand, as well. 'Detective.'

Danny nodded. Compared to the rest of the men, he appeared young and baby-faced, as if daily shaving had not yet become a necessary component of his morning ritual. With his button-down brown shirt and beige sport jacket, he looked relaxed and almost casual. But beneath the parted cascade of his light blond hair his eyes were sharp and intelligent, flitting from one face to the next and missing nothing in between.

They were silent for a moment before Sam turned to Ben. 'The Dresslers would like to return to their daughter as soon as possible. I told them it might help our investigation if you had a chance to look at some of the injuries. They've kindly agreed to give us a few minutes to do that, and have consented for some photographs to be taken.'

Ben nodded. He looked down at Joel. 'I'd like for you to wait out here for us, son. We shouldn't be more than about fifteen minutes.'

'We'll keep an eye on him,' Paul assured him.

'I appreciate that,' Ben said, and he headed through the large double doors with Sam and the two detectives.

The pediatric ICU, Ben noted as they stepped inside, was more tranquil than he recalled. His time as a medical student and resident in such settings had been one of frenzied data gathering, countless procedures, extensive documentation and protracted bedside discussions. It had been a whirlwind of endotracheal tubes and central lines, of ventilators and IV pumps – a seamless blur of medical histories and physical exam findings amid weeks of sleepless nights, as the pager attached to his belt beeped endlessly with its voracious, intractable demands. By comparison, the unit this afternoon seemed hushed, almost silent, as if the patients around them struggled to live or die on their own private battlegrounds, far removed from this physical place in which they lay.

Sam led them toward a room in the far corner. Its sliding glass door stood open, and as they approached a technician maneuvered a large portable motor-driven X-ray machine from the room with surprising grace. He smiled politely at the four of them before steering the contraption down an adjacent hallway. Ben and the officers exchanged glances and then proceeded into the room.

Inside, a young girl lay supine on a gurney. A thin blue hospital gown covered her chest, shoulders, and abdomen, her long black hair disappearing beneath the upper ridge of her torso. The remainder of her small frame was obscured beneath the crisp white linen. She lay motionless, except for the slight rise and fall of her chest in step with the measured mechanical pace of the ventilator. A plastic breathing tube protruded from between her pale, cracked lips, and numerous medication lines hung from an assortment of IV pumps attached to two metal poles at the head of her bed. From beneath the gown, an additional two large plastic tubes emerged, one on each side of her body, and descended into multichambered canisters, which bubbled softly. A bulky dressing covered her right ear.

Sam and the two detectives stood near the wall at the foot of the bed. None of them spoke, and the officers now seemed hesitant, as if waiting for something to happen. It took Ben a moment to recognize that they were waiting for him. To these men, this was a foreign place about which they had little understanding, and the young woman lying unconscious in the bed in front of them – held together by a bewildering assortment of tubes and instruments that doggedly sustained her tenuous existence – was an inexplicable enigma. He could sense their tension, their careful restraint, as if the slightest action might inadvertently tip the scales of recovery against her, as if her broken body might suddenly disintegrate and scatter like ash in the wind. This was *his* world, he realized, or at least it had been at one time in his training. They had asked him to come here to examine her injuries, yes – but they also needed him as a liaison to orient them to what they were seeing and its significance, to broker this space between those who would live and those who would die, and to tell them in which direction to go from here.

He was about to speak when a female voice behind them interrupted the silence.

'Hard to believe she made it.'

They simultaneously turned to encounter a woman in her mid-thirties dressed in blue scrubs and a white lab coat. Her dark hair was slightly disheveled, as if she'd been wearing a cap for most of the day. A stethoscope had been tucked into a side pocket of her lab coat, its earpieces peeking curiously out at them. The clogs she wore on her feet were enveloped by thin blue shoe covers, and there was a large orange stain – Betadine, Ben presumed – on the front of her left pant leg. A single black pen poked out from the front pocket of her lab coat above a hospital ID badge that dangled from a small metal clasp. She thrust out a hand in Ben's direction.

'Karen Elliot,' she announced. 'I've been in the OR with Ms Dressler for a good part of the morning.'

Ben shook hands with the surgeon. Her skin was cool and dry, her grip firm and assertive. He introduced himself, Sam, and the two detectives. 'The case is being investigated as an attempted homicide,' he explained. 'We've received the parents' consent to examine her injuries . . . if it's okay with you, that is.'

'If her parents are fine with it, then so am I,' the physician replied. She stepped to the bedside, retrieved the stethoscope from the pocket of her lab coat and listened to the girl's chest for a moment. She wound the stethoscope into a loose circle, returned it to her pocket, then pulled an otoscope light from its resting place on the wall. As they watched, she pulled back the girl's upper eyelids to shine the light into first one pupil and then the other, noting the response. The otoscope was returned to its wall mount, and the surgeon bent down on one knee to examine the plastic chambered canister to which each of the tubes exiting the girl's chest was attached.

'Could you tell us about her injuries?' Ben inquired.

Dr Elliot lifted the girl's hospital gown to expose her abdomen. The skin along a midline surgical incision site had been left open, the wound packed with gauze. Ben spotted three Jackson-Pratt drains exiting the skin from other areas of the abdomen, their small chambers partially filled with a thin reddish fluid.

'Jesus,' muttered Detective Schroeder. 'You haven't even stitched her up yet.'

'There's no point in it,' the surgeon replied, her

eyes remaining on the patient. 'The first surgery in cases like this is strictly damage control. Get in, do what needs to be done, and get out. The liver and small bowel were lacerated in several places. The spleen was bleeding so badly it had to be removed. The left kidney also took a hit,' she said, pointing to a urine reservoir bag hanging on the side of the bed. Like the fluid in the abdominal drains, the urine had taken on a bloodied maroon color. 'Anyway,' Dr Elliot concluded, 'we'll have to go back in at least once more to take a look at things – to make certain the bleeding from the liver is under control, to take another look at the bowel anastomoses, and to be sure nothing else was missed. So there's no point in closing the abdomen yet.'

Ben nodded. 'What other injuries did she sustain?'

'You name it, she's got it,' she said. 'Bilateral hemo-pneumothoraces, a small right ventricular puncture wound through the pericardium that I have no idea how she survived, multiple small bowel injuries, a grade III liver laceration, grade IV splenic injury requiring splenectomy, left renal laceration, facial bone fractures, tracheal contusion, a left ankle disloc-ation and medial malleolar fracture that was reduced in the OR, multiple soft-tissue avulsion injuries and traumatic amputations of two fingers on the left hand.' She sighed, brushing the hair back from her patient's forehead. 'Most of her right ear is missing. Whoever did this did not intend for her to live.'

'How's her brain?' Ben asked. 'Any intracranial injuries?'

154

The doctor shook her head. 'That's one thing her assailant didn't get around to. She's pharmacologically sedated now, but provided her blood pressure holds and she survives these other injuries, I have no reason to believe she won't wake up once she's weaned off the sedative agents.'

'When will that be?' Ben asked.

'Don't know yet,' she said, glancing at the green digital display of the machine monitoring the patient's vital signs. 'She's still hypotensive, despite the vasopressors. A thousand things could happen between now and then. She could go into DIC, and I'm worried about that liver.'

They were quiet for a moment. Then Ben said, 'Well, thank you for your time, Dr Elliot, and for everything you've done for her so far. If it's okay with you, I'd like to take a few photographs of the injuries. We shouldn't be long.'

'Take all the time you need,' she said. 'This poor girl . . .' She trailed off, her face becoming pinched and hard. She turned away from them for a moment, studying the monitor, one hand on her patient's shoulder. Her fingers touched the thin plastic tubing of the central line that descended from an IV pump before it entered the girl's body just beneath the right clavicle. The surgeon exhaled slowly, then her posture straightened as she turned to face them. 'Take all the time you need,' she said again, and she strode quickly from the room and disappeared through the swinging double doors at the end of the hallway.

Chapter 20

'The patient is a Caucasian female, age sixteen, identified by family as Monica Dressler. At the request of the Jefferson County Sheriff's Department and after consent from the patient's parents, this examination is being performed at Children's Hospital of Pittsburgh, where the patient is being treated for her injuries. The patient is currently intubated and on a ventilator, and she is pharmacologically sedated. She has a right subclavian central line, bilateral chest tubes, an open abdominal compartment following recent exploratory laparotomy, three abdominal J-P drains and a Foley catheter in place. Bulky dressings have been applied to the left hand following traumatic amputations to the fourth and fifth digits . . .

'. . . contusions to the face and anterior neck consistent with blunt trauma . . .

'. . . bandaging to the site of the right ear, which

was severed during the assault and was discovered at the crime scene by Jefferson County forensic . . .

'. . . large avulsion injury to the region of the left deltoid, and similar soft tissue injuries to the left lateral thigh and upper back. Serrations along the wound margins are consistent with a human dentition pattern . . .

'. . . eight puncture wounds to the anterior chest, resulting in bilateral hemopneumothoraces. According to the operative report, the pericardium and right ventricle were also penetrated, and a hemorrhagic pericardial effusion was discovered, requiring a pericardial window via the subxiphoid approach . . .

'. . . an avulsion injury to the right breast. The lateral portion of the areola and underlying adipose tissue have been severed . . .

'. . . penetration of the peritoneal cavity . . .

'. . . left renal laceration from a penetrating wound to the left flank . . .

'. . . report of multiple lacerations to the small bowel, liver, and spleen . . .

'. . . fracture and dislocation of the left ankle with extensive swelling and ecchymosis . . .

'. . . patient is currently listed in critical condition . . .

'. . . Dr Ben Stevenson, board-certified pathologist. A copy of this report was submitted to the Jefferson County Sheriff's Department in compliance with Ohio state statutes pertaining to forensic evidence . . .

'. . . End report.'

Chapter 21

The trip back to Wintersville took considerably longer than the day's earlier journey. After leaving the hospital, Ben had taken Joel to an ice-cream parlor that he'd frequented with Susan during their time in residency training. Ben hadn't felt much like eating, but he'd promised his son this particular part of the excursion as an enticement for Joel to join him on the trip to Pittsburgh. Watching the boy wolf down two scoops of rocky road topped with hot fudge, whipped cream, peanut crumbles and a maraschino cherry had proven to be too much for Ben's already tenuous stomach. He'd chosen to distract himself by looking out through the large plate glass window at the passing pedestrian foot traffic. Dusk was beginning to fall on the city now, and Ben was eager to get home. He pulled his cell phone from his pocket and called Susan to tell her they'd be getting back later than expected, advising her not to wait on them for dinner. 'It's just leftovers,' she said. 'I'll heat something up for you when you get home.' Ben looked across the table at his son as the boy twirled his spoon along the inside bottom of the tall glass, meticulously retrieving the last remnants of melted goodness for his consumption. 'Don't bother,' he told his wife over the phone. 'I don't think either one of us will be particularly hungry.'

He returned the phone to his pocket and placed his open palms on the table. 'You ready, kiddo?'

Joel dropped the long metal spoon into his glass. 'Dad?'

'Yeah.'

'Do you think she'll die?'

'The girl we visited today in the hospital?'

Joel nodded.

'I hope not,' Ben replied. 'It's too early to know for sure. But the doctors and nurses are taking real good care of her.'

Joel peered into the bottom of his glass, then looked up at him. 'But she might die anyway.'

Ben sighed. 'That's right, son. She might.'

The index finger of the boy's right hand traced a line around the outside of his glass where the condensation had formed a small ring on the table. 'Will she go to heaven, Dad? If she dies?'

Ben looked across the table. 'I don't know what happens to us when we die, Joel. Nobody really does.'

'Mom says we go to heaven.'

'I know.'

'But you don't believe in heaven, do you, Dad?'

Ben's gaze drifted to the right as he looked out through the window at the people shuffling by. A pedestrian darted across the street against the stoplight, causing an oncoming taxi to screech to a halt. The cabbie laid on his horn long and hard, yelling an obscenity out the window. The jaywalker turned and flipped the guy the bird.

'Sometimes I don't know if we deserve it,' he said quietly.

Joel was silent for a moment, pushing his napkin around the table. 'Mom says everyone deserves forgiveness. She says it's not up to us to judge each other. It's up to God.'

'Yeah?' Ben smiled, turning his attention back to his son. 'Well, your mom's pretty smart now, isn't she?'

Joel looked back at him blandly. 'She's pretty smart, Dad.'

A bell jingled as the door in the front of the shop opened and two more patrons walked in, the sounds of the city nipping at their heels. The wind gusted briefly through the open entrance, sending Joel's napkin scurrying to the floor.

'Okay,' Ben said, retrieving a replacement from the metal dispenser and sliding it across the table. 'Wipe that chocolate off your face and let's get going. It's getting late.'

'Sure, Dad,' his son replied, smiling up at him. They slid out of the booth, gathered their jackets, and walked together toward the door.

Chapter 22

That night Ben slept poorly, feeling alternatingly either too hot or too cold beneath the covers. After considerable tossing and turning, he'd finally managed to drift off, but he had fallen into a dream in which he was being chased through the halls of the hospital by a large black wolf. He'd fled down long corridors, the floor cold and sterile beneath his bare feet. Behind him he could hear the thing coming, its nails clicking and skittering along the tile. In desperation, he'd entered a room at the end of one of the passages, swinging the door shut behind him and flipping the dead bolt in its track. He stood with his ear pressed up against the door, listening, trying to get control of his breathing. There was no sound from the hallway beyond, only the soft, methodical whisper of the ventilator from the patient lying in the bed behind him. The wild drum of his heartbeat began to slacken in his ears. Then he heard it: a small click as the side

161

rail of the gurney was slowly lowered, the creak of someone shifting their weight in the bed, the soft slap of feet touching the floor. He turned to find Monica Dressler sitting up facing him, her thin legs hanging over the side of the bed, the endotracheal tube still protruding from between her lips. Her eyes were vacant and unseeing, her right hand sifting through coarse black fur. Beside her, sitting at her feet and studying him with its greenish-yellow predatory gaze, was the wolf.

The image startled Ben awake, and he lay there in bed, sweating lightly, bunching the sheet into matted balls with his hands. Finally, he got up, walked across the bedroom in the darkness, opened the door and slipped quietly into the hallway. The house was silent, except for the subtle pulse of the grandfather clock in the living room below. On the left side of the hallway stood the closed door to Joel's bedroom, and beyond that on the right, lost in the shadows, was the door to Thomas's room. No noise emanated from behind either, and after a moment's pause Ben started down the hallway in the direction of the stairs, thinking he'd go to the kitchen to get some –

Suddenly, he stopped. Up ahead at the end of the hall, sitting there in the shadows, was the wolf. Ben could hear its panting, could just make out the outline of its body in the darkness, its long tongue lying flat and slightly protruding through its partially opened jaws. Ben took a step backward, his right hand grasping blindly for the light switch on the wall. Then the thing came for him, rising up from its seated position on its haunches and padding heavily down the short, dim corridor. Ben stood frozen in position, unable to move, bracing himself for the impact of the animal's teeth on his thigh, for the weight of its body pulling him to the ground. His breath came in quick, hurried gasps, the sweat that had begun to dry on his skin now awakening once again and coalescing into tense, tight beads on his arms and back. A small sound escaped him – something between a whimper and a half scream – and although his fingers had finally located the switch on the wall he now felt both unable and unwilling to use it, knowing that to flip it on and to see the wolf in its full form would be too much for his mind to handle.

The creature came to a halt in front of him, and then suddenly and inexplicably, its tail began to swish back and forth in a friendly sign of greeting. The broad head pushed insistently against his left hip, and Ben's hands went reflexively to the sides of its head to ruffle the ears and stroke the long, broad neck.

'Alex, you scared the *shit* out of me,' he said, exhaling slowly, then patting the canine's right shoulder as the dog leaned into him in his usual fashion. The bony tail whipped enthusiastically from side to side, striking the wall with a loud crack.

The second door on the left opened, and Thomas's head poked out into the hallway. 'Hey.'

Ben looked up. 'Hi,' he said. 'Sorry to wake you. Alex just about gave me a heart attack.'

Thomas looked at the two of them without speaking. 'I was going to head down to the kitchen for something to drink,' Ben told him, glad to have someone to talk to. 'Feel like coming?'

'Okay,' Thomas said with a shrug.

'Great,' Ben replied, leading the expedition down the stairs, through the living room and into the kitchen. He flipped on the light, opened a cabinet and pulled two glasses from the shelf. 'What'll it be?' He smiled.

'What've you got?'

Ben opened the refrigerator and perused the options. 'Let's see: milk, grape juice, water, Diet Coke . . .' He frowned. 'There's half a pitcher of unidentifiable pink stuff in here.'

'How about a beer?' Thomas suggested.

Ben turned and looked at him. 'You want a beer?' he asked. To be honest, the option didn't sound half bad right about now.

Thomas shrugged noncommittally.

'Okay,' Ben replied, retrieving two bottles from the back of the fridge. He looked at Thomas. 'You need a glass?'

The boy shook his head.

'Good. Neither do I.' He returned the glasses to the cabinet, retrieved an opener, popped off the tops, and handed one of the bottles over to his son. 'Cheers,' he said, smiling broadly, as he sat down at the table. The bottles clinked together.

Thomas lifted the beverage to his lips and took a long slug, and Ben followed suit. 'Ahh,' he told his son, 'nothing like an ice-cold beer at two-thirty in the morning, eh?'

Thomas smiled thinly and took another sip. 'How is she?' he asked.

'Monica?' Ben let the second swallow of alcohol slide down his throat. The bottle felt light in his hand, and when he looked down he was surprised to see that it was almost empty. 'She's pretty banged up,' he replied, realizing as soon as the words had left his mouth that the euphemism didn't nearly do justice to what he had witnessed today.

'Will she die?' Thomas asked, and Ben was struck by how similar the question was to the one Joel had asked him earlier that day.

'I don't know,' he answered for the second time in less than twenty-four hours. He wondered how many others would be looking to him for the answer to that question, as if holding a medical degree somehow enabled him to look into the future, to retrieve the likely outcomes of people's lives like rabbits from a magician's hat.

Thomas finished off his bottle, and Ben rose from his chair to retrieve another two from the refrigerator, placing one in front of each of them. There was no cheerful salutation or clinking of glasses this time, and they sipped their beverages in silence. Unlike Joel, Ben realized, there would be no questions about God or heaven from Thomas, no discussion regarding forgiveness or salvation. Ben didn't doubt that the questions were there, but his oldest son guarded his inner world much more tightly than Joel, keeping his thoughts and feelings mostly to himself. Over the years it had only gotten worse, the connection between them becoming increasingly distant. It was as if Thomas were standing on a boat that was slowly, almost imperceptibly, drawing away from a pier on which Ben stood and watched. *He could still bridge the gap,* he thought, *if he needed to.* But one day he worried that he would look down to find that the space between them had grown too wide for him to cross.

'I want to see her,' his son said suddenly, his eyes focused somewhere beyond this room that they shared.

'Sure,' Ben replied. 'I'll ask her parents if it's okay if we visit her in the hospital. I'm sorry, son. I know she was a friend of yours.'

Is, Ben thought, correcting himself. She *is* a friend of his.

Thomas nodded, pushed his chair back from the table and stood up. He walked to the counter and placed his bottles in the sink. 'Good night, Dad,' he said.

'Good night, son,' Ben replied. He rose from his seat, intending to place a hand on Thomas's shoulder, maybe even to give him a hug if the boy would allow it. But when he turned around, Ben found himself alone in the room – his oldest son already gone.

Chapter 23

'Thanks for showing us in,' Detective Schroeder said as he and his partner followed the psychiatric unit manager down the corridor toward the elevators.

'I'm sorry he bothered you,' she said. She was well dressed and attractive, and she walked briskly along as she talked. 'Patient confidentiality laws prevent us from providing you with any clinical information.' They stepped into the elevator and she leaned forward and pushed a button.

'It's our job to follow up on these things,' Carl told her. The Sheriff's Department had received a 911 phone call from the hospital's psych unit yesterday. The man, who'd identified himself to the emergency operator as Harold Matthews, had wanted to talk to the detective in charge about 'that girl they found in the woods.' Carl wasn't particularly hopeful, since the call had originated from the psych unit, but he was at least willing to come here to see what the man had to say. It wouldn't be the first unproductive lead they'd investigated in the last few days. Since the second assault, the Sheriff's Department had been inundated with calls from civilians regarding suspicious characters and irregular goings-on within the town. None of these tips had led to anything fruitful. The truth was, there were simply a lot of weird people out there. Usually they settled into the background noise of everyday life. It took something horrific to recalibrate people's tolerance for the odd and eccentric.

The elevator doors slid open and they stepped out into a small lobby. There were two additional doors on opposite sides of the room. The woman had asked them to show their IDs before bringing them up here, and now she ran through a short list of contraband – lighters, cameras and the like. They had none, and the unit manager used her hospital badge to buzz them through the door on their right.

They entered a common area where numerous patients sifted about. There were several small tables at which a few individuals were sitting, their bodies hunched forward as they applied their efforts to jigsaw puzzles, coloring books, and similar activities. In the upper corner of the room was a television, and several of the room's occupants sat on a long couch, studying the screen with varied degrees of interest. Still others meandered about the room, their faces turned downward as they tended to their own private worlds.

'This way.' She gestured, continuing down a hallway

to a small private room on the left. Inside, a large black man sat in the far corner. To the nurses who had seen him brought in to the seclusion room five nights ago – fighting with the staff, punching the door, covered in scratches – this seemed like a different person altogether. The antipsychotic medications had transformed his wild, frenzied state into a more subdued and cooperative demeanor, although he still eyed the detectives suspiciously as Carl settled himself into the only other chair in the room and Detective Hunt took up a position near the door.

'Mr Matthews?' Schroeder began.

The man said nothing, only continued to stare, his eyes flitting back and forth between the two of them, as if they were juicy steaks he might suddenly decide to devour.

'I'm Detective Schroeder and this is Detective Hunt. We're from the Sheriff's Department. We were told you had some information you wanted to discuss with us.'

'You wit' the police?' he asked in a deep resonant voice. There was a hint of a southern drawl to it.

'Yes, we are.'

'Mm-hmm. An' how do I know for sure?'

Carl reached into his pocket and showed him his badge. The man seemed unimpressed.

'Jus' 'bout anyone can git themselves one'ah them. You got a radio, too?'

Detective Hunt pulled back his jacket enough to reveal the small handheld police radio clipped to his belt.

'Mm-hmm.' The big man deliberated for a moment.

'Look, we're very busy,' Carl advised him, beginning to stand. 'If you don't have anything to tell us we really need to—'

'I guess you ought ta know that I killed her.'

That simple statement brought the small hairs on the back of Carl's neck to attention. He sat back down. 'Who do you mean? Who did you kill?'

'That girl in the woods.'

'Now, before you say anything else,' Carl cautioned, 'I need to read you your Miranda rights – just so you understand them.' The man listened patiently until Carl was finished. 'Okay,' the detective continued, 'now, what were you saying?'

'I killed her. Didn't mean to, but I did.'

'The girl in the woods?'

'Mm-hmm.'

'And when did you kill her?'

'Five nights ago. Roun' two in the mornin'.'

'Where did it happen? Along what road?'

'Lockhart Drive.'

'What does she look like? The girl.'

'Pale skin. Long black hair. Little thing.' He paused. 'They been showin' her picture on the TV.'

'You've been watching the story on the news?'

'Mm-hmm.'

'What did you do to her?' Danny asked.

'Don't remember. Sometimes things git dim.'

'Did you rape her?'

'Nah.'

'The body was missing an arm,' Carl said. 'What did you do with it?'

'Didn't do nothin' with it. Body's still under the car.'

'What car?'

He looked back at them. Said nothing.

'Why did you kill her?'

'Couldn't help it. Tried to stop – but I couldn't. Now she's lyin' in the street dead, an' it's ma' fault. 'Cause I can't stop when I git goin'.'

'Where do you live?'

Only silence from the immense figure in front of them.

'Have you killed anyone else?'

He stared back at them. 'I killed lots of 'em.'

'Where did you get those scratches on your arms?' Detective Hunt asked. 'Did the girl do that to you?'

Nothing.

'You don't sound like you're from around here. Where are you from?'

'Tha's all I wanna say.'

'I understand, but can I ask you just a few more questions?'

'Tha's all I wanna say,' he repeated, his large hands clenching into fists on his lap.

'Sure, no problem,' Carl said, pulling out his notepad and pen. 'Do you think you could write it down for us – what you just told us? It helps me remember. Write it down and sign your name at the bottom.'

'Mm-hmm.' He took the pen in his hand and put

it to the paper. They waited while he worked. When he was finished, he handed the items back. Etched on the pad was a crude drawing of two stick figures, one lying on the ground and the other standing over her, hands to his head, his features frozen in a silent scream.

'Is this you?' Carl asked, pointing to the upright figure, and the man nodded.

'You should take me in. Can't stay here. They'll be comin' for me soon, all the ones I killed.'

'We can't take you in just yet,' Danny told him. 'The doctors and nurses need to get you feeling better first.'

'They can't do nothin' for me.' The man dropped his eyes toward a corner of the room. 'I can't stay here.'

'Once you're feeling better, we'll come back and talk to you some more,' Carl promised. 'Thank you for sharing this with us.'

The man's eyes remained fixed in the corner of the room. His lips moved soundlessly, as if in a silent prayer or a conversation only he could hear. The detectives stepped out into the hallway. They walked to the nurses' station and knocked on the door.

'Finished?' the unit manager asked, exiting the station and joining them in the hall.

'Yes, we are.'

'I'll buzz you out then,' she said. They returned to the common area and she held her badge up against an electronic reader on the wall until a lock released, enabling her to push the door open. Once in the waiting area, she repeated the procedure to summon the elevator. 'You can find your way out from here?' she asked.

'Yes. Thank you.' Danny offered her a smile as he and Carl stepped into the elevator.

When the doors closed, his partner asked, 'So, what do you think?'

'He seems pretty disturbed. A few of his facts were correct, although most of them he could've gotten from the television news reports. The street name he gave was wrong, of course, and he didn't contradict you about the missing arm.'

'He said, "Body's still under the car." What do you make of *that*?'

'I don't know,' Danny replied. 'Maybe he's talking about another body – one we haven't found yet.'

'Now, there's an unsettling thought.'

Danny shrugged. 'Said he's killed lots of 'em – that he tries to stop, but can't.'

'He also seems convinced that she's dead. If he's been watching the news reports, wouldn't he know that the girl's still alive?' They reached the first floor and proceeded toward the front of the hospital.

'Let's keep in mind that he's crazy. This is all probably delusional thinking. Still . . . I'd like to know where those scratches on his arms came from.' They exited into the parking lot, squinting into the afternoon sun. 'By the way,' Danny remarked, 'why did you even bother with that attempt at getting a written confession? In his current state in a psychiatric unit, there's *no way* it would've held up in court.'

173

'I wasn't doing it for the confession,' Carl replied. He unlocked the car but stood there looking over the roof at his partner.

Danny paused for a moment with his hand on the latch. Then a dawning expression blossomed on his face. 'Of course. Our killer is left-handed. You wanted to see what hand this guy writes with.'

Carl nodded. 'Did you notice?'

Danny thought for a moment, recollecting the image of the pen poised above the paper. 'Son of a gun,' he said.

'File the paperwork with the hospital to put him on a police hold. When he's ready for discharge, we're taking him in. Mr Harold Matthews gives me the creeps, and I didn't like that picture he drew. He may be crazy, but I don't think we should write him off just yet. We need to be damn sure there's nothing else to it.'

Chapter 24

The office of Dr Aaron Blechman, forensic odontologist, was located on the fourth floor of Children's Hospital. It was situated at the end of a long, dimly lit corridor, as if the room itself had been added to the building as an afterthought. A small sign affixed to the door identified the occupant. Inside, the office was cramped, almost claustrophobic, the majority of the floor space inhabited by a modest oak desk, its surface strewn with a haphazard assortment of books and papers. The afternoon gray filtered through a small window overlooking Forty-Fifth Street and St Mary's Cemetery, just beyond.

'So what you're saying,' Detective Danny Hunt summarized, 'is that the bite wounds from the second victim are identical to those from the first.'

Blechman shook his head. 'Identical, no. The angle of contact with the skin, the depth of penetration, the surrounding patterns of ecchymosis – these will vary from wound to wound. A human bite is a dynamic force. It has many variables.'

'But you think it was produced by the same person,' Detective Schroeder interjected. His face looked strained, as if he were in the process of recovering from a long, tenacious illness. In some ways he was. Fifteen years on the force, two failed marriages, an adult daughter living on the other side of the country with whom he barely spoke. These days he lived for the job. It was all he had left.

'The pattern of dentition appears similar,' Blechman answered. 'Comparison of saliva DNA analysis from the bite wounds sustained by the two victims may provide you with a more definitive answer to that question.'

'We're pretty certain we're dealing with the same perpetrator,' Detective Hunt advised the odontologist, glancing at his partner. 'Unfortunately, the saliva DNA analysis from the first victim failed to yield a match through CODIS.'

CODIS, Ben recalled, was an acronym that referred to the FBI's Combined DNA Index System. The program had been established in 1994 as a DNA database for biological samples acquired in connection with violent felony crimes.

Ben furrowed his brow a bit. 'So the fact that the saliva samples from the first victim's bite wounds failed to yield a match through CODIS means . . .'

'It could mean any number of things,' Carl explained. 'Previous violent felony crimes might have been committed by this guy before the inception of

176

the database in 1994. Or he might have committed prior crimes from which no biological specimens were obtained.'

'Or,' Detective Hunt interposed, 'this could be the perpetrator's first venture into this sort of work.'

Ben nodded. 'Well, it seems to agree with him.'

The room fell silent for a moment, except for the faint sounds of traffic rising from the street below.

'There is something else,' Blechman reported. 'There seems to be a spacing anomaly between the upper left canine and the first premolar. It's what we refer to as a *diastasis* – a small, abnormal gap between the two teeth. It measures about two millimeters.'

Schroeder was jotting this down in his notebook. 'A diastasis,' he said. 'Would this be noticeable to the average person?'

'Not glaringly so,' the odontologist replied. 'The anomaly is subtle. You'd have to know what you were looking for.' He retrieved a plastic dental model from his bookshelf, indicating the involved teeth with the pointed end of a pencil. 'It would be here,' he told them, 'just behind the upper left canine.'

Carl looked at Sam. 'If we could get a hold of the town's dental records . . .'

Sam shook his head. 'I don't think so. Medical and dental information is protected by patient privacy laws. Ain't that right, Ben?'

Ben nodded. The Health Insurance Portability and Accountability Act, established by the US government in 1996, was now well entrenched in medicine.

As a result, access to medical and dental records was tightly controlled.

'A judge might issue a subpoena for the dental records of a specific suspect,' Sam continued, 'provided there was enough additional convincing evidence. But getting a subpoena for the dental records of the entire town is a lost cause.'

'Even in a case like this?' Carl asked.

'*Especially* in a case like this,' Sam replied. 'Catching him is only the first step. We don't want to do anything to jeopardize the DA's ability to prosecute. I'd hate to catch him, only to see him walk on a technicality.'

'If I catch him, he won't be walking anywhere for a while,' Carl muttered to himself, stuffing his notebook into the interior pocket of his suit jacket. He turned to Dr Blechman. 'You'll let us know when the DNA report from the girl's wounds comes back?'

'Of course,' Blechman replied, shaking hands with each of them. 'If there's anything else I can do to help, please let me know.'

They filed out into the hallway and headed for the elevators. 'I presume,' Sam commented, 'that we're all heading to the same place from here.'

A soft bell chimed and the elevator doors slid open in front of them. 'Absolutely,' Ben responded. 'Let's go see how she's doing.'

Chapter 25

The ICU waiting room appeared as if an impromptu town meeting were about to be called to order. Scores of familiar faces milled about, both in the waiting area and in the hallway just outside. The chairs normally situated in the center of the room had been pushed up against the wall to accommodate the standing-room-only crowd. Paul and Vera Dressler were surrounded by a throng of friends and neighbors, each offering their heartfelt support and condolences. A small table in the corner was overflowing with a striking assortment of flowers, whose fragrance and brightness seemed to permeate the room. Children sat together in small clusters, giggling and chattering rapidly to one another, and a collection of teenagers from Monica's high school had gathered at the far end of the hallway, talking quietly among themselves.

As Ben and the officers approached, they were

greeted with careful smiles and warm handshakes. They were pulled into the crowd as one of its own, and were quickly enveloped in questions and conversation. They inquired about the status of Monica's recovery, and were updated regarding planned studies and procedures. Ben was barraged with questions regarding the girl's injuries and prognosis, and when he made eye contact with Susan from across the room, he could tell that his wife had also been tasked with the responsibility of explaining the medical details of the case in a digestible fashion to those who had come here.

In addition to these questions, Ben was asked about the progress of the investigation, about which he simply deferred to Sam and the detectives. *Have any suspects been identified?* they asked. *Are there any leads yet? Do you think Monica was attacked by the same person responsible for killing Kevin Tanner? Do you think this was done by a local, or just someone passing through?* Ben answered them all in the same way: 'I don't know. You'll have to speak with the detectives.' Which was the truth, he decided, more or less.

They had all come to see Monica: this child of the town who had sustained a brutal attack and had been left in the woods to die – this brave girl who had somehow summoned the strength to drag herself more than an eighth of a mile through the mud and underbrush to the side of the road in order to be found. They had come to support her parents, yes; but they all wanted to see her, to sit at her bedside and to pray for her recovery, to will her back to health by their sheer numbers, by the force of their desire to see her well.

It occurred to Ben then, as the faces around him began to blur together into something whole – something unifying – that Monica Dressler represented more than simply one of their own. In many ways, she *was* the town – a physical manifestation of the emotional assault they were all enduring together. To Ben and most likely to others, she represented their will to fight back, their refusal to succumb to the evil that had descended upon them. She had become an inspiration, even as she fought for her life. For if she could find a way to survive this thing, then perhaps so could they all.

Chapter 26

'What do you *mean*, "He eloped"?' Detective Schroeder ran a hand through his dark hair. He was standing near the ambulance entrance next to the emergency department.

'Sorry – hospital terminology,' the security officer responded. 'Patients aren't prisoners, so we don't usually say they "escaped". But in this case, well . . .' He looked back at the automatic sliding glass door. 'We called it in to the police as soon as it happened. They're out there looking for him right now.'

'I *know* we're out there looking for him. I heard it over the radio.' Carl took a deep breath, telling himself to ratchet his anger back a notch. '*How did this happen?* I thought the psychiatric unit was a locked facility.'

'It *is* a locked facility,' the man confirmed. 'You need an ID badge to leave the unit itself, and also one to summon the elevator.'

'I remember.'

'But the patient didn't escape from the psych unit. He escaped from the ER.'

'What was he doing back in the ER?'

'He had a seizure on the unit – a pretty bad one, I guess. The nurse called us to come help them transport him down here. It took a bunch of us just to lift him onto the gurney.'

'Was he still seizing?'

'No, he'd stopped by then. But he was unconscious. I mean, I'm just security – I don't know about the medical stuff – but that guy was dead weight.'

'So what happened then?'

'Once we got him onto the gurney, we left the psych unit, took the elevator to the first floor and brought him to the ER. When we got here it was pretty crazy. They'd just brought in a patient in cardiac arrest. There were no beds available, so the charge nurse told us to put the gurney up against a wall by the ambulance entrance. Then the family of the cardiac arrest guy showed up and started going nuts. The ER staff needed help with them, and since our guy was unconscious we figured, you know' – he shrugged – '*he* wasn't going anywhere.'

'Yeah, sure.'

'But a few minutes later when I looked back at the stretcher he was gone. Just got up and walked out, I guess. *Man*, I've never seen a seizure patient wake up that fast before.'

'If it really *was* a seizure in the first place,' Detective Schroeder grumbled.

'What do you mean? You think he faked it?'

'Right now, I don't know *what* to think,' he called back over his shoulder, heading for his car. 'All I know is that he's out there somewhere, and we'd sure as hell better find him.'

Chapter 27

The junkyard at S&D Auto Salvage off Thistlewood Drive had always been referred to by the younger generation as simply *the Yard*. The quarter-acre lot was enclosed by a chain-link fence topped with an arthritic, twisting spine of barbed wire. A simple glance at the scattered heaps of scrap metal and rust-laden automobile carcasses was enough to make one check the expiration date on their last tetanus shot. A pockmarked sign, yellowed with age, hung at a listless angle near the padlocked front gate, advising would-be visitors that TRESPASSERS WILL BE DEALT WITH ACCORDINGLY – conjuring images of a toothless, barefooted proprietor in overalls with a shotgun at the ready. A mangy, ill-tempered Rottweiler named Rocco patrolled the premises, endlessly pacing the makeshift aisles between the abandoned detritus, as if anything here were actually worth stealing.

The Yard was clearly no place for teenagers, and

as such it was really no surprise that this had become the chosen meeting spot for all sorts of gatherings and events. Ernie Samper's father, an accountant by profession, had inherited the place when his own father had died eight years ago. He should've sold it, for an accountant knows very little about the world of scrap metal and automobile salvage, but he just hadn't been able to bring himself to do it. As odd as it might sound, the place had taken on a certain sentimental value, and so it remained in the family but otherwise sat dormant as the years went by, the cars and decrepit office trailer slowly settling into the dust like everything else within its fiercely guarded perimeter.

'What I don't understand,' Dave Kendricks was saying, 'is how the police let something like this happen so soon after the first murder.'

'They can't be everywhere at once,' Eileen Dickenson pointed out from her seated position on the sun-welted hood of what was once recognizable as a blue Chevy Malibu. 'I don't think it's fair to blame this on them.'

'That's 'cause your dad works for the Sheriff's Department,' Kent Savage commented. He plucked a small stone from the dirt, took aim and hurled it at the left headlight of a Ford Ranger eighty yards away. There was a metallic chink as the stone bounced off the front grille, a foot and a half to the right of its intended target.

'That's got nothin' to do with it,' Eileen responded, glaring in his direction. 'When things go wrong, everyone always wants to blame the police. They're an easy scapegoat. I didn't see *you* offering to walk people home that night.'

'Well, Brian Fowler walked her home, and she got attacked anyway,' Kent retorted.

'He didn't walk her *all* the way home, though, did he?'

'No, he didn't. So maybe we should blame him.'

'I think he blames himself enough already,' Devon said. He reached down with his hand and scratched Rocco behind the right ear. The dog growled and wagged his short, stubby tail simultaneously, apparently uncertain what to make of the unsolicited affection. 'How is he, by the way?' Devon asked. 'Has anyone heard from him?'

The others were silent. Despite multiple phone calls and attempted visits, none of them had seen Brian Fowler in almost two weeks. His chair, along with that of Monica Dressler, sat empty at school as the academic year drew to a close, constant reminders of the two teenagers' absence and the circumstances behind it. If that vacant space was a distraction to learning, none of the teachers had mentioned it. The seats remained empty, day after day. No one dared sit there, and no one dared remove them.

Paul Dalouka spoke up. 'His stepfather told my mom that Brian received permission to finish the school year early.'

The others nodded.

'I don't blame Brian,' Eileen Dickenson commented. 'There's no way he could've known.' She looked around, as if searching for support in her assertion. 'Any one of us would've done the same thing.'

'I agree.' Heads turned toward Natalie Rhodes, who was sitting cross-legged in the dirt. 'A lot of us walked home alone that night.' She looked up at Bret Graham, who was leaning against the hood of a Volkswagen Beetle that had clearly seen better days. 'Your house is, what, four miles from Devon's? Mine's *at least* that far. We both got home safely.' She frowned, her eyes returning to the ground in front of her. 'This isn't something any of us could've predicted.'

'Except it had already happened once before,' Devon replied. He shook his head. 'I never should've let people walk home that night. I should've *insisted* on cabs for everyone.'

'There aren't that many cabs in the entire town,' Thomas pointed out. 'People would've been waiting at your place for hours.'

'*Good*. They could've helped me clean up,' Devon replied, and a slight snicker ran through the group. Rocco stood up and disappeared into the junk maze, resuming his patrol.

'That dog's senile, Ernie,' Russell Long commented.

Ernie Samper smiled. 'Ugly, too. But at least he's got personality, which is more than I can say for the majority of you losers.'

'He patrols a scrap heap,' Russell advised him. 'I just wanna draw your attention to that, Ernie – in case you didn't notice. The dog guards trash.'

'He's hardworking, dedicated and professional,' Samper replied. 'Ya oughta try it sometime.'

'Well, right now he's urinating on a lime-green refrigerator,' Marty Spears noted, adjusting his glasses as he squinted into the sun. They all looked, and indeed Rocco was, the dog's left rear leg cocked skyward in an unbecoming pose.

'That's gonna hurt the resale value,' someone quipped, and they all laughed at this, their guilt and pain momentarily forgotten. The remains of the automobiles within the Yard seemed to study them silently, hunkering their tired, broken frames ever closer to the earth. Somewhere to the east on Route 22 the impatient thrum of newer vehicles could be heard passing along the highway, and the distance from there to here suddenly seemed both very far and very close at the same time.

'Let's get outta here,' Paul Dalouka suggested. 'I'm sick of this place.'

Natalie Rhodes stood up and stretched, her right knee popping softly. 'You stay here long enough, you become part of the heap,' she said, and this was met with some general consensus.

They filed out through the front gate, engaging one another in scattered conversation. Ernie was the last to leave, looping the rusty chain through the gate and locking the padlock behind him. He followed the loose procession up the steep hill of Sycamore Street, and when he reached the crest he glanced back at his father's unlikely establishment, which appeared to fade slightly into the afternoon haze, the dog staring back at him through the metallic skin of the chain-link world in which he lived.

Chapter 28

The days and weeks following the attempted murder of Monica Dressler passed as time often does in the wake of such an event: slowly at first, for those most intimately affected by the tragedy. Shock and disbelief gave way to sporadic fits of incapacitating emotion, the rage and anguish bleeding forth from their bodies like fresh-cut wounds, leaving them raw and vacant and still without answers. They sat alone in the private chambers of their grief, and the passage of time was measured not by the clock on the wall but by the changing faces of the people around them.

The girl's surgeon, Dr Elliot, had turned optimistic, advising Paul and Vera Dressler that their daughter was recovering faster than expected. The large plastic tubes protruding like extra appendages from between Monica's ribs were removed, and the lungs remained inflated – a very good sign, the surgeon informed them. The second exploratory laparotomy had been performed, and after they found that there were no additional injuries and that the bleeding from the liver had completely subsided, they surgically closed the abdominal wall and brought the skin together with sutures. The three abdominal drains were removed, one on each successive day following the second exploratory. The fractured bones of the left ankle had been straightened and secured with titanium plates, and the swelling had diminished significantly. The plastic surgeon had come by to discuss plans for reconstructive surgery of the right breast and the partially amputated right ear. He had every reason to expect, he advised the parents, that the cosmetic results would be excellent. As for the two amputated fingers on the left hand, prosthetics could be utilized, and even the functionality of that hand would remain good, since the thumb, index and middle fingers remained intact.

And yet . . . the girl would not wake.

The sedative agents that had dripped steadily into her veins since her arrival at the hospital had been stopped three days ago. Dr Elliot had advised the parents that it often took time for the body to metabolize the remaining drugs in the system, even once the infusions were discontinued. It wasn't unheard of, she'd told them, for the effects to last many hours or even days. But by now three days had gone by, and still nothing.

Like many in the town, Ben and Thomas had made the trip to Pittsburgh several times now to check on

Monica's progress and to visit with her parents. After her first visit, Susan had elected to stay home with Joel during subsequent trips. 'It's upsetting for me to see her like that,' she'd told her husband one afternoon in the kitchen, 'and I don't think it's good for Joel either to keep going back.'

'Paul and Vera appreciate the support, Susan,' Ben had responded, surprised by his wife's unusual skittishness. 'You might want to reconsider.'

'I can't,' she replied. 'But you and Thomas should go. I think he needs to see this side of things.'

Ben nodded. The day Monica was discovered along the roadside, Susan had confronted Thomas about sneaking out to the party the night before. Her intuition had been right, and after a brief denial their son had admitted to leaving the house against their bidding.

'It was reckless of him to sneak out like that,' Ben agreed. 'I just keep thinking that something like this could've happened to him.'

Susan dragged the dish towel across the counter, shepherding crumbs over the edge and into her upturned hand. She opened a cabinet door and deposited them into the trash can. 'It's hard to know how to deal with children as they get older,' she mused. 'We can't control the choices they make, the people they become.'

'We just have to do the best we can,' Ben said, trying to reassure her.

His wife looked out the window, and as Ben followed her gaze it occurred to him that the world

192

out there suddenly seemed too big, too capricious, too hard and full of sharp edges.

'I just don't want to lose him,' Susan said to herself, her voice wavering near the end.

Ben walked up behind her, cupping her shoulders with his hands. 'Don't worry,' he told her, placing a soft kiss on the back of her neck. 'We won't.'

She turned her head sideways in order to smile back at him, touching the knuckles of his right hand with his fingers. 'I know,' she said, but her eyes were sad and lost in a place Ben didn't quite know how to reach.

Chapter 29

Carl Schroeder sat in the small, crowded conference room with the other men and waited for the phone to connect. Sam Garston sat across from him, Detective Hunt to his left. His junior partner twirled his pen nervously. Carl wished he would stop. It was getting on his nerves. He would have told him just that, too, if the three other men – FBI field agents, newly assigned to the case and now in charge of the investigation – hadn't been there to witness it. Instead, he sat there in silence waiting for his brother, Mike – a computer analyst with the bureau – to pick up the damn receiver on the other end of the line as the speakerphone rang and rang over the quiet hum of the air conditioner.

So far their best lead had been the bite wounds sustained by the victims. Saliva specimens from the wounds had failed to yield a match through CODIS, but there *had* been one important match, which explained the presence of the three FBI agents in the Jefferson County Sheriff's Office today. DNA specimens obtained from the bite wounds sustained by the second victim had matched those from the first. Hence the assailant had been the same person, which meant that in all likelihood they were dealing with a serial killer. The second victim hadn't died, so the perpetrator still had another two murders to go before he truly fit the definition.

The detectives did not intend to wait for those to happen.

The psychiatric patient who'd escaped from the emergency department had been their only real suspect, although Carl still didn't know what to make of him. There was something disturbing in the absolute certainty with which he'd confessed, in the unflappable conviction in his voice, and in the picture he'd drawn of himself standing over the victim, a silent scream plastered on his lips. The FBI had employed the skills of a forensic profiler to assist them in the case, and she'd pointed out that psychiatric patients with fixed delusions can often be quite convincing. Whether those delusions were somehow tied to reality was difficult to say. The problem was, they hadn't been able to locate him. The name he had given – Harold Matthews – had apparently been fictitious, and he certainly wasn't a local. If he was a drifter, Carl thought, perhaps he had drifted on to some other part of the country by now. They might never see or hear from him again. Then again, it was all too possible that they might – and *that* was what worried him.

The injuries from the two victims had been photographed extensively, and color photos of the wounds were now scattered on the table in front of them, coalescing into a grotesque collage of macerated flesh. Silicon castings had been constructed from the wounds by the forensic odontologist in Pittsburgh, and one of the more superficial wounds had left a reliable enough dental imprint for the odontologist to identify an abnormal widening – a *diastasis,* he'd called it – between the upper left canine and the first premolar. It wasn't much of a lead, but at least it gave them *something* to go on. But where did they go from here?

Then an idea had occurred to Carl two days ago while brushing his teeth. He'd returned his toothbrush to its plastic holder and had smiled into the mirror, inspecting his handiwork. *Is there any easily accessible resource,* he'd wondered, *that might be utilized to yield information about an individual's dental pattern?* A general subpoena for the dental records of the entire town was not a feasible option, but what about simple photography? How much information could one get from a close-up picture of a person's smile, for example? He didn't know. Maybe not much, except for obvious anomalies such as missing teeth or a severe overbite. He would have to check with the dental specialist. The other question was how to obtain such pictures, and he thought he had an answer to that. It had presented itself on the computer screen in front of him every time he'd made a routine traffic stop as a patrolman in his earlier days on the force: driver's licenses. There was a face smiling back on nearly every one. Okay, it was true that *some* people didn't smile when they had their picture taken, but *most* people did. At least 70 per cent, he'd guess. He'd looked at enough driver's licenses to know. And the pictures of every licensed driver were on file with the Ohio Bureau of Motor Vehicles. So the question was, how much detail regarding dental anatomy could actually be gathered from those pictures? You'd have to use a software imaging program to zoom in on the smile and adjust the resolution accordingly. You'd have to take measurements and compare them with those obtained by the forensic odontologist. Was it plausible? He'd contacted Mike to find out. The answer was typical for all things technical: it depended on the data.

The software programs to magnify and analyze photographic images were certainly available, and their capabilities were constantly improving. The FBI had been using them for more than two decades for a variety of applications. Photographs for driver's license identification were now taken digitally in every state, which would make them easier to manipulate. Most people partially revealed the upper central and lateral incisors, canines and first premolars when they smiled. Big grinners might reveal the second premolars, and some people revealed the bottom central and lateral incisors and canines, but that was less common. Of course, some people didn't smile at all for the license shot, and some states were now instructing them not to. Presently, Ohio wasn't one of them. So what they'd really be focusing on, Mike had told him, was four to eight teeth along the upper dentition in those individuals who'd smiled for their pictures. In a two-dimensional photograph, the most reliable measurements would be the length of the cutting surface of each tooth and the space between them. How useful that information would be depended in large part on how much of the dental anatomy the forensic odontologist had been able to reconstruct from the photographs and silicon castings of the bite wounds. Hence the plausibility of gleaning useful information depended on the data, but more from the forensic dental analysis than from the numbers crunched by the software programs from the BMV snapshots. The computer work would actually be the more reliable of the two. Computers were predictable. Real life was always the wild card.

With the FBI now formally involved, Mike had been given the go-ahead to review the BMV photos and see what he could find. They'd begun with licensed drivers from Jefferson County. If that didn't yield any positive results, they could expand outward to adjacent counties. It was still a long shot, and Carl knew it. All of this was assuming that their suspect even *had* a driver's license. But at least it had given them a place to start. Now the six of them sat and stood in various positions around the rectangular table and listened to the phone ringing on the other end as they waited for Mike to answer at his lab in Sacramento, California.

On the seventh ring the line was answered: 'If you know the mailbox number of the party you are trying to reach, please press one now,' a courteous voice instructed them. Special Agent Larry Culver swore under his breath. He flipped open his cell phone and began dialing the direct line to a unit supervisor. The rapidity of Detective Hunt's pen twirling bumped up a notch, and this time Carl quietly leaned over and asked him to kindly stop before he was driven stark raving mad. The scattered photographs of the two victims lay on the table in front of the six men and waited patiently for the plodding machinery of justice to respond.

Chapter 30

'How is she today?' Ben asked, as he and Thomas took a seat. The girl's mother, Vera, was at the windowsill arranging flowers in several of the large glass vases that stood sentinel over the motionless figure in the bed beside them. The endotracheal tube was gone, removed two days ago by the respiratory therapist, and the room seemed oddly quiet without the sound of the ventilator to which they'd become accustomed. The room itself was also different, no longer the bright lights, frequent alarms and bustling tempo of the ICU; this was a more sedated step-down unit for less critically ill patients.

'She spiked a fever last night,' Paul Dressler advised them. 'Dr Elliot says it looks like a urinary tract infection. They started her on antibiotics and removed the bladder catheter.' He looked at his daughter. 'She seems better today.'

Ben nodded. 'The Foley catheter makes UTIs inevitable. It's good that it's out.'

'She wears a diaper now.' Vera spoke up from where she stood at the window. 'We change her every few hours. They said we should . . .' She hesitated, glancing at Thomas for a moment. 'I'm sorry,' she said. 'You don't need to hear about that.'

'Has she woken up at all?' Ben asked, moving on to another subject.

'No,' Paul replied. 'Nothing yet.'

'They said she'll probably wake up very soon,' Vera told them. There was a hint of desperation in her voice, her eyes taking in each of their faces in turn. 'Dr Elliot says there's no reason she shouldn't.'

The girl's father sighed. 'They did an MRI of the brain three days ago,' he reported. 'It was completely normal.'

'Well, that's promising,' Ben told them. He tried to sound reassuring. 'These things sometimes just take some time. I'm sure the doctors—'

'"Very soon," is what they said,' Vera repeated, as if Ben had been disagreeing with her.

'Well,' Paul interposed, 'we'll just have to see, Vera.' His wife gave him a contemptuous look, then turned her back on them and began sorting the flowers once again.

They were quiet for a moment before Paul turned to Thomas. 'How's school?'

'Fine,' Thomas said. 'But we all miss her.'

Paul smiled. 'She'd be glad to hear that. You know,'

he said, 'I'm amazed at how many of her friends made it all the way up here to Pittsburgh to see her. Funny . . . she never thought she was that popular.'

Ben rose from his chair. 'I have an appointment with Dr Blechman in a few minutes to go over some findings from the DNA analysis. Mind if Thomas stays with you while I'm gone?'

Paul nodded. 'Happy to have him.'

Ben excused himself from the room and made his way through the hallways in the direction of the forensic odontologist's office. He knew the hospital well, having rotated here during his intern year of residency, but also having spent a considerable amount of time at Children's Hospital during his younger son's own stay in the pediatric ICU in December 2010.

It had all happened so quickly, as he remembered. Joel and Thomas had been playing upstairs – goofing around, taunting one another, racing down the hallway. Even now, as he walked down the hospital's familiar corridors three years later, Ben could still almost hear their footsteps pounding on the floor-boards above him.

'Quiet down, up there!' he'd yelled from the kitchen doorway. 'I'm on the phone!'

Who had he been talking to? He couldn't remember. The boys hadn't quieted down, though. In fact, they'd kicked it up a notch. Ben could hear the sound of small plastic action figures striking the walls. They were *throwing* them at one another. Joel started to shriek in protest to some unseen torture his older brother was likely bestowing upon him.

'Listen, let me call you back,' Ben said. He hung up the phone and started for the stairs. He'd ascended only three steps when he heard the rail from the second floor balcony groan in protest. A moment later, Joel's body came hurtling past him from above.

Ben was completely stunned. All he could do was to watch his son fall. Joel went headfirst, and when he reached the bottom his skull contacted the wooden floorboards with a sickening crack that echoed through the open foyer.

Ben never recalled descending the stairs and running across the room, but he must have done so because at the next moment he was kneeling beside his son, calling out his name, asking if he was hurt, telling him not to move. There was no need for those instructions. The boy's body lay splayed across the floor, quiet and motionless.

A few seconds later Thomas was also there, kneeling next to his father and gazing down at his brother in disbelief. 'Holy crap,' he whispered. 'He fell. I . . . I don't think he saw the rail. He ran directly into it – didn't even slow down. Just hit it and flipped right over. Joel? . . . Joel, are you okay?'

'Go get the phone,' Ben instructed him. 'Call 911. Tell them we need an ambulance. *Go!*'

The ambulance had rendezvoused with a medevac helicopter, which had brought Joel here, to Children's Hospital. His son had remained unresponsive for ten days. They had begun to lose hope. And then, just like that, he had awakened.

'*Thom – as.*'

'Joel. It's Dad, Joel. Open your eyes. I'm right here.'

'Daaad?'

'Yeah. It's me, son.'

The boy's brow furrowed. He ran his tongue across dry, cracked lips. He started to speak, then stopped, reformulating the question in his mind. 'Did . . . did I fall?'

Ben tried to answer and faltered, the words hanging stubbornly in his throat. 'Yes, son. You fell.' He watched Joel try the idea on for size. The boy's eyes searched the room, taking it in for the first time.

'I fell a long way down. Didn't I, Dad?'

'Yes. You did.'

'But . . . but now I'm back,' Joel announced, although his inflection was uncertain, as if he were making a statement and asking a question at the same time.

'Yes,' Ben answered, needing to reassure himself as well as the boy. 'Now you're back.'

'Okay,' Joel said, then closed his eyes for a moment. *Don't close your eyes, son,* Ben thought. *Don't slip away from me again.* He was on the verge of saying something when the boy's lids fluttered open.

'Dad?' The voice was barely more than a whisper.

'Yeah?'

'Were you scared?'

Ben felt his face contort as if he'd been struck. His lips tightened into thin white lines that he pressed firmly together. He looked back at his son solemnly and nodded.

Joel seemed to consider this carefully for a moment, then he looked up once more into his father's eyes and told him, 'You don't have to be scared anymore.'

'—floor?'

'Hmm?'

'What floor?' a female voice asked again, pulling Ben from his reverie.

He looked around. He was standing in front of an open elevator. A young woman was perched just inside, her right hand preventing the door from sliding shut.

'Oh . . . Yes, thank you.' He stepped across the threshold. 'Fourth floor, please.'

The woman reached forward and pressed the button. She appeared to hesitate for a moment, then asked, 'Are you all right?'

'Fine,' Ben replied. 'Why do you ask?'

She smiled at him. 'You were talking to yourself.'

'Oh. Sorry about that,' he apologized. 'I was just . . . thinking of something that happened a few years ago.'

She nodded.

Ben glanced down at his feet, slightly embarrassed. Joel's voice ('*You don't have to be scared anymore*') still echoed inside of his head. He looked up at the woman standing beside him. 'What did I say?' he asked.

'I think you said' – she paused, frowning uncertainly – '"*But I am.*"'

Chapter 31

It seemed that she was always in the woods, in the dark belly of the forest. She ran panic-stricken through the trees, the bramble snatching at her calves and ankles with its greedy carnivorous claws, tearing deep red fissures into her flesh. Her chest heaved with exertion, the dank air filling her lungs over and over and yet never quelling the incessant burning within. Branches grasped at her shoulders as she passed, slowing her escape, trying to pull her to the ground. The voice in her head raced around on its little track (. . . *low and quiet . . . cover myself with leaves . . . distance between us . . . run right by me . . .*) and ended up right back where it had started. She could hear him coming for her, could sense him getting closer, could almost feel the outstretched fingers brushing up against the back of her neck. Her sneakers dug for traction in the wet mud. He was *so close* now. She could hear his breath coming in quick, measured gasps. She couldn't shake him, couldn't hide from him, couldn't outdistance or outmaneuver him. Soon he would be upon her, his fingers tightening around her throat, his teeth sinking deep into her neck.

She glanced backward – saw him barreling through the bushes a few yards behind her. In utter terror, she propelled herself onward, leaping over a thick nest of bramble. Then suddenly, she was falling, her body accelerating downward past a wall of mud and roots that jutted out at her like gnarled, severed limbs. She fell for several seconds, then landed awkwardly, feeling the snap of her left ankle as she struck the bottom of the ravine. The pain was excruciating. She rolled over onto her back, her hands clutching the deformity of her lower leg, and she opened her mouth to scream. Then she stopped, the cry dying in her throat before it was uttered.

He was looking down at her from the lip of the precipice high above, his features unrecognizable in the darkness. There was no sound except for her own ragged breathing and the soft rustle of tree limbs in the wind. The two of them stared at one another for several seconds, and she had time to think, *This is not how it happened before. This is something different.* Then she watched as he got down onto his stomach and swung his legs out over the edge, his feet searching for purchase amid the sporadic knobs of roots protruding from the wall. '*No,*' she whispered, peering up at him as he began lowering himself slowly, one foothold at a time, toward the bottom of the ravine.

There was no option of standing or running, she realized, looking down at the ruined, grotesque angulation of her ankle. She tried to pull herself up into a seated position, but the slightest movement of her leg brought the dull, throbbing pain to a sudden, unbearable crescendo that blanched her vision and caused her to teeter on the brink of unconsciousness. *Maybe that would be better,* she thought to herself. She did not want to be awake when he reached her, could not endure the horror of simply lying here sprawled in the mud, watching him close the distance between them.

'Got to wake yourself up,' a thin voice sounded somewhere off to her left. She turned her head in that direction. In the dim light, she could make out the shape of a female figure lying on the ground about fifteen feet from her current position. The face was turned away from her, but the voice had a familiarity to it that she almost recognized.

'Are you okay?' she asked the girl, for there was something not quite right in the shape of the torso, in the stillness of the chest that did not rise and fall with the usual cycle of breathing.

'*Look! He's already halfway down.*' The girl pointed with her left hand toward the figure above them. Two of her fingers were missing.

'I . . . I can't move,' Monica told her. 'My ankle . . . it's broken.'

The girl turned her head to look up at the night

sky. The top of her right ear, Monica could see, had been torn away, leaving behind a jagged, glistening line of cartilage.

'You're not where you think you are,' the girl said. 'The worst of it is already behind you. You've already made it to the roadway.'

'*What* roadway? I don't understand.' Monica glanced upward. The figure had almost completed his descent. Soon he would be –

'*Wake up!*' The girl's voice was filled with urgency.

Monica shook her head. 'No. I can't just leave you here.'

To her surprise, the girl lying beside her began to laugh. It started softly, then rose in pitch and volume until it filled the night sky above them. A moment later, the figure descending the wall reached the bottom. He turned and quickly traversed the few remaining yards between them. There was an instrument – something long and sharp – in his left hand, and he began to raise it high over his head. Monica turned to look at the girl. 'I can't leave you here!' she wailed.

'*No? You sure about that?*' The girl turned her head so that she was staring directly back at her. The girl's face was a mirror image of Monica's own, only the eyes were dead and vacant. '*You sure about that?*' it said again, as the left arm of the figure looming above them began to swing downward.

'*Wake up!*' she screamed, and she wasn't certain which body she inhabited now – the living or the dead. '*Wake up! Wake up! Wakeup Wakeup Wakeup!!*'

209

The instrument plummeting like a raptor from the sky . . .

And somewhere in Children's Hospital her eyes flew open, staring into the darkness of a room she did not recognize, her body still bracing itself for the blow.

PART FOUR

Pieces

Chapter 32

Ben brought the car to a stop, nestling the right wheels up against the curb. Vehicles crowded the small street on either side, an unfamiliar spectacle in this sleepy community whose inhabitants had grown unaccustomed to the finer points of parallel parking. Half a block down, Tony Linwood was climbing into his parked cruiser. He glanced over, and Ben raised a hand. Tony smiled and waved back.

'Quite a turnout,' Susan commented from the front passenger seat, unbuckling her seat belt.

'Yeah,' Ben replied, taking stock of the swarm of people congregated on the front lawn of the Dresslers' residence three houses down. After eleven and a half weeks in the hospital, Monica Dressler was finally home, and the whole town, it seemed, had come here to welcome her back.

'Dad, can I have a slice of this when we get inside?' Joel asked from the backseat. On his lap, he was holding a pie that Susan had baked this morning in anticipation of the event. It was covered with plastic wrap, but the warm, sweet smell had still managed to permeate the car during their short trip.

'You fat pig,' Thomas whispered from the seat next to him. Joel stuck his tongue out at his older brother, who reached over and pinched his left flank hard enough for Joel to yell out in protest. The pie plate tottered precariously in Joel's lap.

'*Stop it*,' Susan hissed, glaring back at them. She'd been irritable most of the morning. Most likely, Ben thought, it was the prospect of coming here today. Despite Monica's excellent recovery, his wife still found the topic upsetting to talk about. Some tragedies, he supposed, fell too close to home.

'Shall we?' Ben prompted, grasping the latch to his door.

They stepped out into the August sunshine. The air, thick and humid, hung on them like a grumpy child demanding to be carried. Tiny insects weaved in frenzied clouds in front of Ben's face, and perspiration dampened the back of his shirt as he walked with his family up the street. They ascended the front steps and laced their way slowly through the crowd, extending greetings and engaging in brief conversations as they went.

The interior of the domicile was full of friends and acquaintances, and Ben was reminded of the similar reception at Children's Hospital many weeks ago, a time when things had not looked so promising. The somber concern etched into many of those faces was gone now, replaced by a jubilant, almost giddy atmosphere of celebration and relief. They had pulled through this together, it seemed, and at the center of it all was Monica Dressler, who sat on the couch in the family room like a china doll on display, a glass of apple cider resting in her lap. She glanced over at them and waved, the pleasant smile surfacing like a reflex.

'Come on,' Thomas said to his brother in a rare display of inclusiveness. 'Let's go say hi.'

Susan shot them a look but said nothing, taking the pie from Joel's hands.

Ben placed a hand on the small of her back. 'It's okay. Let's find Paul and Vera.'

'I'll need to get over to the hospital soon,' she advised him. 'I still have some patients I need to check on.'

'Sure,' Ben acknowledged, trying not to be angry with her. Standing here amid the din of cheerful conversation, the attack nearly three months behind them and with no similar events since then, he couldn't help but feel optimistic. The fingers of anxiety and dread that had taken hold of him following the murder of Kevin Tanner had loosened their grip significantly, their presence now feeling like a scar from a wound that had almost healed. The worst of it was behind them, he felt, and like almost everyone else here he had chosen to embrace the idea that this town would indeed recover. He was riled by his wife's reluctance to do the same.

A hand fell upon his right shoulder. 'Now, there's

a man who looks like he needs a drink.' Ben turned to encounter Paul Dressler, smiling broadly.

'Hi, Paul. Good to see you.' He looped a hand around Susan's elbow, and she too turned to greet Monica's father.

'Thanks so much for coming,' Paul said. 'It really means a lot to us.'

Susan smiled. 'You must be so relieved to have her home again.'

'We're very grateful,' he said. 'The doctors and nurses took such good care of her. And the thoughts and prayers of everyone here played a major role in getting her home so quickly. Vera and I are overwhelmed with gratitude.'

'How's she feeling?' Ben asked.

'Much better,' he replied. 'She has pain, of course – part of the healing process – but they've given her medication for that. They set her up with a physical therapist five days a week. They have her walking on a treadmill, exercising the muscles in her left hand, working on getting her strength back . . . all kinds of things. They don't take it easy on her, either. She comes home pretty exhausted.' Paul glanced to his right and spotted his wife near the entrance to the kitchen. He waved for her to join them.

'Hi, Susan,' Vera said, walking over and giving Ben's wife a hug. 'I'm so glad you were able to make it.'

'I wouldn't have missed it,' Susan replied, and Ben smiled to himself, recalling the resistance he'd had to contend with at home. 'Paul was telling us about Monica's physical therapy,' Susan noted.

'Oh, yes,' Vera said, rolling her eyes. 'They work her so hard. I honestly don't know if it's good for her, so soon after being released from the hospital.'

'The doctors said it's important,' Paul reminded her. 'We want her to be able to regain as much function as possible.'

'I know,' she said. She turned a conferring gaze toward Susan. 'It just seems a little extreme, is all.'

'I'm sure the physical therapists know what they're doing,' Ben's wife responded, trying to reassure her.

Vera turned her head to study her daughter from across the room. She was sitting on the couch next to Thomas, who was resting a hand on her shoulder and conveying some piece of juicy gossip to her in hushed, conspiratorial tones. Monica listened for a moment, her eyes cast slightly up and to the right, then her face broke into a wide grin and she brought her left hand up to cover her mouth as she laughed. From this distance, the two prosthetic fingers looked natural and uniform with the other digits. Vera turned back to Ben and Susan, who had followed her gaze. Her face was contorted into a mishmash of pain and gladness. 'Thomas has been so good with her,' she said. 'They've become close over these past several weeks.' She smiled, her eyes glistening with moisture. 'It's good to see her laugh.'

Susan nodded. 'Is she saying much?'

The volume of the conversations around them seemed to decrease slightly, as if this were a question on everyone's mind.

Vera's face took on a hard, protective look that

Ben had seen once previously when he and Thomas had visited Monica in the hospital. ('*They said she'll probably wake up very soon,*' Vera had told them then. '*Dr Elliot says there's no reason she shouldn't.*')

'She talks plenty,' Vera advised them. 'She's able to make her needs known to us.' She searched their faces for understanding, and Ben found himself nodding supportively, wanting to place her fears at ease. 'She's been through a lot,' Vera continued. 'The doctors said she'll open up more with time.'

'She doesn't recall much about the incident?' Susan asked, and Ben shot her a reproachful look. This was obviously uncomfortable territory for Monica's mother.

'No, not much,' Vera replied, looking down for a moment at the tan carpeting beneath their feet. She looked up at them again, her eyes weary. 'And given the circumstances, I think that's best, don't you?'

'Yes,' Susan agreed, taking Vera by the hand, her body transforming into a soft posture of empathy – a physical bearing, Ben thought, that seemed to come so much more naturally to women. 'Yes, I do.'

Chapter 33

'Are you sure you're ready?' he asked, positioning his player for the penalty shot. The electronic crowd on the television screen in front of them roared with simulated fervor. 'I'm not gonna take it easy on you this time.'

'Go ahead. Bring it,' she replied, adjusting the Xbox 360 controller in her lap. She used her right hand for most of the controls, but she could still use her functional left thumb on the D-pad and left stick. She'd never been one for video games in the past, but her physical therapist had suggested that thirty minutes a day would help with her fine motor control, and Monica found that the games also helped pass the time, particularly when her friends came to visit. *Anything to take the attention off me,* she thought.

Thomas's striker moved slightly to the right, then his body was in motion and he kicked the ball toward the upper left corner as Monica's goalkeeper made a diving leap in that direction, deflecting the soccer ball up and over the goalpost.

'*No goal!*' she exclaimed as the crowd went wild. '*What a save!*'

'Lucky,' Thomas remarked. 'You anticipated that one.'

'No, I'm just faster than you – even with only one good hand. Here, let's take a look at the instant replay.'

'We don't need to watch the replay,' he said, but the slow-motion video was already under way.

'It looks even better the second time,' she teased him, and he covered his eyes in protest.

'That's two games to none,' she said. 'You ready to quit?'

'Absolutely,' he replied. 'I know when I'm beaten.' He rose and made his way to the kitchen. 'You want anything from the fridge?'

'No, I'm good,' she called out, returning the equipment to the cabinet beneath the TV.

Thomas returned to the living room, a glass of juice in his hand. He sat down on the couch and looked at her, shaking his head.

'What?' she asked.

'You're doing great. Two months ago you were just getting home from the hospital, and now you're kicking my butt in soccer.'

'Video soccer,' she clarified. 'It doesn't take much athleticism to sit in front of the television pushing buttons. It's the real-life physical activity that still gets me.'

He shrugged. 'Little bit at a time. Feel like going for a walk?'

She glanced out through the window and frowned. 'It looks windy outside today.'

He said nothing, just sat there sipping his drink, studying her with those cavernous green eyes.

She sighed, realizing how pathetic the excuse sounded – even to her own ears. Since returning from the hospital, wandering more than a few blocks from the house made her nervous. She could tolerate the trips to her physical therapy appointments, which were indoors and took place in surroundings that were both familiar and unchanging, but being outside was a different animal altogether. For the past eight weeks, Thomas had been helping her with that anxiety, encouraging her to take walks with him throughout the neighborhood during his frequent visits. There were days, in fact, when it wasn't so bad – when she could imagine going out by herself, could imagine returning to the activities she'd taken for granted only five months before. But there were others days – ones like this one – when that degree of comfort and independence still seemed a long way off.

'Okay.' She acquiesced. 'Let me get my jacket.'

They left the house and ventured out into the October afternoon. The daylight hours were getting shorter now, the fall season settling in with its restless, gusting days and clear, chilly nights. Already the leaves were abandoning their perches, casting themselves bravely into the abyss as they fluttered silently and gracefully to the earth. And with the thinning of deciduous limbs came the thinning of activity, as people began to hunker down in anticipation of the approaching winter. Cars sat dormant in driveways, and the few people they passed seemed to move with a stiff, deliberate pace, as if their minds were burdened with other things as they dragged rakes back and forth across modest yards, their hands rising now and then to wipe absently at their noses. A small dog paced them briefly as the two teenagers ambled down the sidewalk, but even he lost interest after half a block, turning back to return to the front steps from which he had risen.

'Seems quiet out here,' Monica observed. 'There are fewer people than I remember.'

Thomas said nothing, only waved to an old man taking out the trash.

'Do you feel like people have changed around here since all this began?' she asked.

'What do you mean?'

'They just seem . . . less sociable . . . more cautious, even with those they know. I feel like people are pulling in on themselves.'

Thomas thought this over. 'I feel like we've been asleep for a long time,' he said, 'and now we're finally waking up. We're opening our eyes and seeing what's out there – what has probably been out there all along.' He stooped to remove a stick from the walkway, tossing it onto the grass to their left. 'It scares people. They don't know what to do.'

They walked on in silence for a while, the wind billowing insistently at their backs.

'It's times like this when we need each other the most,' she said, looping her arm around his and giving him a brief squeeze. He looked at her and smiled, his face calm and impassive as the rest of the world swirled wildly around them.

Chapter 34

'*Excellent! You came!*' Devon greeted Thomas and Monica as they approached the group from across the open field. Their feet shushed through a blanket of gold and burgundy leaves, leaving linear wakes of exposed grass behind them.

'Of *course* we came,' Thomas replied, pulling a pair of cleats out of the duffel bag he was carrying. He sat down on the ground and began removing his sneakers.

'You're in for it this time, Stevenson,' Devon warned him. 'I've got Big Joe on my team.'

Joe Dashel stepped forward from amid the cluster of teens. Joe had played college football for Ohio State during his freshman and sophomore years, but a knee injury had sidelined his athletic career for the final two years of college. With his bum knee, Big Joe wasn't as fast as he used to be, but at 240 pounds he could still pack one hell of a wallop. 'Sorry.' He shrugged. 'He's been asking me all week.'

Thomas gave Devon a disparaging look. 'All week, huh?'

'*Hey, what can I say?*' Devon responded. 'I've got a score to settle.'

Marty Spears ran at half speed onto the field, cutting to the left in a cross pattern twenty yards out. 'Hit me,' he said, and Russell Long threw a spiral pass into his outstretched arms.

Devon looked down at him. 'What d'ya say, T? The teams are all set. We're just waitin' for you.'

'Well, let's do it,' Thomas replied, stuffing his tennis shoes into the duffel bag and getting up from the grass. He turned to Monica. 'You okay?'

'Mm-hmm,' she said with a nod, then took a seat beside Lynn Montague and Cynthia Castleberry.

The boys fanned out across the field, already talking smack before the game had commenced. 'Remember,' Devon called out to his teammates as they prepared to receive the initial kickoff, 'if you catch the ball, lateral it to Big Joe.'

'Okay, here it comes!' Bret Graham yelled, and with a *whumpf* the ball was punted high into the air, turning once end over end as it traveled deep into the other team's territory.

'It's great of you to come,' Lynn commented, leaning over and giving Monica a sideways hug.

'Thanks.' Monica smiled. 'It feels good to get outside. I really missed that, being in the hospital.'

'How do you feel?' Cynthia asked.

'Okay. Not great, but okay,' Monica replied, trying to remain upbeat but honest. The truth was, her days were still overshadowed by pain and stiffness much of the time. Her physical therapy sessions were often agonizing. The medications the doctors had prescribed only went so far to alleviate those symptoms. And, of course, there were the nightmares.

'You cut your hair short,' Lynn observed. 'It used to be down past your shoulder blades.'

Monica reached up with her right hand, fingering the short black locks. 'It was just easier,' she said, 'less to deal with.' She kept her other hand tucked into the front pocket of her hoodie, self-conscious of the two prosthetic fingers, despite the meticulous attention the plastic surgeon had paid to their aesthetic appearance.

'I like your hair this way,' Lynn told her. 'I think it's cute.'

'Thanks.'

On the field, there was an audible crunch as Big Joe made his first hit, sending Bret Graham to the earth like a wet towel. Cynthia winced. 'You okay?' she called out.

'Fine, fine,' Bret assured her, getting up slowly and lifting a hand in her direction. He looked a little dazed.

'Hey,' Devon admonished him. 'No fraternizing with the spectators.'

Monica looked at Cynthia. 'So you and Bret are a thing now?' It was amazing how much she'd missed. There was something profoundly distressing about emerging from such a prolonged incapacitation to find that the world had moved on without her. It was an emotional sucker punch she hadn't quite anticipated.

'We've gone out a few times,' Cynthia told her. 'It doesn't mean we're going steady or anything.' She turned an appraising eye in Monica's direction. 'What about you and Thomas? You two seem pretty close lately.'

Monica blushed, and there was only so much her pale skin could do to hide it. 'We're just friends,' she said. 'He's been very kind to me.'

'Seems like more than that to me,' Cynthia remarked, but she didn't press her further. '*Run, baby, run!*' she yelled as Bret made a mad dash down the sideline toward the end zone.

They watched for a while longer, alternating cheers and protests as the game went on. Paul Dalouka took a hit from Big Joe that knocked the wind out of him hard enough that he elected to sit out most of the third quarter. Monica began to feel her limbs stiffening as she sat there on the grass, and there was a mounting pressure within her bladder that she was able to ignore for only so long. She considered going home, but it felt good to be among her friends in a setting where she was not the frail and beleaguered center of attention. She glanced around. There was no public restroom in the vicinity, just the field, the surrounding woods and a small parking lot to the north. She decided to hold out a while longer, but after another fifteen minutes there were few remaining options.

'I've got to go pee,' she whispered to Cynthia, and

she stood up and made her way toward the woods at the outskirts of the park. She stood at the lip of the forest, peering in. The fall season had already robbed the trees and much of the underbrush of their leaves, making for a less effective visible curtain from the vantage point of the field behind her. She would have to go in a ways to ensure her privacy. She took a step forward, and from beneath the sole of her shoe the leaves and small sticks crackled loudly in her ears. She closed her eyes. *I can do this,* she thought to herself. *I'm just gonna go in a few yards, is all. I'm perfectly safe here.*

She opened her eyes and took another step forward, and another, willing herself to go on. A tree branch jutted out at her, and her hand went instinctively to her throat to protect herself. The pace of her respirations quickened. She was finding it difficult to breath. In her mind, she pictured herself lying in a frozen pond beneath the ice, trapped only inches from the surface as her hands and mouth searched desperately for an opening. Her lips and fingers began to tingle. She could hear her own heartbeat smashing wildly against her chest. To her right, something dark and furry darted across the ground. She followed it with her eyes, and when she looked up he was standing there in the forest waiting for her, beginning to move silently in her direction. She turned to run, turned to escape, but it was too late, too late because he was directly behind her now, the tips of his fingers brushing against her dark black hair, grasping for a purchase, and she opened her mouth to scream and this time she found her voice in time, and she screamed and screamed for them to come and find her before it was too late, before she felt the first slice of the instrument in her chest. There was warmth now sliding down the inside of her leg and she knew she was bleeding heavily but she couldn't find the wound. She stumbled out of the woods and fell to the ground, curling herself into a tight ball, her arms wrapped protectively around her head as she continued to scream, waiting for the searing pain that would descend upon her and the blackness to follow . . .

. . . commotion now, the sound of footsteps running toward her, someone yelling to give her space. She'd made it to the side of the road somehow, and they had found her, lying here in the mud and rain . . .

'Monica.' Someone's voice, a hand stroking the side of her head. 'Monica, honey. You're okay. You're okay.' But she wasn't okay – wasn't okay at all. *Can't they see what he did to me?* She could feel the paramedics hoisting her body into the rig, could feel the sharp pinch of a needle as it entered her arm. *Hang on, girl. You stay with us now, do you hear me?*

'Monica.' Again in her ear, a female voice, calm and reassuring. 'Open your eyes. We're all right here with you. You're safe, honey. It's okay.'

She opened her eyes, and the bright sunlight flooded in. Here was the face of Lynn Montague, and the others behind her. They looked down at her, all of them, their expressions uncertain and apprehensive. 'Do you want me to call an ambulance?' someone asked in a hesitant voice, and Lynn shook her head.

'No. No, she's fine. She's okay.' She continued to stroke Monica's hair, gently brushing away the leaves and broken strands of grass that had taken refuge there. 'Leave us alone. Go back to your game.'

They went, the sounds of their voices fading in the distance, and Monica began to cry. Her body shook, and she turned her face into the grass, drawing her legs up farther into a fetal position. Lynn wrapped an arm around her shoulders, trying to soothe her. 'Shhh, it's okay. You're safe,' she whispered. Monica looked up at her with supplicating eyes. There was something beaten and naked in her expression. 'I wet my pants,' she said, as if she were a young child standing shamefaced in the doorway of her parents' bedroom.

And once again she began to cry.

Chapter 35

'Come in. It's open,' the chief of police called out from behind his desk in response to the light rapping on his office door. He gathered the few papers scattered in front of him, sliding them into a manila folder. As his years of service on the force continued to march along, he was finding himself increasingly trapped in this somewhat depressing administrative office attending to an ever-growing assortment of paperwork. It was certainly one of the downsides of the elected position he'd held over the past twelve years, and it was a chore he would be happy to relinquish once he retired. As far as he could tell, all of those forms over the course of his career – literally *thousands* by now – hadn't ever done anyone any good.

The door to his office opened, and Detective Schroeder stepped inside. 'You got a minute, Chief?' he asked.

'Sure, Carl. What's up?' Sam leaned back in his chair and gestured for the man to take a seat.

Carl pulled a small notebook from his inside suit pocket as he sat down. 'The body they pulled out of the west bank this morning doesn't look like the work of our guy,' he reported.

'No?'

'Single gunshot wound to the right temple. Powder tattooing of the skin. Very close range. Most likely self-inflicted. We've made a positive ID and the wife's been interviewed. Guy lost his job six weeks ago. Wife says he's been acting pretty depressed lately. Almost certainly a suicide, although we're still waiting for the ballistics report.'

'What's he doing washing up on the bank of the Ohio River?' Sam asked.

'The guy lived in Newell, West Virginia, about thirty minutes north of here. Right off the river. We've got a witness says he heard a gunshot near the bridge to East Liverpool two nights ago. He called it in to West Virginia State Police, who sent an investigating officer but found nothing. The most likely scenario is the guy shot himself on the bridge, fell into the river below, and was swept downstream in the current, surfacing two days later on the west bank just south of Brown's Island.'

Sam nodded. 'I suppose he could've still been murdered and dumped in the river, but I agree that a single gunshot to the head doesn't sound much like our guy's work.'

'Nope.'

'So . . .' Sam mused. 'It's been five months since the second attack. Maybe he decided to move on. For all we know, he could be somewhere in southern Arkansas by now.'

'Yeah,' Carl agreed, but without much enthusiasm. 'Maybe.'

'But you don't think so,' Sam observed. It was not a question.

'No. I don't.'

Sam sighed. 'Neither do I.' His face looked tired, carrying within it the accumulating effects of more than a few sleepless nights since this whole mess had begun. 'What about the psych patient who escaped from the hospital? Any word on him?'

'He hasn't turned up yet, although we've certainly been out looking for him.' Carl frowned. 'The FBI's forensic profiler doesn't think he's our man.'

'Why is that?'

'She says that psychosis is not usually the primary issue with serial killers. Let's see, I have a quote from her somewhere in here . . .' He flipped back several pages in his notebook. 'Okay, here it is. "Medically speaking," she says, "psychosis involves a loss of contact with reality. Symptoms include delusions and hallucinations, which are false perceptions of reality. Serial killers, on the other hand, usually have a fairly accurate perception of reality. They often seem normal, even charming, and they understand right from wrong. They just don't care."' Carl looked up. 'The way she explained it to me, Chief, is that psychotic patients get better with treatment and medication. Serial killers don't.'

Sam folded his hands in front of him. 'They can't be fixed.'

'No,' Carl replied. 'Which is why they continue to kill people—'

'Until they're stopped.'

'Right, Sam. Until they're stopped.'

The big man was silent for a moment, his eyes focused on the desk in front of him. 'The Dressler girl give us anything useful yet?'

'Nothing helpful to the investigation,' Carl answered. Following her return to consciousness, he'd visited her twice a week in the hospital. She'd been nonverbal during the first two of those weeks, and his questions had been met with dull stares interspersed with episodes of sporadic sobbing that had escalated, in a few unsettling cases, into outright screams, requiring administration of a hefty dose of sedative by the hospital staff. The girl's nurse had cast a disapproving look at Carl enough times for him to give it a rest for a while. As time passed, however, Monica *had* begun to talk, first in single-word utterances and later in more normal sentences. When she did speak, it was mostly to her parents and friends, and although Carl's face had become a familiar one by now, she'd said very little to him – none of it pertaining to the night she'd been attacked. He'd tried a few more times since she'd returned home, but eventually her mother had asked him, politely, if it wouldn't be better to let Monica recover some more before paying her any further visits. 'I'm sorry,' she'd apologized. 'It's just that

234

she seems to do better on days when you're not here.'

In the office now, Carl and Sam sat across from one another, contemplating the same thing but having no new developments to discuss. It was frustrating, not only because the physical evidence so far hadn't yielded a suspect, but because time was not on their side. Sooner or later their lack of forward progress on the case would most likely cost them another life.

'Still nothing from the BMV images?' Sam already knew the answer to this question. Hell, they'd closed that avenue of investigation more than three months ago. But sometimes it didn't hurt to go over things again.

Carl shook his head. 'Nothing worth pursuing further,' he said. 'Four individuals with driver's license images demonstrating the left upper canine–premolar diastasis we were looking for. One of the four people is dead. Another one is seventy-four years of age and has advanced lung disease. He can't walk from one room of his house to the next without gasping for air and having to rest for fifteen minutes on home oxygen. The other two individuals both have solid alibis during the time of at least one of the two attacks.'

'So it's a dead end.'

'Pretty much, Chief.'

Sam leaned forward in his office chair, which emitted a soft creak of protest but held fast. The leather swivel chair had been brought into the office shortly after he was elected chief of police in 2001 and had served the large man faithfully during his entire tenure. Carl wondered how much life the legs of that chair still had in them, and he couldn't help but imagine the explosive result of their eventual failure.

'The shoe prints from the second crime scene,' Sam said. 'Any further progress on tracking those down?'

'Size eleven men's Nikes. They're from a model that came out a few years back. I checked the . . .'

'How *many* years back?' Sam interrupted him. He was a patient man, but he didn't like ambiguity when it came to the evidence. If one could pin something down more exactly, it ought to be done. Sometimes it made a difference.

'Two,' Carl answered, unflustered. He was used to working with Sam Garston, and had spent many sessions with the chief in this very office during prior cases, the two of them rehashing the evidence incessantly until the pieces eventually began to fit together – sometimes, it seemed, by sheer will alone.

'What model?' Sam asked.

Carl picked up his notepad and flipped back several pages. 'Nike Trainer. Manufactured from November 2011 through July 2012. Sold widely across the US in numerous retail stores, as well as online. Pretty popular. It's a cross-training shoe.'

'Records from local retailers?'

'Six retailers in the area carried the shoe. Two have since gone out of business and there are no records available. Three of the remaining four stores were able to come up with sales records regarding that size and model during the nine months they were sold. Roughly' – he flipped his notepad forward two pages – 'sixty pairs were sold during that time. About one-third of the purchases were in cash.' He looked up from the notebook. 'That leaves a lot of cracks to fall through, Chief.'

'Uh-huh.' Sam shifted in his chair and there was another protracted, disquieting creak from the supporting structure as he did so. He smiled at his colleague. 'How are you getting along with the feds?' he asked.

Carl shrugged his shoulders. 'I've been trying to play nice.'

'I appreciate that. And Detective Hunt? How's he holding up?'

'Danny? I don't know . . . still learning the job, I guess.' Carl returned his notebook to the pocket from whence it had come. 'I think he'll be fine, boss,' he remarked, 'just as soon as he graduates from high school.'

'Just wait till he's old enough to drink,' Sam warned him.

'Tell me about it. These new guys on the force . . . you know: lookin' younger every year.'

Sam nodded in agreement. He looked thoughtful for a moment, his eyes focusing on a spot in the corner of the room he could see just over Carl's left shoulder. *Lookin' younger every year*. Sure. That was bound to happen as one's own years went by with ever-increasing velocity – an occupational hazard of growing old. *But was that all,* Sam wondered, *or was there something else there?* He felt a slight tug in his chest, the pull of an idea that had taken shape while he wasn't paying attention and was now trying to punch its way through to his conscious mind.

'—okay, Chief?'

'What?'

'You okay?'

Reluctantly, he returned to the moment at hand. Detective Schroeder was watching him questioningly.

'Think I lost you there for a moment, Chief.'

'Sorry.'

'Anyway,' Carl said, 'I'd like to stay and chat, but I have to meet with Special Agent Culver from the FBI now, who wants to go over the phone records of every resident in eastern Ohio over the past ten years, or some other equally useless but time-consuming project.'

'Whatever it takes,' Sam replied, and there was something hard in his eyes, like a boy who has been beaten one time too many, and suddenly decides to come up swinging. 'Let's get this guy, Carl. I don't want any more mutilated bodies turning up in this town.'

'Neither do I,' the detective agreed as he rose to go. 'Neither do I.'

Chapter 36

'How's it goin'?' he asked, taking a seat at the table across from her. He'd poured two cans of tomato soup into a sauce pan that was heating on the range.

'Okay, I guess. I'm sore today.'

'Where?'

'My arms, mostly. They've got me doing these exercises with dumbbells now.'

Thomas gave her an appraising look. 'You're a lot stronger than you were when you first came home from the hospital. The physical therapy must really be helping.' He got up and went to the stove, turned off the burner and ladled most of the soup into two bowls. 'The muscles of your arms and legs are getting ripped.' He placed the bowls on the table, filled two glasses with water, grabbed a set of spoons from the drawer, and returned to his seat. '*Bon appétit*,' he said.

'Thanks,' she said with a smile. She basked in his compliment, knowing that what he had just said was true. She *was* much stronger now than when she'd first returned home from the hospital, and her arms and legs had become toned and chiseled from her endless succession of mandatory workouts. Except for the pink ridge of scar tissue that ran the length of her abdomen, her stomach was otherwise tight and flat above the subtle outline of her upper pelvis. From a physical standpoint, in fact, she was tougher and more resilient than she'd ever been.

They ate in silence for a while. It was a Saturday in late October. The weather had begun to turn cold, and it was a small pleasure to feel the warmth of the meal settling into her stomach one spoonful at a time. Her parents were attending a retirement party for one of her dad's colleagues, and they'd left the two of them to fend for themselves for the afternoon. She looked over at Thomas, who had become a semi-regular presence in their household, stopping over most days after school – sometimes with a few of Monica's other friends, but quite often on his own. They would spend those afternoons sitting together in the living room watching television, discussing social happenings among their peers, or heading outdoors for walks and other outings when the weather was nice. It was good for her, she thought. She was being homeschooled for the year, and although this made it easier to coordinate her daily physical therapy sessions and regular medical checkups, she missed interacting with her friends. She found herself looking forward to Thomas's visits and was disappointed on days when he couldn't make it. Still, she sometimes wondered how it could be that one of the most popular guys in school had taken an interest in her – a shy, brainy type who would now struggle with a physical disability for the rest of her life.

'So, what are you doing for Halloween?' he asked, tipping his bowl slightly to scoop up the last bit of soup with his spoon.

She shrugged. 'I don't know.' She hadn't really thought about it much beyond what she *wouldn't* be doing. Trick-or-treating through the neighborhoods in the dark, going to a horror movie or a haunted house – all of those things were *definitely* out of the question.

'Ernie Samper's throwing a party at his house,' Thomas said. 'A lot of people are going, I think.'

She nodded. *A party – just like the last one,* she thought, and a shudder rolled through her body. No, she decided. She couldn't. Even the idea of it made her feel panicky. So many things still did these days. She had a running list in her mind, and she added 'going to a party at night with my friends' to it. Just one more thing she couldn't do – might *never* be able to do – and this thought made her feel isolated and alone. She was a different person now: someone who hid in her house, looking out at the world instead of participating in it; someone who didn't answer the phone when she was home alone, who made more excuses than plans; someone who still dreamed of being chased through the forest, of lying there in the mud as the figure's hand rose above her before plunging downward again and again. There was a piece of her that had been torn away that night, something the surgeons could never replace. She placed a hand over her face, feeling the tears welling up inside her.

Thomas watched her from across the table as she struggled to compose herself.

'It's just that . . . it's just . . .' She made a fist and brought it down hard on the table, causing the spoons to rattle in their empty bowls. The tears rolled freely down her cheeks now, making her appear raw and defenseless in the yellow glow of the overhead light. 'Look at me,' she said. '*I'm a freak.*'

'No, you're not.'

'*Yes, I am!*' She got up suddenly, collecting their bowls and bringing them to the sink, where she filled them with water. The room became quiet except for the sound of the running tap. A few of the neighborhood children were playing ball in the street outside, and their voices filtered softly through the walls of the house and into the kitchen. After a few moments, she shut off the water and turned to face him. The tears were gone, but her eyes were still red and swollen.

'I'm sorry, Thomas. I need to lie down for a while.'

'Sure,' he said. 'No problem.'

'I'll call you later,' she told him, and she left the kitchen, heading down the hall and into her bedroom. She kicked off her shoes and slipped under the warmth of the sheets.

'You sure you're okay?' he asked, hesitating in the doorway.

She turned to look at him from where she lay. 'No. I'm not.'

He came in, pulled a chair up next to the bed. He looked at her blankly, saying nothing.

Monica looked up at the bedroom ceiling, watching the way the light from the window danced and swayed across the smooth surface above her. 'I still dream about it, you know.'

'That night?' he asked, and she nodded.

'I dream about running through the woods, about being chased and finally overtaken. I dream about being left there to die in the darkness.'

He closed his eyes for a moment, as if trying to picture it.

She said nothing, only turned her head to the right so that she could look out at the day through the window across the room.

'In these dreams,' he asked, 'do you ever recognize him? Even the smallest detail might help the police to—'

'No,' she said. 'Nothing. Just . . . a shape. A presence.'

He nodded.

'But sometimes when I wake up,' she confided, 'and even later, in the light of day . . .' She looked at him now, needing to make herself understood. 'I can't help but wonder: *Am I still back there? Am I still lying there in the dirt, and all of this*' – she took in the room briefly with her eyes – 'is something else? A dream, maybe. Wishful thinking. Or perhaps . . .'

'What?' he asked.

She looked down at the shape of her body beneath the sheets, as if assuring herself of its presence.

'Perhaps I never made it out of the forest that night. Perhaps I'm really dead. I mean' – her eyes searched his face as she considered this again for a moment – '*how would I know if I wasn't?*'

Thomas shook his head. 'You're not dead.' He touched her right ear, ran his finger along the line where her own flesh merged neatly with the silicone prosthetic. 'You have the scars to prove it.'

'Don't,' she said, turning her face away from him. 'It's disgusting.'

He withdrew his hand.

'*I'm* disgusting.' Her voice was small and defeated.

'No,' he replied. 'Not to me.'

She turned her head and studied him for a moment, gauging his sincerity. He looked back at her without flinching.

'You're sweet,' she told him, reaching up to touch the side of his face with her right hand, feeling the warm, soft contour of his cheek. 'Why do you come here to see me?'

He smiled. 'Don't you know?'

She shook her head.

'Well, you don't know much then.'

'Do you feel sorry for me? Is that why you're so good to me?'

'No.' He withdrew her left hand from beneath the covers, cupping it gently in his palm. His thumb moved lightly across the two digits that were only partially her own. 'Plenty of people in this town feel sorry for you.' He made a face, crinkling the bridge of his nose. 'You must be sick of it.'

'I am,' she replied. 'I . . . I just want to feel normal.'

'Why would you ever want to be normal? You're better than that.' He closed his eyes for a moment, and when he opened them again they somehow seemed to Monica deeper and greener than before. 'No,' he said. 'I've never felt sorry for you.'

She sat up quickly then and kissed him, before she could lose her nerve. His body stiffened briefly in response, then relaxed. She could feel against her chest the measured rhythm of his heart, as if it were her own – and when he kissed her in return it was at once safe and thrilling and everything she had hoped it would be.

'Could you lie here with me?' she asked after they had kissed for a while, and he did, wrapping her in his arms like a child. And sometime later in the silence that followed, as the light filtering through the window tracked its way across the wall with the afternoon's passing, it occurred to Monica that she was still capable of opening her heart if she wanted to, that her thirst for life might someday be stronger than the sum of her fears, and that there were unexpected events on the horizon – a future far removed from the pain and suffering she had endured over these many months. She did not feel whole again, and maybe she never would. But it was a start – a beginning – and starting, she realized, was the hardest part.

Chapter 37

'What d'ya think, Dr S?' Nat called over from the next room. He was holding a human liver in his hands. It was gray and cirrhotic, shrunken from its normal size by a lifetime of heavy drinking. 'How much ya figure it weighs?'

Ben looked through the doorway of his office. 'I'd guess 875 grams.'

Nat shook his head. 'Too high, Dr S. This thing is pickled. I'm goin' with 680.'

'Well, weigh it and find out,' Ben advised, turning his attention back to the papers in front of him.

'Let's place a wager on it,' Nat suggested. 'An extra two days of paid vacation for me this year.'

'You didn't use all your vacation time last year,' Ben reminded him.

'That's why I need an extra two days this year,' Nat said. 'I thought that shit carried over.'

'Nope. Use it or lose it,' Ben told him. 'You've got enough perks and benefits already.'

'*What* perks and benefits?' Nat wanted to know, the liver in his hands temporarily forgotten.

Ben slapped his pencil down on the desk, exasperated. Trying to get paperwork done with Nat in the other room was like trying to enjoy a romantic, candlelit dinner with a three-year-old at the table. 'Are you gonna weigh that thing, or not?'

'Sure. Yeah. Don't get all crotchety on me, Dr S.' Nat walked over to the scale and placed the item in the metal tray. He paused for a moment, allowing the needle to settle on a number. Ben picked up his pencil again and began to –

'*Oooh*, Dr S. It's 692 grams. You were *way* off.'

'Fine, Nat,' he said, without looking up. 'It's 692 grams. Are you happy now?'

'*Definitely.*'

The blank diagnosis box at the bottom of the form stared up at Ben, challenging him to come up with –

'You owe me another two days of vacation this year.'

That did it. Ben closed the folder on his desk, got up, and headed toward the front of the building.

'Where you goin', Dr S?'

Ben didn't answer. He snatched his coat off of the rack, opened the front door, and headed out into the frigid afternoon. The trees were barren now, their thin limbs stretched like black veins toward the sky. Ben placed a hand on the rail before proceeding down the short flight of steps, recalling the thin, nearly invisible sheets of ice he'd spotted this morning in the parking lot. The wind tugged at the collar of his coat. He pulled the zipper up as far as it would go, hunching his shoulders to protect his neck and the lower half of his ears from the chill.

At the bottom of the CO's front steps, he turned right and made his way along the sidewalk. It was mid-December, and there was snow in the forecast – quite a bit of it, from the weatherman's predictions last night. Ben had noticed this morning that the sky had taken on that thick, bloated look. By early afternoon the flakes had begun to fall, and a good two inches already covered the sidewalk. It crunched beneath his boots as he ambled along. When he got home this evening, he'd have a driveway to clear.

Home. Ben felt his gut tighten momentarily. There'd been trouble between him and Susan lately, although he had difficulty placing his finger on exactly why. Tangentially, at least, it seemed related to the two attacks on the teenagers earlier this year. It had been a stressful time for both of them, and Ben realized that he'd probably made matters worse by being so closely involved in the investigation. It was a topic Susan didn't like to talk about, and any attempt to broach the subject usually ended up in an argument.

Three weeks ago they'd gotten into it again. It had become evident over the past month or two that Thomas's relationship with Monica Dressler had extended beyond simple friendship. They'd been spending increasing amounts of time together, and there was little doubt from their body language and the way that they looked at one another that they'd become romantically involved. To Ben, this seemed like a good thing for the both of them, but after dinner one night Susan had gotten on Thomas's case about it. He'd heard them arguing upstairs in the hallway and had gone up to intervene – a mistake, he realized in retrospect. Susan had snapped at him, telling him to stay out of it. After a brief exchange, he'd found himself standing alone in the upstairs hallway, wondering how in the hell *he* had ended up coming off as the bad guy.

He'd caught up to her in the kitchen.

'What was *that* all about?' he demanded, angered by her dismissiveness.

'I don't know,' she responded harshly. 'Why don't you talk to *him* about it.'

'I'm talking to you,' Ben replied, refusing to be bullied.

Susan turned to face him. Her jaw was set in that manner she had when she decided to really dig her heels in about something. 'I don't think he should be dating that girl.'

'Monica? Why?'

'*Why?* Because she's fragile, Ben.'

'Fragile?'

'Yes, fragile.' She put a hand on the countertop, the other on her left hip. 'She's been through a lot – too much, really. I think he needs to leave her alone. One way or the other, he'll end up hurting her.'

Ben was dumbfounded. 'He's been *helping* her,' he pointed out. 'You don't see that?'

She looked back at him, tight-lipped. 'No. I don't.'

Ben walked to the table and rested his palms on the top of a chair back. 'You know what I think?' he started. Susan simply stared at him, waiting. 'I think you don't like him dating her because it's a daily reminder of the assaults. Monica represents something' – he pointed a finger at her – 'that *you're* having difficulty dealing with.'

'What are you, a shrink now?'

'This isn't Thomas's problem,' he told her. 'It's yours.'

She studied him for a moment. 'Well, you're right about that.'

Ben exhaled slowly through his mouth, trying to dissipate some of the anger. There was no use in them fighting about this. If she could just see –

'Yeah,' she said. 'I guess you know just about everything.'

'Now wait a minute,' he protested, holding up a hand. 'That's not fair.'

'No, Ben,' she'd replied, leaving the room. 'It's not.'

It had been three weeks since then. The next day they'd made their apologies, sure, but things hadn't been the same between them. It was the little things, he realized. They no longer took time to discuss the events of their respective days, for example – focusing instead on coordinating their schedules around the activities of their jobs and children. Their conversations were more formal, less personal, and they'd begun treating one another with the sort of cool politeness reserved for houseguests who've overstayed their welcome. Ben couldn't help but wonder whether this was how it felt to embark on those first few steps down the twisting path toward divorce.

He stopped and looked up at the sky, a pregnant gray canopy lying low above the earth. The precipitation was coming down harder now, the heavy flakes catching in his lashes. Visibility was worsening, the sun already riding low on the horizon. He ought to close up the CO early today, make sure everyone got home before dark. The course of his walk had taken him on a winding loop through the park and an adjacent neighborhood, such that he was now back where he had started. He ascended the steps to the front of the building.

A small plastic bag, partially covered by the snow, leaned up against the door. He looked around, then stooped to pick it up, dusting off the powdery whiteness. In another hour, he realized, it would have been covered completely. They wouldn't have found it until the steps were shoveled the next morning. He opened the bag, peering inside, wondering what sort of –

'Oh my God,' he whispered, the plastic package slipping from his fingers, the blanched, lifeless content spilling out onto the snow. He turned and gripped the wrought iron rail beside him, his body bent at the waist as if he'd been kicked low in the midsection. He could feel his knees buckling, the bile rising high in his throat, the world going dim and distant around him.

Lying in the snow, the palm turned upward in an act of supplication, was what remained of a human hand.

251

Chapter 38

'No fingerprint matches,' Detective Schroeder announced, returning his cell phone to the black leather case clipped to his belt. They were sitting in Sam's office at the station. Outside, the night had fallen, although the snow continued to plummet to the earth with unrelenting intensity. There was already two feet of accumulation on the ground, and the latest weather report was predicting an additional twelve to fifteen inches by morning.

Detective Hunt had been peering out the window. He turned around, his face grim. 'It's gonna be a bitch trying to locate the body in this. Even if we knew where to look . . .'

'We'll search the vicinity around the Coroner's Office,' Sam said. 'Given the manpower we have, it's the best we can do. Although I doubt we'll find anything,' he added.

Carl shook his head. 'The specimen was transported

to the front steps of the Coroner's Office from some-place else. Otherwise, why bother with the bag?'

Ben stood up from his chair and crossed the room restlessly, his fingers pressed to his forehead. A headache had formed behind his right eye, making him feel nauseous and light-headed. He'd dry-swallowed four tablets of ibuprofen thirty minutes ago, but couldn't say they'd made much of a difference. 'What I want to know,' he said, 'is why was it delivered to the CO?'

'Good question,' Carl remarked. 'We were hoping *you* might shed some light on that one.'

'I have no idea,' Ben replied. 'I wish I did.'

The sound of a snowplow could be heard on the street below. It was the only vehicle that had passed this way over the last hour.

'Maybe he was doing us a favor,' Nat suggested from the corner of the room, and all eyes turned to him.

'What do you mean?' Detective Hunt asked.

Ben's assistant shrugged. 'It would've come to the CO eventually, along with the rest of the body. In a way, he saved me the trouble of transporting it.'

'You know anyone who might do that?' Carl asked, one eyebrow raised.

Nat thought this over for a moment. 'Naah,' he said. 'Not that I can think of.'

Danny turned to Ben. 'The bag wasn't there when you left the CO for your walk.'

'That's right,' Ben confirmed. 'It was sitting right up against the door when I returned. If it had been there when I left the building, I'm pretty sure I would've noticed it.'

'So someone watched you leave, knew you were coming back, and placed it there for you to find.'

'Or just happened to deliver it while I was out of the building,' Ben pointed out. 'I doubt it was left there for me personally.'

'Why not?' Sam asked, leaning forward in his chair. 'It seems pretty clear that it's a message.'

'Yeah,' Ben said. 'He's taunting us.'

'Us . . .' Sam placed his big hands on the desk in front of him. 'Or *you*, Ben?'

'For Christ's sake,' Ben replied, working his right temple with the palm of his hand. The headache was worsening, despite the earlier dose of analgesic. 'Why would he be taunting *me*? Just because I'm the one doing the autopsies?'

Sam's face was still, his eyes studying the surface of his desk. 'I don't know,' he said. 'But it's something to think about.' He looked up at the men gathered in front of him. 'Well . . . I don't think there's anything more we can do tonight. Let's call it an evening, shall we?'

'I'll contact Agent Culver in the morning,' Carl told him.

Sam nodded. 'That's fine. Let's get a few boys to shovel a hundred-foot radius around the Coroner's Office in the morning, and have the forensic team go over that area for anything useful. Ben,' he said as the others were filing out, 'can I have a word with you?'

Ben looked surprised. 'Sure,' he said, closing the door to the office when it was just the two of them.

Sam looked across the desk at him for a moment. 'I have a question for you, Ben, and I don't want you to take this the wrong way – but how well do you know Nathan Banks?'

'Nat?' Ben asked incredulously. 'Pretty damn well, Sam.'

'Mm-hmm,' the chief replied. He swiveled his chair to the right so that he could look out of the window. 'He's an interesting fellow, wouldn't you say?'

Ben laughed. 'Interesting. Yeah, I guess you could say that.'

'Left-handed, is he?' Sam inquired, recalling the hand with which the boy had gripped the pen during his completion of the paperwork earlier that evening.

Ben's face lost its humor. 'About ten per cent of the population is.'

'Oh, I know,' Sam said with a shrug. 'It doesn't necessarily mean anything that he is.'

'No,' Ben agreed. 'It doesn't.'

'Still,' Sam went on, 'I wouldn't mind having a DNA specimen for our FBI colleagues to analyze . . . if you think you could get one for us, that is.'

'Sam, I can assure you . . .'

The chief held up a hand. 'I'm sure you can, Ben. Don't make too much out of it. I'm just making certain that we cover our bases.' He rose from his chair and walked to the window. 'We haven't had a snowfall like this in years,' he said. 'Bad timing for this sort of thing.'

'You thinking about postponing the search until some of this melts off?' Ben asked. He was still feeling unsettled by Sam's questions about Nat. He wasn't sure whether to feel insulted, indignant, defensive, or none of the above.

Sam grabbed his jacket and shoved one thick arm through the sleeve as he crossed the room. 'Get home to your family, Ben.' He opened the door, stepping aside for his friend to pass through. 'Someone will find the body,' he said, his fingers on the light switch. 'Sooner or later, they always do.'

Chapter 39

'You Detective Carl Schroeder?' the man asked over the phone.

'I am.'

'This is Sergeant Michael Edwins from the Rock Hill Police Department.'

Carl grabbed a pen from the top of his desk. 'I'm sorry, Sergeant, I'm not familiar with that jurisdiction.'

'We're in Rock Hill, South Carolina, Detective – just a li'l south of the North Carolina border.'

'Okay. How can I help you?'

'Got a man in detention here says he knows yah. Been askin' for yah all mornin'.'

'What's his name?'

'Well, his real name's Clarence Bedford. Born and raised down here in York County, South Carolina. We know 'im pretty well – one of our regulars.'

'I'm sorry.' Carl frowned. 'I'm not familiar with anyone by the name of—'

'Goes by the name of Harold Matthews, though.'

Carl sat forward in his chair. 'You've got him? In custody?'

'For the moment,' the sergeant replied. 'He was picked up for trespassin'. It's a book-an'-release offense.'

'I'd prefer if you hold on to him. Mr Matthews is wanted for questioning regarding the attempted murder of a young girl here in Jefferson County, Ohio.'

'I'll bet he is. Roll in to the psych ward, did he?'

'Yes, as a matter of fact, he did,' Carl confirmed. 'How did you know—?'

'Does it ev'ry time we have a young kid get killed around here. Always confesses to the crime. He's got a long history with us, Detective.'

Carl put a hand to his forehead, laid the pen back down on his desk. 'Is that right.'

'Sure 'nough. He's a bit of a wanderer. Hops on a bus an' leaves town to God knows where ev'ry so often for a few months at a stretch. Always manages to find 'is way back, though.'

'He said he'd killed others. Any truth to that?'

'Clarence hit a boy on a bike with 'is car when he was twenty-three. Said the kid was stealin' a baby that belonged to his sister. Clarence's sister has cerebral palsy. She's in a wheelchair, an' sure as hell don't have no babies. Child he hit was twelve. He died at the scene. Clarence was charged with murder, but it didn't stick none. Turns out he's got schizophrenia. He's crazier 'n a sack of rabid weasels, Detective. Spent a bunch of years in a mental hospital after that. I think he took it hard, though, that kid's death. Still holds himself responsible. Ends up in our local psych unit ev'ry time a kid around here gets killed – sayin' he's the one who did it.'

Carl stood up and looked out at the darkening day through the small window of his office. 'That explains a lot. I'm curious, though – there were quite a few scratches on his body when I interviewed him. Any idea what might've caused—'

'He's a cutter. Cuts on himself to relieve tension.'

'I see,' Carl said. 'Well, thanks for contacting me, Sergeant. If it's okay with you, I'd like to send someone down there to collect some DNA samples from Mr Matthews . . . or Bedford – whatever the hell his name is. Just to be certain.'

'We've got a lab here that can do it for you. Fax me the warrant, and I'll get 'em on it.'

'Thank you. Again, I really appreciate your assistance.' Carl took a deep breath in and let it out slowly, knowing that the sinking feeling in his gut was their only suspect in this case disappearing down the drain. 'By the way, if Clarence Bedford is his real name, why does he call himself Harold Matthews? Does he have multiple personalities or something?'

'No,' the sergeant replied, 'just a lot of underlyin' guilt, I reckon. Harold Matthews was the name of the boy he hit – the one who died at the scene.'

Chapter 40

The week leading up to Christmas break saw the heaviest single snowfall in eastern Ohio since 1950. Forty-two inches of fresh powder blanketed the frozen earth over the course of two and a half days. Schools had little choice but to remain closed from Monday through Thursday while the county plows and salt trucks attempted to deal with the mounting drifts. By the time the precipitation finally ended and the major streets, sidewalks and parking lots were rendered usable, only Friday remained. Drawing on wisdom and experience gained from eleven years on the job, the superintendent of public schools for Jefferson County knew better than to embark upon a futile campaign for the hearts and minds of thousands of children during that one solitary day that teetered precariously on the precipice of a twelve-day winter break. Not wishing to generate ill will among the county's parents and teachers for his lack of both pragmatism and holiday cheer, he proclaimed Friday a snow day as well and became an instant local hero, if only for a day.

It was a wise move. Many families had already left town for an early start to their winter vacations. The Stevensons were among them, with the notable exception of Ben, who'd decided to remain at home. Sam's assertion that it was only a matter of time until the second body was uncovered contributed to that decision, as did the chief's inquiries regarding Nat. It had been disconcerting for Ben, finding himself in the unexpected position of having to defend his amiable, good-natured assistant. And now Ben had been asked to get them a biological sample for DNA analysis. He felt ridiculous snooping around for something like that. More important, he felt like a traitor. Nat looked up to him, respected him, and had an allegiance to both Ben and the CO. In order to accomplish this, Ben would be going behind his back, even if it *was* to prove his assistant's innocence. He didn't like it – didn't like it at all.

There was another thing, as well. Sam suspected that the amputated appendage had been left for Ben personally, as a message. *Or a warning,* Ben thought to himself with a shudder. Either way, it was an ominous sign. If Ben was being targeted by the killer, then his family might also be in considerable danger. He'd been immensely relieved when Susan had agreed to take the boys to visit her parents in Sedona, Arizona, for the holiday. It was difficult to know how much of a difference those two weeks would make, but moving his family to a safe location eased his mind. 'You should come with us,' Susan had suggested, but Ben had declined. It was important that he be available to assist the detectives if and when the body was discovered. Anything he could do to help them catch this guy had to take precedence.

And yet, now that Susan and the boys were gone, Ben was surprised to discover how much he longed for them. His daily activities provided distraction enough, but in the evenings he found himself wandering from room to room, Alexander the Great padding steadfastly behind him. 'It's quiet in the house without them, isn't it?' he'd asked the dog, who had swished his tail back and forth in commiseration.

'How are you two getting along?' Susan had asked him that evening on the telephone.

'Alex and I have been watching a lot of movies,' Ben advised her. 'How's Sedona?'

'It's beautiful,' she told him. 'Arizona's spectacular this time of year. Dad's taking us hiking tomorrow. I'll email you some pictures.'

'Great,' Ben said, trying to sound more chipper than he felt.

There was a pause on the line. 'You okay?' she asked.

'Yeah.' Ben reached down and ran his hand along the side of Alex's broad neck. 'I miss you guys, that's all.'

'You could still catch a flight out to join us.'

'I can't,' he told her. 'Not right now.'

'Now might be the perfect time,' she suggested. 'Nothing will turn up until the snow melts.'

'And if there's another murder between now and then?'

'There won't be.'

Ben sighed. 'You don't know that,' he said. 'I've been telling myself for months that this guy has probably moved on. Thing is, I never really believed it. And now this. He'd just been waiting for the right opportunity, Susan – waiting this whole time.'

And mostly, Ben realized, that's what it came down to now: an act of waiting. Waiting for the snow to melt. Waiting to discover what was lying out there somewhere beneath those infinite drifts. Waiting for another dismembered body part to materialize on the front steps of the CO. Waiting to see where the investigation would lead, how the pieces would fit together, and whose life might be claimed in the interim. *Waiting,* he thought as he said his goodbyes to his family for the night and hung up the phone. Waiting like a sentenced man, standing blindfolded and rigid before the firing squad. Waiting and listening for the hammers to fall.

Chapter 41

The blizzard that had blanketed most of Ohio and western Pennsylvania the week before Christmas had been followed by ten days of frigid temperatures. During that time, the afternoon highs had peaked above freezing for only a few hours on two separate occasions. As a result, the snow that had fallen two weeks previously had had little chance to melt. Except for the sidewalks, parking lots and roadways that had been cleared by necessity, the majority of the waist-deep drifts across backyards, fields and forests remained untouched, as if the storm had occurred only the night before.

As one might imagine, this had several ramifications. Ski shops enjoyed an unprecedented surge in business, most notably in the sale of snowshoes and cross-country ski equipment. Local fire departments spent several days digging out hydrants from the mounds of snow under which they'd been buried. Sturdy backs and snow shovels were put to the test clearing driveways and reestablishing usable patches of backyards for small dogs to do their business. Emergency departments attended to a whirlwind of fractures and other injuries sustained by unsuccessful attempts to traverse icy sidewalks and parking lots. And for anyone under the age of twenty (and for many people over that age, as well) the most important derivative of the weather was the nearly unlimited sledding opportunities that presented themselves. Hundreds of thousands of children across the region, all on winter vacation, took to the hills for an exuberant, screaming, accelerating descent down snow-covered embankments on cheap plastic vessels. It was the purest joy many of them would ever know.

These were not the only recreational activities. Bret Graham had convinced his uncle to let him borrow his snowmobile for the day, and by 10:30 a.m. he was zipping across fields of untouched powder, the reverberating growl of the revving engine following in his wake like a snarling mongrel on a tattered leash. He held fast to the handlebars, turning them back and forth as he cut a random, serpentine path through the snow. Eventually, he brought the vehicle to a halt behind 403 Crawford Avenue. He let the engine idle for a moment, then killed the switch. Dismounting, he trudged a few steps across the yard to the rear patio and rapped loudly on the back door. At first there was no sound from within the house. Then he heard light footsteps approaching from the inside hallway, and Cynthia's face suddenly appeared in a pane of glass. She looked at him inquisitively for a moment, then spun the dead bolt and opened the door.

'What in the hell are you doing out there, Bret Graham?' she asked with a wide grin. Her voice was melodic and feathery. Just the sound of it kicked his heart rate up a notch.

He smiled back. 'I'm here to take you snowmobiling, darlin'.'

She looked past him at the machine parked and waiting for her. It listed a little to the left in the soft snow. 'I don't know, Bret Graham.' (She liked to say his full name, as in, 'I'm dating Bret Graham,' or 'Bret Graham is taking me to the movies tonight.') 'That thing doesn't look safe.'

'*Doesn't look safe?!*' he repeated with an exaggerated scowl. 'What do you *mean* it doesn't look safe?'

'It looks sketchy,' she replied, crossing her arms in front of her. 'Do you even know how to drive that contraption?'

'*Do I even . . .*' He let the words trail off at the end. 'Shoot! Why, you're safer on the back of that so-called contraption with me at the wheel than you are standing right here in your own house!'

'I doubt that,' she said.

'You do?' He shook his head in mock disbelief. 'Well, go put that snowsuit of yours on and let me show you what it's all about.'

'Yeah?' She was finding it increasingly difficult to hold back the excitement in her voice.

''Course,' he responded with complete confidence, as if any other course of action was beyond discussion.

'Okay,' she said, her face lighting up with anticipation. She leaned through the open doorway and planted a quick kiss on his unsuspecting lips. 'Bret Graham is taking me snowmobiling!'

'That's right.'

'Wheee!!' she exclaimed, and ran back to the foyer to fetch her gear. Bret stepped cheerfully inside to wait for her, acutely aware that on the other side of the threshold the sun was shining, the snow was soft and inviting, he had an adrenaline-packed rocket ship parked at the ready and he was here to pick up his girl. When you're sixteen, it simply doesn't get any better than that.

When she returned, they made their way through the snow and climbed aboard. Cynthia straddled the seat behind him, wrapping her arms tightly around his waist. 'You sure this thing is safe?' she asked once more.

'No, I am not,' he told her, starting the engine. 'But that's why I'm bringing you along. If we crash, I want something soft to land on.'

'Oh, yeah?' she said. 'Well, here's something soft to land on!' She scooped up a large handful of snow and jammed it into his face.

'Oh, that was *not* cool,' he advised her, wiping the slush from his eyes. He could feel some of it already winding its way down the front of his neck. 'You'd better hold on, girl! You're in for a wild ride!'

'No. Drive slowly.'

'Right,' he said, and gunned the engine. The vehicle lurched forward, nearly throwing her off the back.

'*Whoa! Take it easy!*' she yelled into his ear above the din of the motor, the ground already becoming a blur as it sped by beneath them.

The snowmobile whooshed along, cresting small hills with enough velocity to propel the craft into the air for brief moments of time. On the last rise, they took leave of the earth for a full second and a half before setting down with a soft jolt in a spray of dove-white powder. The vehicle scampered down the decline, then hooked a right as Bret directed the handlebars toward a stretch of trees.

'*No! Not the woods!*' Cynthia yelled into his ear, but her voice was no match for the volume of the engine.

They shot through the trees, which stood a sufficient distance apart for Bret to negotiate a wild, careening slalom around their broad trunks. Cynthia dared to look over his shoulder once and, immediately regretting it, buried her face between his shoulder blades for the remainder of the journey. The motorized vessel yawed to the left and right with each turn. Seventy yards ahead of them, the woods gave way to another vast, open field of untouched snow. At the edge of the woods, Bret could see that the ground fell away slightly, and his plan was to accelerate to a speed that would enable them to enter the field in mid-air. He pressed down on the accelerator with his right thumb, gunning the vehicle in that direction.

'*Whoooo-hoooooo!!!!*' he bellowed to no one in particular other than the silent trees whizzing by.

The vehicle never quite made it. Five yards from the point where the woods met the field, they struck something large buried beneath the snow. The nose of the snowmobile dipped sharply, and in an instant both occupants were tossed over the handlebars and into the air. Cynthia's arms remained clasped tightly around Bret's waist, and as a result the two of them flew through the air in perfect unison. It took less than two seconds for them to reconnect with the earth, but during that span of time each had an opportunity to wonder just how badly they were about to be injured. Their bodies made a three-quarter turn, head over heels, as if performing a somersault for a gymnastics competition. Both of them were athletes – Bret wrestled and ran cross-country, Cynthia had played soccer since she was five – and neither of them made the mistake of sticking out an arm or a leg to try to break their fall. They stayed tucked – chin down, body loose – and went with the roll. When they struck the earth, they met with a cushion of soft snow in an open field. They rolled twice, the snow crunching quietly beneath them, then came to rest.

The snowmobile sat idling at the outskirts of the woods, nose pitched forward and partly buried in the snow. For ten seconds neither of them spoke.

Taking stock of his physical condition and finding nothing alarmingly out of place, Bret was the first to break the silence. 'Cynthia,' he said, rolling over to get a better look at her. 'Are you okay?'

'Ugh,' she responded, her face buried in the snow.

He rolled her onto her side. 'Is anything broken? Are you able to move your arms and legs?'

'I think . . . I can move everything but my right arm,' she replied slowly.

'Does it feel broken?' he asked, the guilt already flooding through him in great, rolling waves. 'I'm sorry,' he added. 'That was really stupid of me.'

'I think . . . I might be able . . . to move it a little.' She winced.

'Wait! Don't try to move it! It's probably broken.'

'No, hold on a second,' she said. 'It was just sort of numb for a second there. I think I can move it. Let me see . . . if I can . . .'

Her right hand shot up and smashed an ice-cold fistful of snow into his face for the second time that day. At least half of it found its way into his gaping mouth. Bret sputtered in shock and surprise, falling backward.

'There's a little present for you!' she squealed. '*Bon appétit!*'

'*Wha – ?*' Brett spit out a mouthful of snow. 'I . . . I can't believe you just did that!'

'Believe it, sucker!' she taunted him. 'You deserved it. You could've gotten us *both* killed.' She looked back at their downed craft. 'What in the hell did we hit, anyway?'

'Hell if I know,' he said. The rear end of the snow-mobile was pointing at a 45-degree angle toward the sky. 'Hey,' he said, giving her a serious look. 'Thanks for not being mad. Most girls would—'

'First of all,' she said, interrupting him, 'who says I'm not mad? You're going to have to make it up to me, you know.'

'And second?'

'Second of all, I'm not "most girls". Just keep that in mind.'

'Yes, ma'am,' he replied smartly. 'Anything else?'

'Yeah,' she said, leaning over and giving him a kiss on the cheek. 'Let's get the hell out of here . . . that is, if that death-mobile of yours isn't destroyed.' She was already making her way in the direction of their maimed vehicle.

Bret pushed himself up into a standing position. His legs held. Nothing seemed to be broken. They'd made it through unscathed. That was good. Still, he felt guilty. He shouldn't have been going that fast. If she'd been injured, he didn't know wha –

That was when Cynthia screamed. The stark sound of her cry pierced the silent midday air. It leapt into the woods and came scampering out again like a spooked creature trying to escape. He was so stunned that for a moment he could only stand there, gaping at her. Then his feet were moving, seemingly of their own volition, and he was running toward her as fast as he could through snow cresting his knees.

'*What is it?!*' he called to her, closing the distance. She neither answered nor screamed again – only stood there, body rigid, looking down at the wounded snow-mobile. Making his way through the deep drifts was maddeningly slow, and Bret had time to think that he wished she would scream again, just so he would know that she was mentally still with him. A single scream and silence; somehow, that was worse.

'What is it?' he asked again, but by the time he'd completed the sentence he was standing beside her, and he was able to see quite clearly for himself. His girlfriend stared at the snow, at the spot where the nose of the vehicle disappeared beneath the powder, at the thing they had struck that had sent them hurtling through the air in the first place. Thankfully, most of it was still hidden below the surface. The part that was sticking out was enough, though – enough to know what they had found. From beneath the snow, as if awoken suddenly from a deep slumber, a single forearm jutted accusingly toward the sky. The skin was bluish white, only a few shades darker than the surrounding snow, and the appendage ended abruptly at the wrist in a macerated curl of muscle and bone.

They had discovered the third victim.

PART FIVE

Discoveries

Chapter 42

The young body – as yet unidentified – lay on the metal autopsy table and attempted to tell its story. There was no doubt the boy had been murdered. A long incision began just above the right clavicle and followed a slightly diagonal course across the anterior neck, ending just inferior to the left angle of the mandible. The incision had been deep, severing the internal jugular veins bilaterally, as well as the right carotid artery. Mercifully, the boy would have bled out in less than a minute, and had undoubtedly lost consciousness within the first thirty seconds. Hemorrhaging had been massive, as demonstrated in striking detail in the color photographs of the crime scene police had taken of the uncovered body lying crumpled in the snow amid a shredded carpet of scarlet contrasted on the dove-white backdrop.

Judging from the nature of the wounds and the zealous dismemberment of the body, there was also little doubt that the perpetrator of this crime was the same individual who had attacked the two previous victims. There were several human bite wounds that appeared to have occurred postmortem, and Ben was fairly certain the dental patterns from these wounds would match those sustained by the others. Mutilation of the body seemed to be a strong motivational component for the assailant. In this case, the victim's facial features had been stripped away using an abrasive surface – *something akin to a cheese grater* was the first thing that had come to mind. As before, several of the victim's digits had been amputated. They had either been cast within throwing distance of the body or had been stuffed into various orifices for Ben to discover during autopsy. The left hand, of course, was already accounted for.

The facial mutilation would make it difficult for family, once they were located, to ID the body. Confirmation of the child's identity would most likely rely on fingerprints and dental records. Based on the anatomy, Ben estimated the victim to be about ten, maybe eleven – *not too much older than Joel,* he realized with a dull sort of horror.

So far, no one locally had been reported missing over the past few weeks. It was possible the boy was a runaway. According to Detective Schroeder, twenty-three runaways fitting the victim's general age and gender had been reported missing from a 250-mile radius over the past six months. To Ben, that number seemed high, but when he'd asked Schroeder about it the detective had been nonplussed.

'Lot of kids decide to leave home and strike out on their own. The family environment in many of these cases is' – he shrugged – 'less than ideal. Sometimes remaining at home is the more dangerous of their limited options.'

Ben looked through his open office door at the body lying on the table. Detective Hunt stood over it snapping off a few additional photos. 'Not in this case,' Ben said.

'No,' Schroeder agreed from where he sat on the other side of the desk. His hair had grayed significantly over the past nine months, Ben noticed, and his eyes appeared to sag a bit more around the edges. The detective tapped his pen lightly on the corner of his notepad, then flipped to a fresh page. 'Any idea about the time of death?' he asked.

Ben folded his hands in front of him on the desk. 'It's hard to pinpoint,' he began. 'The body was buried in the snow, which causes some minor moisture damage to the superficial tissues but retards the decomposition process.'

Schroeder nodded. 'Except for tracks left by the snowmobile and its occupants, the snow cover in the vicinity where the body was located was untouched. There were no surface tracks leading either toward or away from the scene. Which means,' he continued, 'the victim wasn't brought there from someplace else. He was murdered at the spot, presumably before or during the last snowfall, and was simply left there to be buried by the gathering accumulation.'

'From a timing perspective, that coincides with the

delivery of the package I received on the front steps of the CO,' Ben said. 'That was on the first day of the storm. The hand was cold and virtually bloodless, but no significant decomposition had occurred.'

'Which means that once again,' Carl noted, 'he killed this one in broad daylight.' He shook his head. 'It's gutsy of him, I'll give him that.'

'Maybe there's a part of him that wants to be caught,' Detective Hunt suggested, entering the office and, with no other chairs available, selecting a spot against the wall behind Ben's desk on which to lean his thin frame.

Ben turned to him. He had to look back over his left shoulder slightly. 'Sorry about the cramped quarters, Detective,' he apologized. 'There're a few stools in the autopsy room, if you'd like to grab one of those.'

Danny waved away the offer. 'Don't worry about it, Doc.' He smiled. 'Once I make senior detective, the department's going to give me my own chair to sit on. Chief Garston promised. Until then, I've learned to do some of my best thinking standing up.'

'It's because the blood's rushing away from your brain,' his partner observed, giving him a flat look. Carl was growing weary of this case. He'd more or less been in a bad mood since it had begun.

'Is that a picture of your family, Dr Stevenson?' Danny asked, ignoring the insult. He gestured toward a framed photo Ben had sitting on his desk. It had been taken two years ago during a white-water rafting trip in West Virginia. In the posed shot, they stood shoulder to shoulder on a huge rock along the banks of the river, oars hoisted triumphantly over their heads as the water churned and sprayed in the background.

'Yeah,' Ben said, handing him the picture. 'We're a good-lookin' group, ain't we?'

Danny smiled. 'What river is that?'

'Lower Gauley.'

'Ever try the Upper?'

Ben shook his head. 'That's quite a bit beyond our experience level,' he said. 'People die on the Upper Gauley, Detective.'

Carl was glaring at his colleague. The anger had been building inside him during most of this inane conversation. Over the past few months he'd gradually come to the conclusion that having Danny Hunt as a partner was like trying to run a marathon with your shoelaces tied together. The kid slowed him down, often seemed not to appreciate the seriousness of their work and showed more interest in chitchat than in examining the facts of the case in front of them. *I really ought to have a word with Sam Garston about the kid's overall conduct,* Carl thought. Danny was a nice enough guy, he supposed – but he sure as hell wasn't cut out for detective work.

'Are you finished?' he asked his partner coldly. 'Because I'd like to talk about the case now. That is, if it's okay with you.'

Danny nodded, handing the picture back to Ben. He reached into his suit pocket and pulled out his notepad. 'Sorry,' he said, eyes cast downward onto the pages in front of him.

'Thank you,' Carl replied. He turned to the doctor. 'What do you make of the face? Was he trying to make it difficult for us to ID the victim?'

'I don't think so.' Ben frowned. 'He also amputated several of the kid's digits, but I don't think it was an effort to avoid fingerprinting. He left some of the fingers intact. In addition, all of the amputated digits were either found with the body itself or simply tossed aside in proximity to the crime scene.'

'So why destroy the face? Does that suggest any significance for psychological profiling?'

'Psychological profiling is not my area of expertise,' Ben replied. 'But provided we think this is the same guy – which we do – I'd say no. The faces of the other two victims were damaged, but their general features remained intact. It doesn't fit his MO.'

'Which is?'

'Judging from the injuries to the bodies, I'd say that each one has been progressively worse.'

'You think he's getting better at desecrating them?' Detective Schroeder asked, glancing toward the metal table in the next room.

'No,' Ben said. 'I think he's experimenting – seeing just how creative he can get. I think his enthusiasm for this sort of work is growing.'

There were a few more questions, but they were mostly formalities. By now, they all knew what they were dealing with. In a way, they each shared a certain intimacy with the killer, wading through the aftermath of each successive massacre and getting to know him by the tattered pieces he left behind. Detectives

Schroeder and Hunt thanked Ben once again for his time. 'If you discover anything else that might be of assistance,' Carl reminded him unnecessarily, 'please give us a call.' Ben assured them that he would.

The detectives took their leave and made their way across the parking lot to the unmarked cruiser out back. 'You know,' Carl said as they pulled the doors closed against the bitter chill, 'you really ought to try concentrating on your job for once.' He popped the key into the ignition and started the Chevy, but left it idling in neutral. 'I mean, what in the hell was *that* all about back there? Is this case boring you? You'd rather go white-water rafting with the doc this weekend?'

'Sorry,' Danny replied. 'I wasn't trying to irritate you.'

'You think I'm out of line?' Carl challenged. 'You think I shouldn't be irritated?' He dropped the car into reverse and backed away from the building. He tried to let go of his frustration, telling himself he was overreacting, that the stress of the case was getting to him. Still, it was hard to let the anger go once it had taken hold of him. 'I mean, why don't you try getting your head out of your ass and start acting like you really care about solving this thing. I could use a little help here. You think you could manage that?'

Danny remained quiet, looking out through the passenger window. His right hand fidgeted with the armrest. Carl watched him for a moment, then shook his head in exasperation. There was no fight in the boy; that was the problem. If anyone had given

Carl the type of verbal flogging he'd just dished out, he would've told them to go to hell; it wouldn't matter *who* they were. Instead, the kid just sat there and took it.

He guided the car out of the parking lot and shot down the street in the direction of the station, the tires screeching slightly on the asphalt as they accelerated. Neither of them spoke for the remainder of the trip. Small homes and businesses streaked past them on either side. It wasn't a huge town: one high school, a couple of gas stations, a few bars and restaurants for evening entertainment. Not much, really. But it was *theirs* to protect, *theirs* to safeguard. The thing was, nobody around here had been outwardly vocal about the delay in catching this guy. No one had stood up and said, '*Why ain't the police doin' their job? That's what I want to know!*' It simply wasn't that kind of place. These people were Carl's friends and neighbors, and he knew most of them by name. For the most part, they were decent folks. People trusted that their Sheriff's Department was doing everything in its power to put an end to this. The town seemed to have faith in that, and most people understood that a barrage of criticism wouldn't make the department's job any easier. That made it all the more frustrating for him that the investigation had failed to make any real headway since the last attack. The DNA sample from Clarence Bedford, the escaped psychiatric patient, had not matched any of the DNA left behind on the bodies by the perpetrator. And just like that, their most promising suspect – their *only* concrete suspect – had been swept off their list, leaving them with no one. That setback left Carl feeling angry and ashamed, and ready to bite the head off anyone who he judged wasn't doing their part to get this case solved. That's where Danny came in. The kid needed someone to light a fire under his ass, and by default Carl had been the one to do it. *If I hurt the kid's feelings,* he thought as they pulled into the station ten minutes later, *well, tough shit*. If it yielded something useful, it would certainly be worth it.

For his part, Danny had sat quietly in the front passenger seat during the short ride, gazing thoughtfully out through the window at the parade of storefronts and side streets they passed. He cared very little about the rebuke he'd just received from his partner. His hide was considerably thicker than Detective Schroeder presumed. Nor did he need a fire to be lit under his proverbial ass, as his partner imagined. He had taken the case seriously from the start, and had logged more hours than anyone during this investigation, sifting through the BMV photos until their images appeared before him even in sleep. He'd carefully reviewed the evidence over and over, looking for something to stand out from the background noise. The results of his efforts had been as frustrating to him as they had been for Carl. He didn't know why this should be the case. Hard work had always paid off for him in the past. Maybe he'd simply been thinking about it too much, trying to will something to happen when it clearly wanted to take its own sweet time coming to him. If that was so, the price of patience had been another dead child. That had pushed him back into a state of action once again, no matter how futile those actions might turn out to be. It was what drove him to bring his own digital camera to the autopsy review today. The body had already been thoroughly photographed by the crime scene investigators at the time it was originally discovered. Extensive pictures of the injuries were also taken during autopsy. Every wound had been well documented. It had not been necessary for him to repeat the process today. And yet he had felt the need to do so, if for no other reason than to involve himself as intimately as possible with the available evidence. And so, for twenty minutes he had remained with the body in the autopsy room while his partner and Dr Stevenson talked further in the pathologist's tiny adjacent office. When Danny had finished, he'd returned the camera to its carrying case and had joined the others in the next room. And then . . .

'The bodies of the victims took quite a beating,' he observed now offhandedly, breaking the silence as they nosed into a parking spot.

'You just noticing that, are you?' Carl responded.

Danny barely registered the remark. His tone was thoughtful: 'One hand and multiple fingers amputated. Deep stab wounds. Genitals amputated on the first victim. Most of the face abraded away on this last one.'

'Yeah. It's amazing how you're putting all of this together,' Carl replied.

'You can't inflict those sort of wounds with your bare hands.'

'I think we've already established that there was a weapon involved.'

'Several, most likely. Pretty tough to abrade someone's face away with a regular knife.'

'Uh-huh.' Carl killed the ignition.

'And the amputations; you ever tried cutting through bone with a knife, even a really sharp one?'

'I've done some hunting.'

'So you know it isn't easy, especially if you're going to do a bunch of them in a short enough period of time to minimize your chances of being caught in the act.'

'Is there a point to any of this?' Carl asked, impatiently. 'Or are you just playing catch-up?'

'While I was photographing the injuries today,' Danny replied, studying the palms of his hands, 'I was just thinking about what type of weapons – or specialized tools, if you will – might be necessary to carry out something like that.'

'And?'

'And I noticed a lot of them either lying around in the sink or stored away in drawers in that very room.'

'Now, wait a minute.' Carl stopped him. 'If you're implying that the doc or his assistant might have had something to do with this, you're way off the mark. If you'd been paying attention, you'd remember that we actually checked on that, mostly because we had nothing better to do. Both of them have solid alibis during at least one of the three attacks. And the DNA analysis from the assistant didn't match the biological samples obtained from the bite wounds.'

'True. I'm just saying that the Coroner's Office would make a nice source for acquiring some of the necessary instruments. I'll bet some of the tools might not even be missed. Or perhaps,' he said, 'they might have even been returned without anyone noticing. Think about it. What a great hiding place for a murder weapon: in an autopsy room in the midst of scores of similar instruments used to dissect cadavers on a daily basis. Hell, they might even have been cleaned by the CO staff between murders.'

'Interesting theory,' Carl replied. 'But they keep that place locked up when there's no one there. No security guard with an extra set of keys. Who would that leave? The secretary? You think she's got the strength to carry out those kinds of attacks?'

'No,' Danny answered. 'Besides, most of the stab wounds have upward trajectories – more consistent with a male attacker. Women tend to hold the weapon over their head and stab downward.'

'Generally, yes,' Carl agreed. 'So would that imply a break-in? We could check, but I don't recall the Coroner's Office reporting any break-ins over the past year or so.'

'No, they didn't.'

'So, according to your theory, we would be looking for someone with access to keys to the CO, but not necessarily the staff itself. Friends, family, lovers. That sort of thing?'

'Right.'

'Well . . . we could check into it – talk to a few people and see if anyone fits the profile – but I think it's a real stretch. I wouldn't get your hopes up, Sherlock Holmes, but I do appreciate your willingness to get your head back into this invest—'

'There's one other thing,' Danny said.

'What's that?'

'The bite wounds. I can't stop thinking about the bite wounds.'

'What about them?'

'Well, for one thing, it just seems . . . I don't know . . . so animalistic. So savage. I find it the most upsetting factor, don't you?'

'The *whole thing's* upsetting, as far as I'm concerned,' Carl said. 'I mean, that obliterated face today was pretty disturbing. But we're in a gruesome business, kid. You've got to get used to stuff like that.'

'I know.' Danny was studying his hands again. 'But I was photographing the bite wounds today.' He looked up and smiled thinly, a little painfully. 'I had to focus in pretty close to get the detail clear enough.'

Carl sighed. 'Yeah?' With the ignition off they'd lost the heater, and the late December Midwest cold was starting to settle into the passenger compartment. He wanted to get into the station where it was warm instead of sit out here and listen to his junior partner go on about things he could've discussed during their conversation with the doctor at the CO.

'Do you remember that abnormal gap between the upper left canine and the first premolar that the dental expert identified from the silicon castings of the bite wounds? He called it a diastasis.'

Carl nodded. 'Of course. We looked into it. Nothing panned out.'

'Well, it looks to be consistent with at least one of the superficial impressions left on the skin of this body, too. It's clearly evident, provided you know what to look for.'

'Which means the guy who killed this kid is the same one who attacked the other two. As suspected.'

'Right.'

'So? I don't see how that moves us any closer than where we already were.'

Detective Hunt stopped studying his hands and looked up at his partner. He looked a little ill. Carl wondered if he might be coming down with his first winter cold of the season. Probably end up getting him sick, too.

'I noticed the diastasis twice today,' he said. 'Once while I was photographing the body, and a few minutes later in the doc's office. I don't think it would've even registered in my mind if I hadn't gone through all those BMV photos this past summer. I just looked across the desk and there it was. I had to get a closer look to be certain, but yeah – plain as day.'

'What are you talking about?' Carl asked, but something in his gut had begun to stir, and he thought he knew what his partner was about to say next.

'The photograph on the doc's desk,' Danny replied. 'The one of the whole family posing for a snap-shot on the riverbank. Big smiles all around.'

'Who?' Carl asked. His mouth suddenly felt dry and unpleasant, as if he had been eating old mothballs extracted from his grandmother's closet.

The young detective held his gaze. His face was as still and solemn as the autopsy room they had just vacated.

'Oldest boy,' Danny said, and with that he stepped out of the car and headed into the station, where it was warm.

Chapter 43

Sam Garston sat back in his chair. The two detectives exchanged glances, but neither of them spoke further. Their phone call had caught him in the middle of dinner. Was he available to speak with them? 'Of course,' he'd said. 'What's up?' Perhaps it was better if they spoke in person, Detective Schroeder had suggested.

'Well, I'm not heading out again unless it's an emergency,' Sam had replied, glancing out through the kitchen window at the sleet that had begun to fall. 'You boys might's well meet with me at home, if it needs to be tonight.'

And so the two younger men had driven through mostly deserted streets and had trudged up the walkway to their boss's front door.

'Cold out tonight,' Carla observed, ushering them in. 'Interest you men in some hot coffee? Freshly brewed.'

Neither one of them had to think twice about *that*.

Having heard them out, Sam now turned his head to the right, his eyes studying his own living room wall. It was sparsely populated with photographs he'd taken over the years, mostly from the few vacations he'd managed during the course of his adult life. Those vacations had been short and all too infrequent. He and Carla had simply been too busy most of the time, distracted with a parade of unending duties and obligations. Their world had been small and neatly packaged, just the way they liked it. He just hadn't thought of it that way until recently. Lately, though, Sam found his thoughts turning with increasing frequency toward retirement, and he wondered with a sort of tentative excitement what it would be like to return to a place in his life where his options once more seemed far greater than the sum of his responsibilities. It wasn't far off now; he could feel it. In the meantime, there remained a few unresolved matters that demanded his attention.

'We'd better be damn sure about this before we start hauling people in for questioning,' he said at last. 'If we're wrong, the situation will be . . .' He searched for the right word. 'Irreparable.' He looked at them both to make certain they understood. 'Ben Stevenson not only has a close working relationship with this department, but he also happens to be a personal friend of mine.'

'A fingerprint match would clinch it,' Schroeder noted.

'No. I don't want the boy brought in for fingerprinting until we're reasonably certain.'

'A search warrant of the house would likely yield sufficient prints from the kid's bedroom,' Danny suggested, 'in addition to anything else we might find.'

'I'm not serving Dr Stevenson with a search warrant of his home based on an observation *you* made from a photograph,' Sam told him, shooting an irritated glare in Detective Hunt's direction. He tried to tell himself that it wasn't Hunt's fault. He was simply doing his job – a job Sam himself had assigned him to do. *You have to follow the evidence where it leads*, he reminded himself, *no matter whose door it takes you to*.

'Why don't we petition a judge to order the release of the kid's dental records, now that we have someone specific we're interested in?' Danny suggested.

Sam considered it for a moment. 'There are three local dentists in town,' he replied. 'We don't know which one he goes to. We'd have to ask the judge for a court-ordered release of records from all three. That's going to raise some local interest. It's the kind of thing that's hard to keep quiet in a small town.'

'How likely is it, anyway,' Carl wondered, 'that he's had recent dental imprints made, and that a physical casting would be available to send to the forensic odontologist. It would be a gamble that might very well turn up nothing.'

'I don't know, Chief,' Danny sighed. 'A limited search warrant of the home may be the most straightforward approach here – just to get fingerprints from the kid's room and to take a quick look around. If we're right, we've got him. If we're wrong and the

292

prints don't match, we apologize to the doc and trust that, given the gravity of the investigation, he'll understand.'

'I'd really like to avoid that if we could,' Sam responded. 'I mean, what's your degree of certainty here? I know Thomas Stevenson. He's a good kid: smart, athletic, very likable . . .'

'Fits the profile,' Carl observed.

Sam traced his thumb across the leather armrest of his chair. 'You really think he's responsible for murdering and desecrating those kids, for attacking Monica Dressler? You think he's *capable* of that?'

'We won't know unless we check it out, Chief,' Carl said. Truth be told, he was somewhat surprised by his boss's reluctance to pursue this lead.

'But what does your *gut* tell you?' Garston asked. 'You think he actually did it?'

Carl shrugged. 'Lord knows, I don't want it to be him any more than you do. But just because we don't want it to be so, doesn't mean it isn't.'

'Why don't you try the high school,' a thin voice proposed from the kitchen, and Carla Garston's frame appeared in the doorway. They all turned to look. 'I'm sorry,' she told the detectives. 'I know I'm not supposed to be eavesdropping. But after twenty-eight years of marriage, I can say with relative certainty that my husband will end up discussing this with me later tonight anyway. It saves him the trouble, if you think about it.' She raised her hands in a half shrug, as if to say, *Gentlemen, let's not quibble on the details*. 'I hope you'll excuse the interruption.'

'What do you mean, "try the high school"?' Sam asked, nonplussed by his wife's interjection.

'For prints,' she responded, drying her hands on a dish towel.

'Carla, do you have any idea how many sets of prints would be covering that place?' her husband asked incredulously.

'Not that many,' she replied. 'You just have to limit your search to a finite area.'

'Such as?' Detective Schroeder asked.

'The door to his locker, of course.' She disappeared into the kitchen for a moment as she returned the towel to its rack near the oven, then rejoined them in the living room. 'School grounds are county property. That should alleviate your search warrant predicament. Plus, the building's empty for winter break. You could be in and out of there without disturbing a soul, except for maybe the janitor who could locate it and unlock the door for you.'

They looked at each other, each considering the idea and finding it basically sound.

Carla shrugged. 'Seems like a good starting place, anyway,' she said. 'Care for a refill on that coffee, Detective Hunt? Detective Schroeder? I still have half a pot here that will go to waste if you don't drink it. Sam's doctor says he's not allowed to have caffeine before he goes to bed. He's been struggling with a little insomnia lately.'

'I don't think the detectives need to hear about *that*, Carla,' Sam advised her. He shifted uncomfortably in his seat.

'It's no secret,' his wife replied. 'With the bags you carry around under your eyes some days, I'm sure any detective worth his rank could deduce as much just by looking at you.'

'I'll take some more coffee, ma'am,' Danny Hunt said with a grin. 'I can drink a whole pot and sleep like a baby. Got used to it in college, I guess.'

'I should've known you were a college boy.' She smiled at him and refilled his cup. 'No wonder you're so smart.'

Danny was twenty-seven, and still had the tendency to blush an embarrassing shade of magenta when the situation called for it.

'Criminal justice major, I presume?' Carla inquired.

'No, ma'am. Philosophy with a minor in biochemistry.'

'Ahh. All the makings of a fine detective,' she said, turning to refresh Carl's mug as well. With the pot empty and a reasonable course of action now decided upon, she excused herself to get ready for bed.

Chapter 44

'Thanks for the pictures.' She spoke into the cordless phone cradled between her neck and shoulder. She stepped into her bedroom and closed the door for privacy.

'You're welcome,' he replied.

'I wish I was there with you.' Monica went to her computer and scrolled through the digital photos Thomas had e-mailed her that afternoon. Her favorite was a picture of him standing on a rocky outcrop overlooking the impressive expanse of a valley far below. Thomas was turned at an oblique angle to the camera, such that half of his face was highlighted by the light of the setting sun, while the other hemisphere was lost in shadows. The rocky landscape had taken on a deep ruddy crimson complexion, and the soft orange sky hovered in the background like an artist who chooses to add a few remaining strokes to a work he knows is already finished, simply because he cannot bear to pull himself away. She touched the photo with her thumb, stroking the side of his face. 'When do you come home?'

'Three days. You think you can wait until then?'

'Nope.'

'Well, you'll have to go find some other guy then.'

She smiled. 'I don't want another guy. I want you.'

He was quiet for a moment, and Monica crossed the room, sitting down on the side of her bed. She ran her fingers across the sheets, thinking about the day they had lain here together, his deeply tanned arms wrapped protectively around her while the afternoon unfolded splendidly around them.

'What've you been doing since I've been gone?' he asked.

'Nothing exciting,' she said. 'Schoolwork and physical therapy, mostly. They've got me jogging on a treadmill now. Three days a week for thirty minutes.' She grimaced. 'I hate running.'

'You shouldn't. You're good at it.'

'How would you know?' she said, a reflexive note of challenge in her voice. 'You've never seen me run.'

There was a slight pause. 'No, but you're good at everything,' he told her. 'I'll bet you're fast as hell when you want to be.'

She had a brief image of herself hurtling through the woods, her breath coming in ragged, terrified sobs – and then it was gone.

'Not fast enough,' she said, standing up and walking to the window. She pressed her fingers up against the glass. The front yard was still blanketed in heavy drifts.

Tree branches spread their naked fingers toward the sky.

'Listen, I've gotta go,' he said. 'Hang in there. I'll be home in a few days.'

Don't go yet, she felt like saying. *We can talk for a little while longer, can't we?* She pressed her lips together and remained silent.

'I'll call you tomorrow,' he promised. 'Okay?'

'Okay,' she replied, her voice faltering a bit on the last syllable.

She listened to the receiver until the connection was lost, until the mechanical voice on the other end told her that if she would like to make a call she could hang up and try again. She thumbed the off button and placed the phone on the desktop beside her, but remained standing at the window for a long time, looking out at the bleak afternoon. Except for a few parked cars, the street outside was vacant, devoid of the children who so frequently played there. These days everyone was being careful. Her eyes wandered across the stillness of front yards and driveways, overturned sleds lying lifeless and abandoned in the snow. From her vantage point behind the protective pane of glass, the scene suddenly struck her as offensive, almost obscene – as if she'd unexpectedly come across a dirty magazine sitting on the dresser in her parents' bedroom. She had the urge to turn away, to pretend she hadn't noticed.

'It'll be okay,' she told herself, but she wondered now if it ever really would be – for any of them.

These days she wondered about that a lot.

Chapter 45

It was Monday afternoon. The cold snap had finally decided to relinquish its hold on the region, and the snow and ice that had collected on the frozen ground almost a month ago had now, at long last, initiated its inevitable metamorphosis toward oblivion. Trillions of rivulets of muddied water set out on their sluggish, unhurried journeys into sewer drains, streams, ponds, reservoirs and even into the porous flesh of the earth itself. The white landscape that had maintained a constant presence during the past few weeks now gave way to patches of brownish, puddled muck. Tree limbs, unencumbered of their heavy loads of frozen precipitation, stretched out their wooden spines as if straightening themselves at the end of a long day of stooped, hunchbacked labor, and the spines of many of the town's residents bent to shoveling sidewalks newly freed from the thick layer of ice that had rendered the concrete walkways nearly impossible to clear only a day before.

So it was that Sam Garston found himself sitting in his office watching the snowmelt dribble past his window in large pregnant drops from the station's roof down onto the sidewalk below. He had gotten a call from the lab less than an hour ago. Several of the prints they'd collected from the Stevenson kid's locker that morning had matched those found on two of the three victims. (The body of the last victim, having been buried in the snow for several weeks, hadn't yielded any salvageable prints at all.) 'Was there any question about the match – any doubt in the analyst's mind?' Sam had asked. 'Not much,' the man on the other end of the phone had replied. The error rate of the software program they used for such purposes was about one in 1.6 million. That didn't leave a whole lot of room for wishful thinking.

That had been enough to request a search warrant of the Stevenson residence, which Judge Natalie Grossman, presiding over the Jefferson County Courthouse that day, had granted them. Detectives Schroeder and Hunt had gone to pick up the document and would be contacting Sam in his office as soon as they had it in hand. He'd already notified Larry Culver from the FBI of their findings and pending search of the home. The bureau would send its own forensic team to assist them with evidence collection. The Stevenson boy would be arrested on-site and taken in for questioning. The rest of the family would also need to be questioned, however painful that might be for Sam personally. It was important to ensure that the boy had acted alone.

The call from the crime lab regarding the fingerprint match had invoked in Sam an unpleasant surge of nausea that he'd been unable to shake over the last fifty minutes, despite a generous swig from the bottle of Maalox he kept in the lower right-hand drawer of his desk. That, mixed with the onset of just a touch of mild chest pressure, made him wonder (with no small degree of concern) whether he might be in the process of having himself one of those all-American heart attacks he'd heard so much about over the years. *Why not?* he asked himself. He'd put in his time at a few greasy spoons in his day. He was certainly due for a few rounds in the ring with the ol' Massive Coronary. If so, perhaps he'd be staring up at the inside of a closed casket before the week was through. 'Now *there's* a nice thought,' he muttered, as he watched a piece of melting ice abandon its grip on the gutter above him and tumble unceremoniously like the corpse of a dead bird to the concrete below. He took another swig from the bottle of antacid in his right hand, wincing at the thick, nasty artificial sweetness of it. *Heart attack.* Just the idea caused him to break out in a light sweat.

This is one of the many unpleasantries of the job, he thought: finding out that someone you knew, someone whose parents you'd had dinner with on more than one occasion and whose father was not only a colleague but also a friend, had wandered onto

301

the wrong side of the law. (Hell, in this case 'wandering onto the wrong side of the law' was a monumental understatement now, wasn't it?) And yet, when Sam thought about the fury that had been unleashed on those young souls . . . When he thought about the heartbreaking agony sustained by those children's parents . . . *Indeed,* that *was the worst of it,* he reminded himself. *Not this.*

As for this part – the arrest and its aftermath – Sam was merely fulfilling his responsibility, wasn't he? It was a responsibility that'd begun when he'd entered the training academy as a young man. Back then, it had only been an idea, a concept – words he had uttered with the rest of his class during a graduation ceremony almost forty years ago. Still, he'd never suspected the measure of sacrifice the job would ultimately demand of him, or the personal casualties that would be sustained along the way. Now, decades later and near the end of his career, he could look back and finally take stock of the full weight of those casualties. His restless nights and the half-empty bottle of Maalox he now clutched in his hand were only the beginning. The uncomfortable pressure that had taken up residence in his chest this afternoon was also a part of it. But most of all, there were certain tragedies he had witnessed – their images stuck in his mind like desert burrs, caked with the dirt of time but sharp and tenacious nonetheless – that served to remind him that the world, or at least the human race, was indeed broken in some fundamental and perhaps irreparable way. *That* was the true measure of payment the job had exacted upon him over the years.

The phone on his desk began to ring. It would be Detective Schroeder, notifying him that they'd obtained the search warrant. The final act of this investigation was about to commence, and Chief Samuel J. Garston of the Jefferson County Sheriff's Department, having served steadfastly and dutifully on the force for the past thirty-eight years, two months and fourteen days, realized he wanted nothing to do with it.

I do solemnly swear, he thought to himself, reaching for the phone, *that I will faithfully and impartially execute the duties of my office . . . to the best of my skill, abilities, and judgment; so help me God.*

It was Carl Schroeder on the line. The conversation was brief, a simple confirmation, and Sam hung up the phone within thirty seconds. He grabbed his coat off the rack and opened the door to his office. The chest discomfort he'd experienced earlier was subsiding, at least. There was that much. Hopefully, it had been nothing too serious. So help him God.

Chapter 46

Detectives Schroeder and Hunt were the first to arrive at the Stevensons' residence. There was one car in the driveway – Susan's gray Saab – but after a protracted series of knocks on the front door it became clear that the house was empty. This wasn't completely surprising, since it was the middle of the day and both of the physicians would presumably be at work. Officers were immediately dispatched to the hospital where Ben worked, and to the medical office Susan shared with a colleague. On the off chance that Ben was engaged in official duties at the Coroner's Office, a car was sent to that address, as well. The building would need to be secured and thoroughly inspected regardless, since its numerous drawers, racks, and countertops could very conceivably host the weapons used in one or all of the murders. Chief Garston pulled into the driveway a few minutes after Schroeder and Hunt, and two additional cruisers arrived shortly thereafter, along with a van from the forensic investigation unit that had been dispatched to assist with the search of the premises and related evidence-gathering. The congregation of law enforcement vehicles and personnel quickly filled the Stevensons' driveway and spilled out onto the narrow road servicing the suburban neighborhood.

Mary Jennings, who lived just across the street in a modest two-story split-foyer, noticed the accumulation of sheriff's deputies and emergency vehicles from her kitchen window as she was preparing lunch. In a state of concern, she picked up the phone and dialed Susan Stevenson's cell phone. As circumstances would have it, the voice that answered was neither across the street in the house now surrounded by police officers, nor at her medical office three miles away, but rather almost two thousand miles away, on the other side of the country.

'Hey, Mary. What's up?'

Susan sounds particularly nonplussed, Mary thought, *given the fact that half of the Jefferson County Sheriff's Department is walking around on her front lawn.* 'I just wanted to make sure everything's okay,' she replied. 'There're a bunch of cop cars sitting in your driveway. I thought maybe you guys might've had a break-in this morning.'

There was no response from the other end of the line, and Mary wondered if perhaps they'd been disconnected. 'Sue?' she asked tentatively. 'You still there?'

At first she thought that, indeed, she'd lost the connection. But as she listened she realized that the line was not completely dead. She could hear something in the background: the muffled voice of what sounded like a convenience store clerk ringing up a purchase (*'Will that be all? Can I get you anything else today?'*) beneath the subtle static of the open line. She began to take the receiver away from her ear when she heard – or at least thought she heard – a reply on the other end.

'—any?'

'Hello, Susan?'

'Mary, you there?'

'I'm here,' she replied. 'Sorry. I thought we'd lost the—'

'How many?'

Her brow furrowed. She had no idea what her friend was referring to. 'How many *what*?' she asked.

'Cops. Sheriff's deputies, Mary.' Susan's tone sounded strained and impatient. 'How many police officers are at the house?'

Still, the question bewildered her. It seemed to Mary that this was among the *least* important details of the situation. 'I, uh . . . I don't know. Let me check.' She went back to the window and peered through the glass. 'I assume you're not at home,' she said.

Susan left the question unanswered. Instead, her neighbor repeated her initial query. 'How many, Mary?'

Mary counted the vehicles and the people whom she could see. Most, but not all of them, were in uniform. 'Five – no, six – cars,' she reported. 'One white van. Looks like about . . . I don't know . . . twelve to fifteen officers. It's hard to say. Some of them are still sitting in their cars. It looks like they're waiting around for something. I thought . . . I mean, I know

it's a horrible thing to say and all,' she continued, 'but
. . . I thought maybe they were waiting for an ambulance.' *Or a hearse,* she thought, but omitted this last
part. In the back of her mind, she'd been worried that
perhaps Ben had suffered a heart attack or even a
cardiac arrest. Susan's husband had been looking like
he'd been under a lot of stress lately. He'd seemed too
gaunt, too . . . *haunted* was the word that popped
into her brain. Her body gave an involuntary shudder.

'—en there?'

'I'm sorry, sweetheart. What was that?'

'Is Ben there?' Her voice sounded tense but
controlled, almost – as ridiculous as the idea seemed
– as if she'd been expecting this development all along.

'No,' she said. 'I don't see Ben's car, and I don't
see him. Maybe they're waiting for him to get home.'
A thought struck her then, and she was unable to
keep the alarm out of her voice. 'Oh, God, Susan! I
hope it's not the children! I hope nothing's happened
to one of the kids!'

'The kids are with me,' Susan replied.

'*Oh, thank God!*' she said. '*Thank God* for that,
honey.'

The voice on the other end was quiet for a moment,
then responded: 'Yes. Thank God for that.'

For perhaps five seconds neither one of them spoke.
It was a short pause, but within it, Mary was struck
with the impression that a decision had been made.

'I have to go now, Mary,' Susan said. 'Thank you
for calling. I can't tell you how important your phone
call was, or how much I appreciate it.'

307

'Oh, you're welcome, honey,' she replied, modestly brushing away the compliment yet pleased with herself for having been such a good friend and neighbor to the Stevensons, and to Susan in particular. Contacting her to make certain that she and her family were okay had just come naturally to Mary. It was the kind of thing neighbors used to do for each other all the time when she was growing up – and in the Midwest, she was proud to imagine, something neighbors *still* did for one another, no matter how disconnected and self-absorbed the rest of the country had become.

'You've always been a good friend to us, Mary. That friendship has meant a lot to me personally over the years. It still does. Regardless of everything else, I hope we can still have that.'

'Of course we can, Susan. You know you can come to me no matter what. If there's anything I can do – anything at all – you just let me know.'

'Thank you, Mary. Goodbye.'

There was an audible click as the line was disconnected, and Mary returned the phone to its receptacle. She stood in the kitchen for a few moments, turning the conversation over in her mind. She realized that she'd learned very little about what was going on across the street at the Stevensons' residence. Nevertheless, she decided that she had been able to offer them assistance, and for that she felt grateful. Humming quietly to herself, she went about setting the table for lunch.

Chapter 47

The face of the sheriff's deputy who appeared in the doorway of Trinity Medical Center's pathology lab that afternoon belonged to Tony Linwood, a friend of the Stevensons'. Looking up from his microscope, Ben recognized the deputy immediately.

'Hello, Tony,' he said, smiling. 'Nice to see you.'

'Doc.' Tony nodded. His youthful, often animated face appeared neutral, his body language guarded.

Ben, who had begun making his way around the large desk to greet him, registered the officer's tone and stopped, his fingers resting lightly on the varnished wooden surface.

'What brings you all the way down to what we in the business lovingly refer to as the "bowels of the hospital"?' he asked.

Tony's feet shifted slightly, a little restlessly. 'Chief Garston has requested your presence, sir.'

Ben felt his stomach clench. *Not again,* he thought.

309

And so soon? He couldn't face another one so quickly after the last autopsy. He simply couldn't.

'Has there been another murder?' he asked apprehensively.

'I'm not at liberty to discuss things with you further, sir. I've just been asked to come get you.'

So formal. So guarded. Suddenly, a thought occurred to him: *What if my presence is needed not as the medical examiner, but as the father of the victim?* A moment of panic seized him, and he was struck with the nearly overwhelming urge to rush at the deputy, grab him by the front of his uniform, and demand to know what was going on. ('*Is it one of my boys, goddamn it?! DID HE KILL ONE OF MY BOYS?!!*') If he'd taken such an approach, it wouldn't have gone well for him – family friend or not. When Deputy Linwood had received the call over the radio, the dispatcher had said, 'Possible suspect in a 187, needed for questioning.' One-eighty-seven was the radio code for homicide, and in a town that almost never saw such a crime, Tony had little doubt which series of murders the dispatcher was referring to. Any sudden rush by Dr Stevenson would have resulted in Ben lying face-first on the floor with the full weight of the deputy's knee pressing into the back of his neck.

Fortunately, Ben suddenly recalled that the boys were with their mother and grandparents in Arizona, and thus well out of harm's way. Which left him with one residual thought: *Who's it going to be this time?* He released a sigh of resignation. 'Okay, let me get my keys.'

'You can leave your car here, sir,' Tony advised him. 'I have instructions that you're to come with me.'

Ben frowned. 'I can just follow you, Tony. It's not a problem.'

'I'm sorry, sir. I have specific instructions.'

Ben paused for a moment, considering. '*I have instructions that you're to come with me,*' Tony had said. '*I'm not at liberty to discuss things with you further, sir.*' He'd never received a police escort to any of the other crime scenes. So, what was going on here? He was having difficulty making the pieces fit.

'Tony – Deputy Linwood,' Ben said carefully, opting halfway through his sentence for the more formal address. 'Am I under arrest for something?'

'No, sir,' the officer responded. 'Not at this time.'

Chapter 48

The trip in the police cruiser was a short one, and none of them spoke. There had been a second sheriff's deputy waiting for them just outside the lab, and the officer sat in the front passenger's seat, with Tony at the wheel. Ben was relegated to the back, where the doors could be opened only from the outside. A thick Plexiglas divide separated him from the officers, and his knees were smashed up against the back of the seat in front of him.

He had no idea whether sheriff's deputies worked in unison, or whether two officers to a car was the norm. He suspected the former, however, and wondered whether the second officer had been dispatched in case there had been a scuffle. It was hard for him to imagine – *ridiculous, even* – fighting with the police. What did they want to question him about? He wasn't guilty of anything that he could think of. And yet, here he was, sitting in the back of a cruiser like a common criminal.

It didn't take Ben long to figure out that they were headed for his house. Still, when they rounded the bend in the road and his driveway came into view, he was absolutely stunned by the number of police vehicles parked outside. The cruiser came to a stop several houses up the street. It was the closest they could get given the veritable parking lot of official-looking vehicles stationed along the modest residential street. Several of his neighbors stood on their lawns and front steps, gawking at the spectacle.

'Wait here,' the sheriff's deputy in the front passenger seat, unfamiliar to Ben, instructed him. (*As if I have a choice,* Ben thought to himself.) Tony remained in the car, hands still gripping the steering wheel, although he'd already turned off the engine. Ben considered asking him again what this was about, but decided against it. If he was truly wanted for questioning regarding what appeared to be a fairly big deal, then perhaps the less he said, the better. He shook his head. He was already starting to think like a defendant. Boy, *that* hadn't taken long.

He looked out through the dirty side window next to him. He could see Sam Garston approaching the car, accompanied by the deputy who'd ridden with them from the hospital. Sam looked grim and irritable. 'What's he doing in the back of the car?' he barked in their direction. 'Let him out.'

Tony jumped out of the driver's seat and opened

the rear passenger door. Ben pulled himself into a standing position beside the cruiser.

'I'm sorry as hell to have to do this to you, Ben,' Sam said, drawing one of his large hands across the angle of his lower jaw.

'*I certainly hope so,*' Ben countered, not waiting for the man to finish. 'Whatever this is about, Sam, I can assure you there's no need for this sort of . . .'

'Ben?'

'. . . *freak show* . . .'

'Ben?'

'. . . *I mean, I've got neighbors, for God's sake!* What're they supposed to—'

'Ben, shut up,' Garston said flatly, and that *did* shut him up. Like a slap across the face.

Sam paused a moment, waiting for another outburst. The two deputies standing next to them glanced at one another, but said nothing. When he was certain that Ben was listening, Chief Garston continued.

'As I was saying, Ben, I'm sorry as hell to have to do this to you, but before we proceed any further I have to go over your Miranda rights with you.'

'*My Miranda righ*—' Ben began incredulously, but the large man in front of him continued speaking as if he hadn't noticed.

'First,' he advised him, looking Ben directly in the eye to ensure that he was listening, 'you have the right to remain silent. Anything you say can and will be used against you in a court of law.'

Ben felt as if he were hearing these words from a great distance. Sheriff's deputies continued to mill

314

about in his driveway and on the front lawn of his house. It seemed to Ben that their movements were slow and surreal, almost as if they were floating from place to place. To his immediate right, his next-door neighbors watched the exchange between him and the officers with fascination. Ben knew them both: Harry and Samantha Caddington. Susan was their family physician. Three years ago, she'd visited their son every day in the hospital while he was being treated for Hodgkin's lymphoma. She'd sat with them for countless hours at the boy's bedside during the worst of the illness. They both had. Now, Ben noticed, they wouldn't even meet his gaze.

'Second,' Garston continued, 'you have the right to an attorney. Are you listening, Ben?'

'Yes,' he responded through numb lips, his voice dull and metallic in his own ears.

'If you cannot afford an attorney, one will be appointed for you.' Sam paused for a moment, taking a breath. He appeared to be sweating lightly, despite the cold weather. 'Do you understand these rights as they have been read to you?'

'Yes, I understand them,' Ben said.

'Good. Now, listen to me. You're not under arrest, Ben. But we do need to ask you some questions.'

'Okay,' he replied weakly. It was all he could manage.

'We also have a search warrant for your house and property.'

'A search warrant,' Ben said, trying to make sense of the words. The term seemed strange and foreign

315

to his ears, as if from a second language he was only just beginning to learn.

'Yes. Now we've been authorized to forcibly enter the house, if necessary. But it would avoid a bit of damage to your front door if you happened to have a key on you.'

Ben fished around in his right front pocket and brought out a small key ring, which he handed to one of the officers.

'Good,' Sam commented, nodding his head. He reached into the inside pocket of his jacket and produced a piece of paper. 'You have the right to inspect the search warrant, Ben.'

'It's okay. I trust you, Sam.' He glanced again at his neighbors to the right, who hastily averted their eyes and began inspecting the concrete construction of their own front steps.

'You shouldn't,' Sam said. 'Not right now. As your friend, Ben, I advise you to take full advantage of your rights. Here, go ahead and read it.' He handed the form to Ben, who let his eyes wander over the language. It was written in fairly plain English, but the words seemed incomprehensible at the moment. He handed it back.

'Can we please get out of the street?' he muttered.

'Of course,' Sam replied. 'Let's go.'

He turned and led the procession to the front door. The officer who'd been given Ben's keys fiddled with the lock for a moment. 'It should only be the dead bolt,' Ben advised him, and he nodded. A moment later, there was the sound of the latch retracting into the cylinder. The officer placed his hand on the knob.

WHOOOOOO-WHOOO-WHOO-WHOOO!!!!

The deputy glanced at him, eyebrows slightly raised. 'Dog?' he inquired.

'Oh, yeah,' Ben said. 'Alex. Alexander-the-uh . . . He's our' – *security system,* he was about to say – 'Great Dane.'

'Great Dane?' the officer repeated. From behind the door the howling continued.

'WHOOOO-WHOOOOO-WHOOOO-WHOO-OOOOO!!!"

'You'd better let me put him in the basement.'

The officer with his hand on the doorknob looked at Sam, who nodded. 'I'll go in with him,' the chief advised them. 'Everyone else stay here for a moment.'

The deputy stepped back and raised his right hand in a gesture as if to say, *Be my guest.*

Ben turned the knob and pushed the door open just enough to squeeze through. 'Hold on, let me get his collar on,' he called back to Sam. Ben grabbed the choker chain from where it hung on the wall and slid it over the dog's massive head. He placed a finger through the metal ring and guided the dog toward the interior door leading to the basement. As he moved the dog away from the front entrance, Sam took the opportunity to slide inside, closing the door behind him. He followed the two of them down the hallway.

Ben stopped at the door to the basement, but did not open it. He turned toward the chief. 'What's going on here, Sam?'

The man stared back at him. He looked sick – pale and slightly ashen. 'It's serious, Ben. A . . . a nasty thing.' He shook his head. 'I wish to hell it wasn't.'

'Tell me. Can you do that? Please, talk to me.'

The chief sighed. 'Put the dog in the basement. We have to get started here. I'll bring in the others and we can talk.'

Ben opened the door, flipped on the light switch, and ushered Alex down the steps. Closing the door, he moved to a chair at the kitchen table. He tried to brace himself for what was to come next. He knew himself to be innocent, and he wasn't concerned about self-incrimination. That left Susan or one of the boys, and he didn't see how *any* of them could be involved in anything remotely serious. He knew them too well for that. You live and interact with the people in your family through all of the joy and nastiness (*'It's serious, Ben. A . . . a nasty thing.'*) that life has to offer. Along the way, the fabrics of what began as separate individuals are woven together into something new – something organic and inseparable. And the only thought that came to him now was this: *Please, don't let me lose them*. If one of them had died, or had suffered some devastating injury, he wasn't certain he had the strength to face it. *Please, don't let me lose them,* he prayed silently to himself, or to God if He was out there and felt like listening. In this moment of confusion and disorder, it was the only sentiment that seemed to matter.

'Okay,' he said, his dark eyes watching the officers fan out across the house – *his* house – and one hand gripped the edge of the table for whatever stability it had to offer. 'Tell me what this is all about.'

Chapter 49

'No. You're clearly out of your fucking mind.' Ben looked blankly at Detective Schroeder, who remained standing next to the sink, one hand resting on the granite countertop.

The detective returned Ben's gaze with infuriating equanimity. 'The evidence is pretty convincing, Dr Stevenson.'

Get your filthy hand off that countertop, Ben wanted to scream at him. *My wife cooks there!*

'The evidence is wrong,' he said instead.

'The boy's prints were on the bodies of two of the victims.'

'The boy's prints . . .' Ben echoed, his voice dry and hollow, trying to make sense of the words. Suddenly, his son – his oldest son, whom he loved with unflinching purity and tenacity – suddenly *his son* had become simply 'the boy' to this man standing in front of him.

'The boy has a name,' he advised the detective. 'I strongly suggest you start using it.'

The three of them – the two detectives and Sam Garston – were silent for a while, allowing the shock of the news to dissipate slightly before proceeding further. They could have waited an eternity as far as Ben was concerned. A few minutes' respite wouldn't make a bit of difference to him.

'Ben,' Sam started. 'You and—'

'I want *this one* to get *out of my house*!' Ben thrust an index finger in Carl's direction.

'I'm sorry, Ben,' Sam replied. 'This is Detective Schroeder's case. He has the right to question you.'

Ben turned to Detective Hunt, the only one of the three officers who'd taken a seat at the table, and who thus far had not uttered a word. 'Aren't you also investigating this case?'

The detective nodded solemnly.

'Fine,' Ben proclaimed. '*You* stay.' He gestured once again toward the senior detective. '*This one* goes.'

None of the men budged. Carl Schroeder continued to stare at him, as if Ben were some sort of interesting insect he was considering adding to his collection.

'Listen, Ben,' Sam replied, 'that's not the type of tone you want to take during this interview.'

'It's *exactly* the type of tone I want to take!' Ben's eyes flashed once more in Schroeder's direction. 'I have nothing to hide – *nothing!* – and neither does my family. I am willing to cooperate with you, and I am willing to answer questions. But I *will not* sit here and listen to this man call my son a murderer!'

Silence filled the kitchen. In the adjoining rooms, nearly oblivious to their presence, teams of forensic crime scene examiners scurried about like beetles, fastidiously foraging for their esoteric treasures. Ben could hear them rattling about, conversing quietly with one another. He realized, of course, that he was behaving ridiculously. Carl Schroeder was simply doing his job. They all were. The chief and his team of investigators had followed the evidence to where they thought it led. They had made an egregious mistake, of course – that much was clear – and they would soon discover just that. In the meantime, was there really any cause for Ben to . . . (*doubt*) . . . to respond in this manner? It made sense to remain calm and to cooperate with them as much as possible. Didn't it?

And what if they're right? a voice spoke up inside of his head. *What if they're right, Ben? Have you even bothered to consider that?*

Of course he had. He'd considered the idea for a fraction of a second before tossing it properly out through the front door where it belonged.

Is that right?

Yes, that was right. They could lay out all of the circumstantial evidence they had in their possession – make whatever wild accusations they wanted. They *would not* make him doubt the innocence of his own son. *They would not.*

Because you know your boy. You know what he's capable of. And what he isn't.

Damn right, he knew his boy. After almost seventeen years, he ought to, by God. If his son were

321

involved in anything remotely *close* to what they were suggesting, Ben would know about it. Wouldn't he?

Sure, the voice said. *How could you not? After all, you've been through so much with him – with both of them.*

Yes, he had. Susan, too.

Like the stint Joel spent in the hospital after falling over the rail of the upstairs balcony. Times like that.

Of course. Times like that.

Right over the rail, he went. An accident.

Yes. Such a terrible accident had a way of bringing a family togeth –

Because it couldn't have happened any other way – right, Ben? The boy couldn't have . . . been pushed . . . or thrown, for example.

Thrown? That was ridiculous.

Because you were right there. You saw it all, and you would've known, wouldn't you? You would've known if something like that had happened.

But he hadn't seen it. Not the entire skirmish. All he'd witnessed as he ascended the staircase was Joel's body falling to the floor below.

And that's it, right? Nothing else. Nothing you might've caught in your peripheral vision and chosen not to see?

No, nothing.

Because you know *your boy. You know what he's capable of.*

Yes. He did. Didn't he?

He looked up at them. They were watching him, all three of them, waiting for him to deny it again.

322

From the look in their eyes – *Even Sam? Yes, even his friend Sam* – he could tell that the question was already settled in each of their minds, and that the only fool in this room . . . was him. Yet he couldn't bring himself to accept what they were alleging. None of it made any sense to him. None of it at all.

'Call, Susan,' he said finally. 'They're visiting her parents in Arizona right now. Call my wife, and she'll tell you just how crazy this all is. Call her. You'll see.' And he gave them the number.

Chapter 50

The desert sun beat down on the metallic hide of the automobile as the car tracked its course across the barren landscape. In the rearview mirror, another vehicle could be seen cresting the horizon. She found it hard to resist the urge to accelerate. Instead, she allowed the cruise control to do its job, keeping them at six miles per hour over the posted speed limit. She couldn't afford to get pulled over. Not now. And yet, time was short, wasn't it? How much time did they actually have? She didn't know – *couldn't* know for sure. Not knowing made her want to place her right foot on the accelerator and floor the motherfucker, and again she resisted the urge. If she panicked, it would all be over.

Another thought occurred to her, a saner thought: stop. Stop now, either here or at the next exit (wherever that might be in this veritable wasteland of sand and sporadic scrub brush). Stop now and put an end to it before a horrible situation became much, much worse. In the backseat, two children slept – one hardly qualifying as a child any longer. If she took the next exit, found a gas station or a convenience store – anyplace with a landline (there'd been zero bars on her cell phone for the past forty minutes) and maybe another human being – she could make a phone call and just stay put. Allow it to end. She could allow herself to choose the only reasonable course of action.

Which was diametrically opposed to what she was doing now. She could try to convince herself that she was somehow protecting them, but . . . was she, really? She had known for a long time, she supposed, that this would end badly. She had known ten years ago, when he was six, when he would simply sit for long periods of time – hours, sometimes – watching them, his small face devoid of expression. It wasn't normal; she didn't need to be a child psychiatrist to know that. The thought had occurred to her that perhaps he was experiencing some type of seizure – *absence seizures,* they called them. But his eyes, intelligent and aware, suggested differently. To be absolutely certain, she'd taken him to a pediatric neurologist. 'Why does he do that?' she'd asked, but after a half-dozen tests and a few thousand dollars in medical bills the specialist had deemed her son healthy.

'Nothing wrong that I can see,' he'd tried to reassure her. 'He's an intelligent, curious child. These episodes' – he'd shrugged, getting up from his seat and placing one chubby hand on the exam room's doorknob, apparently eager to move on to the next patient – 'are just part of his development. He'll grow out of them. Something else will take their place.'

And Thomas *did* seem to grow out of them, too – for a while, anyway. She had taken comfort in the fact that his general demeanor, as well as his interactions with others, had seemed to normalize over the next two years. And while his affect was never what she would consider completely normal, at least he had seemed more willing to engage in the world around him. It was around that time, however, that she'd discovered the wood rat.

Ben had installed a small shed in the back of their yard the year before. He'd needed just enough storage space for the lawn mower, a few sawhorses, some planting pots, the circular saw and a couple of shovels and assorted hand tools. It wasn't a big structure, but it had a roof, four walls and a sliding aluminum door with a latch that her husband usually kept locked.

She'd been working out back in the garden one late spring afternoon when she'd noticed that the door to the shed was standing slightly ajar. Normally, she wouldn't have thought twice about it; but they'd been having some trouble with rodents getting into the trash lately, and the sight of that partially open door had brought with it the thought of what an *absolute mess* she'd have on her hands if the rats got in there and decided to chew through the four bags of topsoil she'd purchased last week. She went to the shed with the intention of simply closing that door and, as an added measure of caution, perhaps to pause for a quick inspection of the interior to ensure that no critters had taken up residence inside. When she arrived at the door, she threw a quick look inside and then started to slide the door closed on its plastic track. Then she paused, for an unpleasant stench seemed to waft through the structure's open doorway. *Oh, God. Something has found its way in there,* she thought, *and has probably died in the process.* She wasn't particularly enthusiastic about going in after it, either. But Ben – the usual cleaner-upper of such disgusting, odiferous delights – was out of town for the weekend and wouldn't be back until Tuesday. God only knew how nasty that smell was going to get between now and then.

She reversed course and threw the door wide open, letting in the maximum amount of light to illuminate her ensuing inspection. She'd hoped, perhaps in vain, that the enhanced flow of fresh air would also dissipate most of the offensive odor. What she saw inside the shed amid the flood of sunlight was, in essence, unremarkable. Tools leaned lazily against the corrugated aluminum walls in their usual positions. The lawn mower sat dormant, patiently awaiting her husband's return. Even the bags of topsoil appeared unmolested, their white bodies congregated in the corner of the shed like a small crowd of curious onlookers. Nothing seemed out of place, and there was no dead animal lurking in the recesses that she could see. Still, the smell was as pungent as ever – even more so now that she'd stepped inside.

She made her way to the back of the shed's interior, allowing her nose to guide her rather than her eyes. It was here that the smell was most powerful, and she got down on her hands and knees to inspect the corners of the small enclosure, to push the bags of topsoil aside.

She found nothing.

Susan returned to her feet, hands placed squarely on her hips, as she continued to scan the inside of the shed from top to bottom. The stench was so noxious that she was forced to pull the front of the her T-shirt up over her nose, the smell of her own sweat and – yes, let's be honest here – body odor preferable to the alternative olfactory assault. No matter how hard she looked, however, she was unable to identify the source of the odor.

Well, I've given it an earnest try, she told herself. This would be a job for Ben when he returned. It was one of the divisions of labor in their marriage. She had carried Thomas in her intractably expanding uterus for nine months, and was now three months pregnant with her second child and repeating the process all over again. She had been plagued by frequent episodes of nausea and vomiting during the first trimesters of both pregnancies, and by varicose veins and intermittent lower back pain at the end of her third trimester with Thomas. She had already pushed one child's enormous head out through the smallest of orifices, and her body had been permanently altered by that experience in ways she would never feel completely at ease with. Now it would be her husband's turn to retrieve dead things from the tool shed. It still wasn't exactly a fair division of duties – he was getting off much too easy – but right then she was more than happy to cash in on her investment in their nuptial arrangement.

Susan exited the shed and slid the door closed behind her, glad to be free from whatever fetid thing still lingered inside. She was on the verge of crossing the lawn and returning to her gardening – perhaps, in retrospect, it would've been better if she had – but the obnoxious smell still hung in the air, even with the door to the shed closed and latched, and she remembered thinking to herself, *What if it's not inside the shed at all, but behind it?*

Even then, she'd considered letting the matter go. It wasn't her responsibility to go on a half-day scavenger hunt looking for this thing. The days that she truly had to herself, with her husband out of town and Thomas off with his friends, were few and far between. She ought to be enjoying the day, not traipsing around the yard searching for clues like some veterinary medical examiner. *The hell with it,* she decided. *I'm going back to my goddamn garden.*

And yet a moment later she found herself peering around the rear corner of the shed. The front of her shirt was once again pulled up over the bridge of her nose like a bandana, as if she were more intent on robbing a stagecoach than exploring her own backyard. That was when she spied it, the source of the odor. At first, she wasn't quite certain *what* she was seeing – the mass of flies swarming around it was so thick. She took a step forward and shooed them away with her hand. The majority of the airborne insects retreated a short distance, although they still loitered in the area, waiting for her to depart and leave them once again with their prize. At her feet lay a large Tupperware container, its underside pointed toward the sky. It sat in a small patch of dirt behind the shed, facedown on a two-inch-thick section of lumber, which completely sealed the container's only opening. Along the edges on all sides, a series of nails had been driven through the container's plastic lip and deep into the wood beneath.

Condensation had accumulated on the inside of the chamber, making it difficult to clearly make out the details of the amorphous form inside. Its dark outline was perfectly still, its body nearly filling the confines of the small compartment. There was no doubt about one thing, however. Whatever had been purposefully imprisoned inside the container was quite dead. The reek of its decomposing corpse wafted up through multiple punctate holes in the plastic, obviously created with one objective: to allow the passage of air in and out of the container so the animal could breathe. And that was where her eyes kept returning – to those small air holes designed to prevent quick suffocation. Obviously, the animal had been meant to die. But it had been meant to die slowly.

She'd backed away in revulsion, moaning slightly. In doing so, she managed to trip over her own feet, and she sat down hard in the grass a few yards from the makeshift death chamber. If there had been an upturned nail in the grass, she would've sustained a significant enough injury to land her in the emergency department, but she was lucky in this regard – all of the available nails had been used for other purposes. The flies took this partial retreat as a sign to resume their swarming, and they did so with new enthusiasm, desperate to get inside. One of them flitted onto her forearm, and she swatted it away in a spasm of disgust. She pushed herself backward along the ground, crab-walking away from the pitiful shape in front of her as fast as her adrenaline-laced appendages could carry her. All the while, her eyes kept returning to the air holes.

Die slow, thing inside. Die slow. The thought sloshed around inside her head like a rotting jellyfish, and suddenly she turned clumsily over onto her hands and knees and vomited in the grass. The stink of it mingled with that of the dead creature only a few yards away, and the axis of the earth seemed to tilt unpredictably as she vomited again, abdominal muscles clenching each time the spasms passed through her bent frame. Small beads of sweat broke out on her back, her shoulders, her forehead. Her hands balled into small fists as she clutched the grass, afraid that if she let go now her body would simply slide away from the earth and into the blackness that surrounded her. She remained that way for a long time: eyes shut, fingers dug into the soft dirt for purchase, flies buzzing in her ears, the ground shifting dangerously beneath her.

When the worst of it was over, she simply lay

motionless in the grass, waiting to recover. A rogue fly landed on her calf, and she twitched it away. She wasn't certain how long she lay there. She had the place to herself, and no one came out to ask if she was okay. During that limitless space of time, she thought of many things, but mostly she thought of Thomas. She thought of her strange, dark boy staring at her from across the room at the age of six. She did not wonder whether he had done this, for in some deep, primitive part of her brain she knew with a mother's simple certainty that he had. Instead, she wondered about the insignificant details: *Where did he get the hammer?* From the shed, of course. *Where is it now?* She was fairly certain that if she went back to look for it, she'd find it hanging in its usual spot on the wall. *He returned the hammer, but left the animal. What does that mean? Why didn't he try to hide it?* The question made her want to cry, for what it meant to her was that her son was broken in some deep, irreparable way. She thought of the neurologist, with his thick-rimmed glasses, bow tie, and doughy body: '*These episodes . . . He'll grow out of them. Something else will take their place.*'

It had. Something else had taken the place of those vacant stares. And the question before her was, *What now?* She asked herself whether she should confront him, and if so, how. Should he be punished? Perhaps punishment was too mild a response. Should he be hospitalized? What does a parent, or a physician for that matter, do with a . . . with a sociopath? For that was what she was dealing with here, wasn't it? Normal people do not nail animals inside of a Tupperware container to watch them die. What's more, normal people do not do something like that and just walk away when it's over without shame or guilt, without hiding the evidence.

She allowed the analytical part of her brain to work it through. Medical school had provided her with enough basic knowledge of psychiatry to know that sociopaths – the more correct term these days was antisocial personality disorder – are essentially unaffected by all attempts at treatment. The fundamental problem was that they lacked the basic human ability to identify with others. They were unable to mentally place themselves in the position of another creature, be that a person or an animal. It wasn't that they necessarily didn't understand right from wrong; it was simply that they lacked the ability to care. Eating an apple and torturing an animal carried with them the same level of unrest within the conscience: none. In fact, it was as if the conscience – the ability to *care* about right and wrong – were anatomically absent from the brain. The same was true for the absence of mercy – not because mercy was something such individuals chose to withhold, but because it was a faculty they simply did not possess. The condition couldn't be medicated away or repaired by psychotherapy or psychoanalysis, any more than those treatments might be expected to regenerate an absent arm or leg in an amputee. Over the centuries, medical treatment had become quite adept at fixing parts of the body that were broken: a shattered bone, or even a shattered mind; but it had never been very good at *creating* something, especially something as amorphous as a conscience, in situations where it never existed in the first place.

Likewise, from a rational point of view, the idea of punishing her child for this atrocity seemed somewhat pointless. Perhaps punishment would at least teach him that every action has its consequences. But if he had no ability to appreciate that the action was wrong, reprimand was unlikely to keep it from happening again.

What other options did that leave? Sending her son somewhere to be locked away? Following him around every moment of every day to ensure that this sort of thing – or worse – never happened again? Impossible. She sat in the grass, legs crossed in front of her and arms wrapped protectively around her knees. She sat there for a long time, some ten yards from the dead wood rat in its plastic cell, and searched herself for an answer. It wasn't a situation she'd ever imagined encountering, and now that it was here she had no idea what to do with it. She could still smell the stench of the thing: its furry body bloated and rotting in the sun, tiny feet torn apart and matted with blood from useless attempts to claw its way out. She felt another hitch in her stomach and turned to the side to retch once again. This time nothing came. She had emptied herself completely.

She wiped her mouth with the back of one dirt-grimed hand and stared at the container nailed to the board with its respective cloud of flies. The sight of it repulsed her, made her want to distance herself from it as much as possible. And yet, she realized now that it was also a part of her. She owned it as much as her son did, for wasn't there an inseparable connection between mother and child? From the moment of conception, the two are linked by body and blood, and that visceral intimacy continues well beyond childbirth. It becomes a part of who you are, as indissoluble as the color of your skin or the tempo of your heart. She was vaguely aware that it was somehow different for fathers, who seemed to be able to disconnect themselves at times from the lives of their children, or at least to compartmentalize their thoughts and feelings in accordance with their various duties and responsibilities. She'd never been able to accomplish that degree of mental separation. She was a mother above all else, and for better or worse, she felt inherently tied to the lives of her children. She had difficulty describing it any more clearly than that, but understood it perfectly and without reservation. And what it meant was that the thing in the container was *hers* as much as it was Thomas's. And now she was responsible for taking care of it.

She got up, crossed the yard, entered the house, and retrieved a pair of latex exam gloves from the modest supply of medical equipment she kept on the upper shelf of her bedroom closet. She wished for a mask to cover her mouth and nose, but lacking that, she grabbed a bottle of Vicks from the bathroom medicine cabinet and smeared a generous amount of the vaporizing gel on the skin between her upper lip and nose, then covered her lower face with a handkerchief that she knotted behind her head. She returned to the shed and grabbed two large, black heavy-duty garbage bags that Ben kept for the disposal of raked leaves and other yard debris. Then, quickly, before she could think about it further, she walked around to the rear of the shed, snatched the contraption off the ground – it was heavier than she'd anticipated, although she preferred not to think about why – and tossed it into the open bag. Angry flies zipped around her head, but she did not pause this time to swat them away. Instead, she wound the opening of the bag around itself several times, tied it with an overhand knot, dropped this bag into the next with her discarded gloves, and repeated the process.

She walked with her (*What was it? Discovery? Prize? Package of shame?*) to the Saab parked in the driveway out front, popped the trunk, lowered the thing in, and slammed the lid closed again against the smell that still seemed to permeate through the tightly bound, double-bagged plastic cocoon. She barely remembered the twenty-minute drive to the local dump, barely remembered tossing it into the gaping mouth of excavated earth, and barely remembered standing there for a moment, watching it from above. She did recall, all too well, that after a few watchful moments, the bag appeared to move, just slightly, as if she had been mistaken and the thing inside was not quite dead yet. That had been enough for her. She turned quickly, showing it her back, and drove home in a cold sweat that clung to her body for the remainder of the day, even after a hot shower and fresh clothes. Weeks later, despite all of her efforts to eradicate the smell, the car still seemed to stink of the thing, although Ben never took notice. Perhaps it was only an olfactory memory. If so, she owned that, too.

The next time she saw Thomas, she said nothing about the incident. In fact, she found herself avoiding him. She wondered whether he'd gone looking for the animal, found it missing, and had realized she must've discovered it. She also wondered if he cared, and she imagined that, most likely, he did not.

A week later, she encountered Thomas alone in his room, lying on his bed and listening to music on his headphones. The bedroom door had been closed. Susan was carrying a basket of laundry in her arms. She rested the basket on one thigh, knocked lightly on the door, and when there was no answer, opened the door and entered the bedroom, assuming it was vacant.

When she saw that he was there, she paused in the doorway, not wanting to go farther inside, not wanting to be alone with him, even for the few seconds it would take to leave the clothes on his dresser. More than the encounter itself, she was disturbed by the realization that she was so uncomfortable in his presence. *No matter what he has done,* she reasoned with herself, *I am still his mother.* That role hadn't ended that day behind the tool shed, and although her discovery had forced her to see her son as something different from what she'd previously perceived him to be, the basic dynamic of their relationship hadn't changed. *Had it? No,* she decided. He was still her child, after all, and she had an obligation to look after him. How to fulfill that duty under the current circumstances was something she had yet to figure out, but the responsibility was there, the same as if he'd been born with cerebral palsy or mental retardation.

She motioned for him to remove his headphones so she could talk with him, and he did so with the normal reluctance of an eight-year-old boy. She stepped inside the room, set the basket of folded clothes on the floor, and closed the door behind her.

'I found the dead rat behind the shed,' she told him matter-of-factly, 'the one you nailed inside the plastic container.'

She didn't know what she'd been expecting his response to be. Denial, perhaps. Or anger. Lying. She was even prepared for tears. What she got instead was: nothing. He lay on his back in bed, his head propped up on one hand, and regarded her blankly, waiting for her to continue – waiting for her to say something of some significance.

When he made no reply, she continued. 'You tortured and killed that poor, helpless creature. I want to know why.'

He continued to regard her, his face devoid of emotion.

'Are you sick, Thomas? Do I need to put you in a hospital? Is that what needs to happen here?'

Nothing. His green eyes remained disinterested. It was unsettling, the way he looked at her with that empty, dispassionate gaze. His response scared her, probably because it confirmed what she'd already feared.

338

Suddenly she wanted to slap him. She wanted to cross the room, grab him by the shoulders, and shake him violently back and forth until some emotion – *any emotion* – registered on that face. She wanted to scream, '*Fuck you for what this means! Fuck you for putting me in this position!*' Instead, she picked up the basket of clothes and dumped them on the floor. It was a meaningless, pathetic act.

'You listen to me carefully,' she told him. 'I won't tolerate anything like this again. *Ever*. If you have a problem, you need to deal with it. If you need help dealing with it, I will get you help. But you need to ask for it. You need to show me that you want to get better. Because if you continue down this path, it will not end well, Thomas. I guarantee you that.'

The boy said nothing in response, showed nothing discernible in his expression. She turned and left the room, moving down the hallway and descending the stairs to the family room, nearly tripping over her own feet as she went. Her vision blurred slightly as tears of frustration threatened to spill over her lower lids, and she made a beeline for the front door, needing to take a walk and get away from the house for a while. As she passed by in the hallway, Ben glanced up from the kitchen table, where he was sorting through bills.

'What's the matter?' he called to her.

'Nothing,' she said. It was the first time she lied to him regarding their son, but it would not be the last. 'I'm going for a walk.'

'You want company?' he asked.

Sweet, sweet Ben, she thought to herself angrily. *So well-meaning, and yet so completely oblivious.* She tried to remind herself that it wasn't fair to cast him in that light. How was *he* supposed to know? She considered taking him up on his offer, considered asking him to join her. But she knew that if she did she would end up telling him the whole story of the wood rat and their oldest boy's newfound hobby. That would start a chain of events beyond her ability to control, and she wasn't ready for that yet. She wasn't ready to involve him. She needed time to think, and to observe what happened next. Yes, she would keep her horrible knowledge to herself for the moment. It seemed like the course of action with the least number of variables, and right now that strategy made sense to her. Perhaps it was the only thing that did. She had no way of knowing then how that decision would change the course of the years to come, or how the simplest decisions are sometimes the most important ones.

'No thanks,' she'd called back to her husband as she grasped the knob on the front door. 'I need to be by myself for a while.'

All of that seemed like such a long time ago. Life moved on, as it always did, and she watched her boy grow older and more mature with the passing years. For nearly two years after the incident with the wood rat, she'd discovered no further evidence of similar behavior from Thomas, and she dared to imagine that her confrontation had paid off – that he had somehow gotten better. It wasn't until shortly after

340

his tenth birthday that she noticed the home-made signs stapled to several telephone poles in their neighborhood. *Lost cat*, they read, identifying the wayward feline as Mr Tibbs, who was orange with a broad white stripe along his underbelly. *Reward if found!!* the sign promised, and gave a phone number and address to contact. The address belonged to Susan's neighbor three houses down.

The first thing she'd done after reading the sign was to return home and look behind the tool shed. She didn't think there would be . . . well, she didn't know *what* she thought, exactly. But of course there was nothing there. That night she'd casually mentioned during dinner that she'd seen the signs alerting people to the missing cat, and she'd watched Thomas closely out of the corner of her eye for a response. He barely seemed to have heard her, which offered her little relief. *What if he hasn't gotten better at all?* she wondered. *What if he has only gotten better at hiding his true nature?*

Several days passed. That weekend, while Ben and the boys were off at one of Thomas's baseball games, she decided to pay their neighbor a visit. There was a cake-decorating class Susan was thinking about attending that summer, and she wanted to know if the mother, Annie, would be interested in joining her. They talked for a while, and as she was getting ready to leave, Susan mentioned that she'd noticed the signs regarding Mr Tibbs, and she inquired as to whether he'd been found.

'Not a sign of him.' Her friend shook her head.

'He was always an outdoor cat. Liked to wander through the woods out back, I suppose. Liked to stalk birds, too, although I don't know what he'd do with one if he ever caught it. Sometimes he stayed out all night. I never paid it much mind.' She offered Susan a thin smile. 'He always showed up at the back door for breakfast and dinner, though. That guy could eat. Most afternoons he slept inside on the windowsill.' She pointed toward the vacant sill, which looked sad and deserted in the cat's absence. 'Sally's been pretty upset about it. She sure loved that cat.'

'He'll show up,' Susan assured her, trying to sound more optimistic than she felt.

'I hope so,' Annie said. 'I hope he didn't get hit by a car or anything. If Sally came across him in the roadway, I'd have a pretty traumatized little girl on my hands.'

'Don't think that way,' Susan responded, reaching over and squeezing her friend's hand. 'Cats are very resourceful animals. They know how to stay out of harm's way.' She tried on a smile and found that it almost seemed to fit.

When she arrived home, she went to the tool shed, wanting a second look around. She found the door to the shed locked, just as it should be. She retrieved the key from the kitchen, removed the padlock, slid the door open and stood inside. The interior was stagnant, and smelled vaguely of the combined scent of oil and earth. Being there reminded her immediately of the day she had discovered the wood rat. Recently cut grass clung to the wheels of the lawn mower. The bags of topsoil she'd purchased two years ago for her gardening were long gone. In their place was a spade-tip shovel, leaning against the far wall. Its tip was caked with dirt. She ran her fingers thoughtfully along the wooden texture of its long handle. The tool seemed to be the only thing out of place in the neatly arranged shack. Acting more on instinct than anything else, she picked up the shovel, exited the shed and proceeded into the woods behind their house. It took her twenty minutes to find the recently dug grave, and only two minutes to exhume the body. Her right hand automatically went to the back hip pocket of her jeans, pulling out the heavy-duty black plastic bags she'd absently brought with her. She had no recollection of grabbing the bags from the shed, but she'd obviously done so. She must've known all along what she was bound to find.

She double-bagged the animal as before, barely taking notice this time of what had been done to it. She made the trip to the dump and disposed of it in a manner that, if discovered, would not lead to her son. She returned home, showered and took a nap. Ben woke her from a dreamless slumber when he arrived home an hour and a half later.

'You okay, honey?' he asked, brushing the hair back from her eyes and feeling her forehead with the back of his hand. 'You were sweating in your sleep. Are you sick?'

'No,' she responded, looking up at him, her thoughts still muddled with sleep. *But your son is,* she almost added, but again chose not to, leaving him out of this for the second time. God only knew why. 'Just tired,' she muttered, and rolled away from him, trying to find her way back down into the merciful nothingness from which she'd been disturbed.

PART SIX

Terms of Survival

Chapter 51

Early May. Dr Ben Stevenson pulled the dark blue Honda into the parking lot and killed the motor. The lingering caress of winter had grudgingly slipped away two weeks ago, giving way to warm sunshine, a multi-colored tapestry of blooming things and the frenzied flurry of insects eager to begin the new season. Normally, the nicer weather would have lightened Ben's spirits, which tended to be darkest during Ohio's cold, grim, intractable winters. This year the change of season only heightened his sense of loss. It reminded him that life went on, and subtly suggested that wounds, however deep, might someday heal, and that loss, however poignant, was but a temporary condition that would fade ever so slightly with each successive year.

He climbed out of the car and closed the door, glancing behind him as he crossed the parking lot. No one watched from the driver's seat of an unmarked police car. They'd stopped following him two months ago, and *even that* had saddened him. *Have they given up that quickly*, he wondered, *or have they just decided I have nothing further to contribute?* If their assumptions coincided with the latter, they were right. He was in the dark as much as they were – perhaps more. *There must be leads they are pursuing,* he told himself. There *have* to be. A mother and two children cannot simply disappear from the face of the earth without a trace. *Could they?* No. Surely, there must be something.

On the day they'd disappeared, Ben had been detained for further questioning. For eight hours they'd interrogated him, asking the same questions over and over in a thousand different ways, trying to get him to contradict himself, not believing he hadn't known. 'You mean to tell me,' Special Agent Culver had asked, looming over him behind the chair in which Ben sat, 'that you examined the bite marks on those victims, photographed them, discussed them with the investigating detectives, and *never noticed* that they matched the dental architecture of your own son? I mean, *look at the pictures*!' He'd thrown photographs of Thomas down on the table all around him, framed pictures that had been prominently displayed in Ben's own home. 'You don't see that gap between the upper left canine and the first premolar – the one we've been focused on throughout the investigation? *You don't see that?!*'

The truth was, he hadn't. Or more precisely, he'd seen it every day, and had never made the connection – had never *allowed* himself to make the connection. During medical school, one of Ben's mentors – a surgeon with the last name of Zaret – had been fond

348

of telling his students, 'The eyes cannot see what the mind does not know.' If you don't consider the possibility of a particular disease, in other words, you won't recognize the signs and symptoms for what they truly are. 'You have to think about it here,' the scrub-clad surgeon would say, pointing to his forehead, 'before you can see it here,' he'd finish, the index finger descending to the level of his eyes.

Ben shook his head. He hadn't seen it – hadn't allowed himself to see it. But what if he had? Would he have been able to intervene somewhere along the way, before it became too late for all of them? And what about Susan? How much had she known, and when? Why had she not come to him with that knowledge? More important, why hadn't she done anything to stop it? And the question he kept asking himself more than any other: why had she chosen to run?

He wondered if perhaps she'd been trying to tell him all along, and that he simply hadn't been listening. Bits of conversation stuck out in his mind like thistles, catching him when he wasn't looking, wounding him with their missed significance.

'. . . *I don't think he should be dating that girl. One way or the other, he'll end up hurting her* . . .

'. . . *Why don't you talk to* him *about it?* . . .

'. . . *You have* no idea *about the measures that I am prepared to take* – that I have already taken – *to safeguard the lives of those children* . . . *I would do anything* – anything – *for them* . . .'

'. . . *Mom says everyone deserves forgiveness. She*

says it's not up to us to judge each other. It's up to God . . .'

'. . . We have to take care of each other. Just as we always have . . .

'. . . I just don't want to lose him . . .'

Ben recalled how, after the first murder, he'd asked his wife – nearly pleaded with her – to take the boys away for a while. Their safety was the most important thing, he had argued.

'It won't make any difference,' Susan had told him, and now he realized why.

The sliding glass doors of the hospital's front entrance retracted dutifully. He crossed the lobby, turned right at the first intersection and proceeded down the familiar hallway leading to the west stairwell. He passed several people in the corridor but said hello to no one. These days, that was best. He was a well-known presence in this town, but he walked the streets and buildings alone, like the ghost of a soul who has not yet realized that he is dead. People studied him with sideways glances, drew their children close in his company, and gave him wide berths as they passed. His son had decimated this town like a disease, an infection, a plague of one – and at the very least Ben was guilty by association, although there were many within Wintersville who claimed that his culpability ran far deeper than that. As a result, he was not only unwelcome here – he was suspect. And he would have left this place months ago if there were anywhere else for him to go.

But it was here, within this town, that he had lost

them. For although Susan and the boys had been on the other side of the country when they disappeared, he had lost them long before that – in the lines of communication that had fallen short, in the clues that had gone unnoticed, in the innumerable opportunities he had had to stop this, if only he had listened carefully to the messages all around him. No, he couldn't leave – couldn't abandon the only tangible connection with his family that remained, couldn't walk away from the things they had once touched, the rooms they had once occupied, the place they had once called home.

Distracted by these thoughts, he almost ran into her as she exited the gift shop.

'Monica,' he said, but she grimaced and stepped backward as if he were contagious, as if he might suddenly reach out and try to grab her.

Ben looked at her anyway, trying to see her as his son might have seen her. It was true that Thomas had pursued her through the woods, had torn apart her body, had left her lying there in the rain to die. She would never be the same because of it, would never be truly free of what his boy had done to her. But was it possible that Thomas had also come to care for her, to love her in some perverse way? *Was he capable of that?* Or had he only been toying with her all along – fascinated with Monica because of her survival, a living display of his handiwork. At the same time, Ben wondered what she might have once seen in him, if there was some shred of goodness and kindness she had discovered hidden within his son, a saving grace within his deep pit of damnation.

'I . . .' He faltered, searching for some means to connect with her, for some way to ask her about the things he was thinking. 'How are you?'

She stared back at him without answering, her body poised in a defensive position.

'I heard that your father was in the hospital.' Ben stumbled onward. 'Pneumonia, is it? I . . . I just want you to know that I've been thinking about him. I hope he's feeling bett—'

'You stay away from my father,' she responded with such vehemence that for a moment Ben thought she was on the verge of striking him.

'I'm sorry,' he said, stepping past her and continuing down the hallway. 'I didn't mean to . . .'

'You stay away from both me *and* my family,' she called after him.

Ben reached the end of the hall and placed a hand on the doorknob leading to the basement.

'*Do you hear me?*' Her tone was loud and defiant within the tiled passageway.

Ben pushed the door open, stepping into the stairwell. It was quiet in here, but the sound of Monica's voice carried through the open door as it swung slowly closed on its pneumatic piston. Her words snapped at his heels as he hastened down the concrete steps toward the floor below. '*You stay away from us. Do you hear? You and the rest of your twisted family. You stay away from us all!*'

Chapter 52

Sam Garston drove by the residence for the third time that day, stopping at the entrance to the driveway. Ben's car was parked in front of the house, and Sam pulled the cruiser in behind him and turned off the engine. He sighed. He had no business here, he knew. Ben was no longer under formal investigation. There was no piece of news they had to discuss, no change in the situation between them. *So, why do I keep coming here?* Sam asked himself. *What am I looking for? What do I expect to find?* Perhaps nothing, he thought as he stepped out of the vehicle and approached the front door, the soles of his shoes clicking lightly on the warm pavement. As odd as it sounded, Sam still considered himself Ben's friend – one of his *only* friends, he realized. Perhaps he came here more as an ally than an adversary, to see how Ben was holding up under the strain of the last several months. He had seen the way people in this town treated him – their collective judgments raining silently upon him without mercy or reservation – and although Sam had difficulty blaming them, he also couldn't help but feel empathy for the man. There was no one Ben could talk to now, no one in his corner. And so he had stopped by once again to check up on him, to let him know there was someone in this town who still worried about him, who was available if Ben wanted him to be.

He ascended the steps and rapped three times on the door.

From inside came the heavy rush of a hurried approach down the front hallway. For a brief moment, Sam was struck with the certainty that Thomas had returned. In his mind, he imagined the door swinging open, the boy's face staring back at him as the long, sharp instrument in his hand fell in practiced and determined swings into the side of Sam's neck – an arch of pulsing blood jetting upward into the fine spring air.

Something large hit the door with enough force to make it shudder on its hinges, and Sam took a reflexive step backward, his right hand falling instinctively to the grip of his firearm. Then the guttural bellows of the dog erupted from the other side of the thick wooden slab that separated them: 'WHOOOOOOH!! WHOO! WHOO!! WHOOOHHWHOOH!!'

'I've already had to replace that door once,' someone commented from the driveway behind him, and Sam spun around quickly, beginning to pull the weapon from its holster.

'*Hey, take it easy,*' Ben exclaimed, dropping the

long-handled shovel he was holding and showing Sam the palms of his hands.

Sam reseated the weapon. 'Don't sneak up on me, Ben.'

'I wasn't trying to,' Ben assured him. 'I mean,' – he looked around – 'this is *my* property. I may not be welcome anywhere else in this town, but I do believe I have a right to be *here*.'

Sam descended the steps and joined him in the front yard. He nodded at the shovel. 'Doing some planting, are you? A little yard work?'

'The thought occurred to me recently that I ought to dig a moat.' Ben stooped to pick up the shovel, then leaned it against the house.

'You still having trouble with the neighborhood kids? I told you before I can go talk to their parents.'

'No, it's fine,' he said. 'It's mostly harmless pranks. I've had to replace two broken windows from rock-throwing, but that's really been the worst of it. It's probably best to ignore them.'

'Well, I don't tolerate vandalism in this town. You let me know if you want me to put a stop to it, and I will.'

Ben nodded.

'How you holdin' up otherwise?'

'Fine.'

'I heard you quit the CO.'

'Yeah,' Ben said. 'I couldn't do it anymore. Too many bad memories there.'

'Nat's gonna miss you. That kid really looks up to you.'

'He comes by the house every once in a while.' Ben smiled.

Sam looked out at the quiet suburban street. A young boy on a bicycle pedaled past. 'You ever hear from Susan?' the chief asked, unable to help himself. 'She ever try to contact you?'

'Nothing,' the other replied, and Sam, who'd based a large portion of his career on the ability to separate truth from dishonesty, knew that Ben wasn't telling him everything.

'You know, the best thing for all of them would be to turn themselves in,' he said. 'We know they crossed the border into Mexico, and we have people tracking them down even now. It's only a matter of time. This won't play out for long.'

Ben looked as if he was about to respond to that, but chose instead to change the subject. 'How's the ticker?'

Sam smiled confidently. The five days he'd spent in the hospital following a heart attack on the day Ben's family had disappeared were already receding in his memory. 'Good as new,' he declared, and tapped his chest with his right hand as if to demonstrate.

Ben nodded. 'I guess one way or the other we're all on borrowed time,' he observed as they made the short walk together to the parked police car in the driveway.

Sam considered this for a moment, then opened the door of his cruiser and lowered his large frame inside. 'I'll let you get back to enjoying your weekend. You give me a call if you want to talk.' He offered

Ben a discerning look. 'I'm sure you'll contact me if you hear anything from them, won't you, Ben? You don't want to allow yourself to become an accomplice in all of this.'

'I already am,' the man in front of him replied, turning his back on the chief and heading for the front door of the only refuge he still had left. 'I already am.'

Chapter 53

Ben stood looking down at the wooden crate submerged in the earth, the sweat rolling freely down his flushed face. It had taken him thirty minutes this time to dig his way down to it. He was getting better at it, his arms becoming accustomed to the stony soil and the way it resisted his efforts.

The long-handled shovel lay at his feet. He wondered why he had carried it with him to the front of the house to answer Sam's visit. It had been an instinctual move, but he wasn't sure it had been the right one. The big man had a curious nature, his eyes missing nothing. Perhaps, on some level, Ben wanted to be caught – although he didn't think so. More likely, he had brought the tool with him because the best way to hide something is not to hide it at all. People never look carefully at what's directly in front of them. He had learned that lesson over the past year. He had learned it well.

He got down on his hands and knees, reaching his arms into the hole. The tips of his fingers dug for purchase at the corners of the lid, and then he was lifting it upward, casting it aside on the grass next to him. Inside the crate was a blue duffel bag wrapped in plastic, and he brought it to the surface. He got to his feet, removing the bag from the plastic and carrying it – almost gingerly – into the house.

In the kitchen, he placed his possession on the table and unzipped it. Inside was his passport, a map of Mexico, ten thousand dollars in small bills and a series of postcards he'd received sporadically in the mail over the past two months. On the kitchen table was another postcard, one that had arrived in his mailbox three days ago. The front displayed a photograph of an old church rising up from amid a lush tapestry of variegated gardens. *Villahermosa*, it said. *La Esmeralda del Sureste*. Beautiful village. The emerald of the southeast. On the back was Ben's name and mailing address – nothing more. No brief personal note or return address. But the message had been clear enough: *We are here. We are safe. Come if you want*.

The first card, he remembered, had come from the town of Tampico. It had arrived in his mailbox two and a half months after they'd disappeared. He had been sitting right here at the kitchen table sorting through mail when the thing had slid out from between two larger envelopes onto the flat wooden surface in front of him. He'd turned it over in his hands, curious but not yet realizing its significance. Then his body froze when he saw the soft slopes and curves of the handwritten letters – unmistakably Susan's writing. He'd stared at those letters for a long time, as if he were an astonished biologist encountering a novel species of animal for the first time. Eventually, he'd turned the card over again to study the front. *Tampico,* it said in pink cursive writing overlying a picture of a white sand beach, the shimmer of the setting sun reflecting off the water's surface. '*Tampico,*' he'd repeated to himself, the word sounding surreal and otherworldly in his own ears. The urge had fallen upon him to leave at that very moment, to purchase a plane ticket and to just go – to leave everything behind, bolting in the direction of the only contact he'd received from his family in more than two months.

Several considerations, however, had prevented him from doing just that. The most significant concern being, *What if they're just passing through?* What if he got there to find that his wife and children had already moved on? And how would he go about finding them in the first place? Would he wander the streets asking people in English – the only language he spoke – whether they'd seen an American mother with two boys fitting Joel's and Thomas's descriptions? Tampico was a tourist destination. How many families vacationing there fit that exact picture? No, it wouldn't work. He'd needed something more to go on.

For the time being, therefore, he had decided to wait, imagining that since Susan had sent him one postcard advising him of their whereabouts, more were sure to follow. Six weeks passed without further contact. Each day he'd stalk the mailbox, certain that *this* would be the day, and each day his heart would sicken with despair when he rummaged through the bills, catalogs, and assorted junk mail to find . . . nothing.

Then one day it came. A second postcard. On the front was a picture of a large pyramidal relic, above it the name *El Tajín*. Entering the name into an electronic search engine on his desktop computer identified it as a famous archeological site to the north of Veracruz, Mexico, along the Gulf of Mexico some 250 miles south of Tampico. They had moved on. This time, he decided, he would go after them.

Another concern had worried him, though. *Would he be followed?* Both the Sheriff's Department and the FBI had been keeping tabs on him since Susan had taken the boys and run. If he suddenly purchased a ticket to Mexico, it was likely that someone in law enforcement would know about it. Traveling by car would be better, he decided one evening, a large map of the United States and Mexico sprawled on the kitchen table in front of him. He sat back to ponder the details, absently running his hand across the top of Alex's broad head. Suddenly, he realized something else he hadn't considered. What would he do about the dog? On the one hand, Alex was the only family he had left, the only one who hadn't deserted him. On the other hand, traveling with a 180-pound Great Dane was not exactly the best way to keep a low profile. Finding accommodating hotels would be a persistent problem, and he doubted whether he'd even be allowed to bring the dog across the border. Eventually, he'd turned to the only person he felt he could trust with the responsibility.

'No problem, Dr S. You leave that glandular freak to me.'

'I may be gone for a while, Nat. I'm not sure when I'll be coming back. Are you sure you can handle—'

'You leave me a good supply of beer and keep payin' the electric bills, and you can take a six-month trip to China, as far as I'm concerned.'

There was something else to discuss. A postcard from *Villahermosa* had come only a week after the last one, as if Susan and the boys had to leave their prior location unexpectedly. Ben could think of several possible reasons for their hurried relocation, but the one that kept surfacing in his mind involved his oldest son, a long sharp object and the remains of yet another mutilated body discovered in his wake. In his mind, he could see the gaping holes left behind – flesh torn away by human teeth – and he wondered to himself once more: *What sort of creature am I chasing? And what will I do when I find it?* Then Nat's voice was pulling him back to the moment.

'Yo, Dr S. You still with me?' Nat searched his face with eyes that did not yet seem to understand that the world is full of predators, and that they are often much closer than we allow ourselves to believe.

Ben pulled the first postcard from his back pocket, the one from Tampico. 'I need to ask you another favor,' he said.

'What's that?'

'I'm expecting some additional correspondence

362

from the same friend who sent me this.' He handed Nat the postcard. 'If any more of these show up in the mail' – he tapped the card with his index finger – 'I need to know about it. I'll call you periodically to check in with you.'

Nat looked up at him skeptically. 'A *friend* is sending you these.'

Ben nodded slowly. He felt stupid for taking this chance – he was making himself incredibly vulnerable – but it was the only way he would know if they moved on again. He *had* to trust someone, and strangely, that someone turned out to be this lanky twenty-two-year-old standing in front of him.

'And I imagine you wouldn't want me to mention anything about this friend to, say . . . Chief Garston, for example.'

Ben's face remained flat, devoid of expression – or so he hoped. 'Chief Garston would not be interested in this friend, Nat. I wouldn't bother him with it.'

'No,' Nat agreed. 'I can't imagine bothering him with stuff like that.'

'Thank you,' Ben said, unable to recall a time when he'd uttered those words with greater sincerity. He had begun to leave, but what Nat said next made him pause in mid-stride.

''Bout time you went looking for them.'

Ben turned and looked back at his assistant. 'Is it?'

Nat's face was still, his eyes clear and earnest. 'I would,' he responded.

'And when you found them?' Ben asked. 'What then?'

Nat shrugged. 'Don't know. I guess I'd try to bring them home.'

'I don't think he's salvageable,' Ben said. 'He won't stop. More innocent people will die because of him.'

'Maybe there's nothing you can do about him then,' Nat mused, 'and maybe there is. But there's more to this situation than just Thomas. This is about what's best for all of you. Isn't it?'

Chapter 54

She opened her eyes in the dark, the fragments of a dream she could not quite remember slipping from her shoulders like a tattered shawl. Something had awakened her – a dog in the street, perhaps, yapping incessantly into the predawn hours. She listened. There was scratching to her right near the large dresser she shared with Ben. Alex must have entered their room last night, pushing the door open with the top of his head, curling up on the floor beside them. She should get up and let him out. She should –

A chair shifted near the corner of the room, and she froze, her eyes straining to penetrate the darkness. *Someone is in here with us*. Someone had broken into the house and . . . no . . . that wasn't quite right. Where was she? She forced herself to wake up more completely, to push herself the last few inches to the surface, and as she did the reality of her situation came tumbling back in on her – a nightmare that was not a nightmare at all, but rather the nightmarish truth of her existence. A phone call from a neighbor ('*There're a bunch of cop cars sitting in your driveway*') . . . a hasty stop at the bank to withdraw as much cash as possible . . . a frantic car ride across the desert . . . the tense, heart-pounding moments at the border crossing . . . and now . . . a motel room, in a city she could barely recall. And how many others before this? How many days spent etching out the terms of their survival in the thin veil of anonymity, how many nights spent lying on a dilapidated mattress in a run-down motel room as the paint peeled imperceptibly from the walls of their lives and she wondered how much more of this she could stand?

The soft scratching noise began again, and this time she tried to focus more concretely on where it was coming from. Through the slightly parted curtains, a vague hint of light illuminated the room in amorphous, ghostly detail. Someone was sitting in the chair by the small table near the foot of her bed. That was where the sound was coming from – a steady, methodical scratching of a pen across some flattened medium. As her vision adjusted to the light and the shadows coalesced into more discernible detail, she realized it was Thomas. He had been sitting there and watching them with his dispassionate eyes while they slept. *What is he doing?* she wondered. The sound of the pen's scratching went on and on.

She observed him from the bed. Here was the boy for whom she had sacrificed everything to protect – whose secret she had locked away in her heart as if it were her own. *And at what cost?* she asked herself. *At what cost to all of us?* The life they had once known was over now, and days that lay ahead were as shapeless and lonesome as the room around her. During those first desperate weeks after crossing the border, escape and concealment had been the only strategies she'd allowed herself to contemplate. *But what now? What comes next? What purpose will define the course of our lives from here?* The silence of her reply was loud and stifling in her ears, the sound of the stone slab of a tomb closing above her.

The scratching stopped, and her oldest son's body sat rigid and motionless for a moment, as if caught in a trance. She maintained her breathing as before, slow and steady, as if she were still asleep. She wondered if he could make out her open eyes from across the room, and she allowed her lids to slide halfway shut, a compromise between seeing and being seen. She could hear the ceaseless rhythm of her heart drumming along in her ears, could feel the mounting tension in her body, and she wondered to herself: *When did I begin to fear him?* For that was what this was, wasn't it? That was the manner in which she'd come to perceive him. She feared him, and resented him, and hated him for having placed them in this position – she and Joel, both. He had forced her to choose, and Susan realized on some level that she had chosen wrong. She had failed him as a mother, and had certainly failed Joel. In trying to protect them, she had done her children more harm than good, and now they were all paying for that transgression – each in their own way.

Thomas stood up from the chair and walked to the bed, standing over Susan and her youngest son as they lay defenseless beneath the covers. She closed her eyelids to mere slits, watching him through her lashes. She could have reached out with a tentative hand and touched his leg.

He stood there for what seemed like a very long time. The sun was beginning to crest above the horizon, the room becoming faintly brighter with every passing minute. A rooster crowed in the distance, and then fell abruptly silent in mid-intonation, as if quieted by a farmer's axe. Thomas leaned over and placed a hand on Joel's shoulder. Susan's muscles bunched beneath her skin, the adrenaline flowing freely as she readied herself to act. She could no longer control her respirations, which slid in and out of her with increasing rapidity.

Thomas withdrew his hand from his brother's shoulder, returning to a full upright position. He studied Joel for a moment longer, then turned and crossed the room to the door, flipping back the dead bolt and opening the door just wide enough to allow himself to pass through to the exterior walkway beyond. There was a soft click as the door swung shut behind him.

Susan slipped out from beneath the covers, stood and crossed the floor to the window, pulling back the curtain several inches so that she could peer outside at the second-story exterior walkway and through the rails at the parking lot below. She could see the top of Thomas's head as he descended the stairs. She turned her attention back to the room – to her sleeping son, to the suitcases standing to attention in the corner, to the plastic cups and napkins on the table beside her. She drew the curtain back farther, letting in some additional light. There was something else lying on the table, the thing on which Thomas had been scribbling, and she picked it up now for a closer look.

It was a photograph she had taken of Joel and a young Mexican girl of roughly his same age. There had been times over the past few months when their lives had fallen into transient normality – brief moments and unexpected encounters when the suffocating reality of their situation was temporarily lifted. This picture had captured such a moment, a fleeting friendship Joel had made with a young girl in the time it had taken Susan and Thomas to acquire gas and a few groceries. She'd allowed Joel to stay with the car while they shopped, and when she returned she'd been surprised to find them playing on the withered, sun-beaten grass, the two of them laughing and giggling as if they were the closest of friends rather than strangers who became acquaintances for the space of fifteen minutes at a roadside convenience store in rural Mexico. It had saddened Susan's heart to see the way her youngest son interacted with the girl, for it made her realize how starved he must be for social relationships like this one.

She had put the groceries in the car, and had sat there watching them for another twenty minutes, wishing there was more she could offer him. When it was time for them to go, she'd gone back inside and purchased a disposable camera to take their picture.

She looked down at that photograph now, clasped in her hands, and the only face smiling back at her was the girl's. Above the neckline, Joel's face had been scratched away by the dark lines of Thomas's pen.

She stood there breathing deeply, the hurt and rage coursing through her body in alternating currents. Did he care so little for them that he would destroy even the few small tokens that brought them joy? He'd done it out of pure maliciousness, she decided, to spite them regardless of the sacrifices they had made to protect him. It was . . .

No, she corrected herself. *This was something else she was seeing here*.

She thought of Thomas sitting there at the table, watching them as the pen in his hand scratched back and forth across the face of her youngest child. There had been no spite or maliciousness in his expression, only a detached, calculating manner she had seen several times before. She recalled the way he had stood over them, one hand resting lightly on Joel's shoulder as if . . . as if to say . . . goodbye.

Outside, a car trunk slammed, and she turned to look out of the window. Thomas was heading back across the parking lot. In his left hand he held a lug wrench from the spare wheel compartment, the prying tip at its distal end catching the early morning sunlight along its black metallic surface.

'*Joel. Joel, wake up,*' she hissed, going quickly to the bed and shaking him roughly, casting aside the covers.

'What . . .' he replied, his voice still thick and muddled with sleep.

'*Get up,*' she urged, dragging him from the bed. 'We've got to go. We've got to go *right now.*'

'Where's Thomas?' Joel asked, looking around the room.

'He's coming,' she replied, snatching the extra set of keys from the pocket of her jeans. She went into the bathroom, turned on the shower, pushed the doorknob's button lock, stepped out of the bathroom, and closed the door behind her. 'Thomas is coming, but I don't want him to hear us leave. We're leaving without him. Do you understand?'

'Why did you lock the bathroo—?'

'Don't worry about that. I don't have time to explain.' She glanced at her clothes in the corner of the room. She would have to leave them here, remaining in her T-shirt and pajama bottoms. There was no time to get dressed. There was no time for anything.

'I want to get my—'

'No, Joel. *We have to leave now.*' She opened the door and poked her head out of the room. She could hear Thomas's footsteps on the stairs, heading up toward them. He would be on their level in less than ten seconds. Halfway down the corridor in the

371

direction of the stairs was a small alcove with a soda machine and an ice box. If they were quick about it, they could hide there until Thomas passed them along the walkway.

She pulled her head back inside the room and looked at Joel. 'Very quiet,' she said. 'Not a word.' Her son nodded, and she took his hand in hers. 'Follow me.'

They slipped out into the hallway and closed the door gently behind them. The sound of Thomas's tennis shoes on the steps was getting louder. His head would clear the level of the floor and they would be in his line of sight at any moment. Susan sprinted down the corridor to the alcove, pulling Joel along. Their bare feet were nearly silent on the concrete flooring. She could see the top of Thomas's head come into view as she leapt into the alcove, dragging Joel with her. The large soda machine jutted out from the wall on her left, and they pressed their bodies against the space to the right of it, allowing it to shield them from view.

Susan wrapped her left arm around Joel's body, pulling him toward her. In her right hand she held the key to the car, the short tip protruding from between her index and middle fingers. She would punch with that hand, she told herself, if it came to that. It wasn't much of a weapon – and certainly didn't match what Thomas was carrying – but it was the only one she had. The element of surprise would afford her one good shot, and she thought quickly about where to place it.

Then the sound of his footsteps passed them along the walkway. A moment later, she heard him open the door, step inside, and close it once again.

'Let's go,' she whispered, and the two of them left the alcove and headed for the steps, taking them as rapidly as their bare soles could tolerate. They reached the bottom and hustled across the parking lot. Susan pressed the button on the remote to unlock the doors in anticipation of their arrival, and the car chirped responsively.

Shit, she thought, and on the second story above them a door suddenly opened and Thomas appeared at the railing.

'Mom,' Joel said.

'Get in the car,' Susan ordered, running around to the driver's side of the vehicle.

'But Mom . . .'

'*What?*'

'He's coming.'

Susan looked up. The spot where Thomas had been standing a moment before was now empty. Her eyes shot to the stairwell.

'Get in, Joel,' she said, dropping into the driver's seat and fumbling to get the key into its slot in the ignition. The passenger door opened and Joel climbed inside. Through the open door Susan could see Thomas as he appeared at the foot of the stairwell, taking the last three steps in a single leap.

'*Close the door!*' she yelled, and Joel swung the passenger door shut. The fingers of her right hand felt numb and clumsy as she jammed the key home in the cylinder. Still, it wouldn't turn. In her peripheral vision, she could see her oldest son sprinting toward them across the parking lot.

She grabbed the steering wheel and yanked it counterclockwise, freeing the key to turn in the ignition. The engine sprang to life just as Thomas reached the car and the door on Joel's side began to open once again. '*No!*' she screamed, dropping the transmission into gear and mashing her right foot down on the accelerator. The vehicle lurched forward, wresting the door from Thomas's grasp, and when it shut this time Joel locked it. The engine raced, but the vehicle moved slowly, as if it were being held back by invisible wires. In the rearview mirror Susan could see him, still running, still coming for them. For a frantic moment, she realized that he was gaining on them.

'The handbrake,' Joel reminded her. Her right hand grabbed the handle, and her thumb pushed the release button as she slammed it downward.

The car sped up, sending them flying out onto the street. She hooked a left, scraping the right front quarter panel on a parked vehicle as they negotiated the turn too widely. When they reached the next intersection, she went right, barely slowing as the right rear wheel jounced up over the curb. She straightened out the steering, then gunned the automobile in the direction of the closest highway.

'Slow down, Mom! You're gonna crash!' Joel yelled, reaching across himself to snap home the buckle of his seat belt.

Susan forced herself to back off on the gas. She

was shaking uncontrollably, but she couldn't bring herself to stop the vehicle until they'd covered another twenty miles. Then she got off at the next exit and eased the car to the shoulder, placing it in park and killing the engine. She leaned back in the seat and closed her eyes, attempting to pull herself together. Joel was quiet beside her, looking out through his window.

'I . . . I know this is very confusing for you . . .,' Susan said haltingly. She began shaking again, and willed herself to stop, reminding herself that her son needed her. 'It's been . . . it's been confusing for me for a long time,' she said, and she took a deep breath and let it out. 'I owe you an explanation, and an apology.'

A car passed on the otherwise vacant early-morning stretch of highway to their left, and Susan turned abruptly in her seat to watch until it disappeared from view. She looked back at the nine-year-old in the seat next to her, his light brown hair still tussled and wild from the night's sleep, a pillow mark fading on his face.

'I can't explain everything right now,' she said. 'But I want you to know . . . I want you to know that I'm sorry.' She began to cry then, the tears large and shameful and naked on her face, and she refused to lift a hand to brush them away. She deserved each and every one of them. 'I want you to know that I'm sorry for bringing you into this, Joel. You're a good kid, and I love you. You . . . you never deserved this.'

She tried to go on, but she couldn't. The grief and fear and regret were all muddled up inside of her, and the more she tried to talk the more she wept, until at last her son placed a hand on her forearm to quiet her.

'It's okay, Mom,' he said, and she looked at him and nodded, allowing herself to accept his forgiveness for the moment. Joel leaned over and gave her a hug, and she held him tightly against her, closing her eyes and mouthing a silent prayer of gratitude that he was safe – that they both were – for the first time in months.

A few minutes later, she started the car, readying them for the next leg of their journey. 'Mom,' Joel said, and she smiled over at him, smoothing his hair with her hand.

'Yeah. What is it, honey?'

His freckled face was earnest but hopeful. 'Can we go home now?'

Epilogue

Ben sat at his desk, the calendar laid out in front of him. Susan's attorney had called this afternoon, advising him that a review hearing had been scheduled for three months from now. *Will you be available to attend?* the lawyer had wanted to know. 'Of course,' Ben had replied. He glanced at the year in the upper right-hand corner, listening for a moment to the quietness of the house around him. *Five years,* he thought to himself. Was it really possible that his wife's incarceration was finally drawing to a close? He could feel the weight of those years pressing upon him – years he had long since become accustomed to carrying. It was hard to imagine what it would feel like when that burden was finally lifted.

His mind turned back to the day they'd been reunited. Sam had shown up on his front steps only two days after his previous visit. This time, Ben had met him at the door – instead of in the driveway with a shovel.

'Back so soon?' he asked, making no effort to conceal his irritation with Sam's frequent, unsolicited appearances.

'We've got them, Ben,' the chief told him. 'Susan and Joel turned themselves in at the US border yesterday evening.'

Ben stood there in the doorway, trying to make sense of what he'd just heard. He'd been planning on leaving for Mexico the following day.

'They'll be arriving at the airport late this afternoon,' Sam advised him. 'They're being accompanied by federal marshals. We'll need you to come with us to pick up Joel.'

Ben looked down at his hands, at the postcard he was holding between his thumb and forefinger. He reached back and stuffed it into his rear pocket. 'Susan and Joel are coming home? You found them, Sam?'

'Well.' The big man frowned, considering this briefly. 'Technically, they found us.'

'And Thomas?' Ben asked, but Sam had shaken his head.

'We haven't located him yet,' he'd replied. 'But we will. Don't you worry about that. We'll find him. Sure as rain.'

For her part in the affair, Susan had been sentenced to eight years in state prison. Her attorney had been optimistic that she would be released much sooner, and indeed it now seemed that *that* time might be coming to an end. They'd stayed married during all of this, although Ben wasn't sure if anything substantial remained to hold on to. He supposed it depended on how much mercy and forgiveness they had left for one another.

As a single parent, Ben had raised Joel as best he could. His youngest son was experiencing life as a teenager, becoming more independent with each passing year. There were times when one of Joel's mannerisms – a certain facial expression or tone of voice – reminded Ben of Thomas at a slightly younger age, and although they were painful to witness, he was also grateful for those moments, for they allowed him to remember his oldest son as the boy he still loved, separate from the affliction that had eventually consumed him.

He stood up now, stretched and glanced about the room. Thomas's old bedroom had been converted into a study, and it was here where Ben liked to work. The posters had been removed years ago, but the tape had left an indelible mark on the paint. The minor blemishes could have been touched up with a brush, he imagined, but Ben preferred to leave them as they were, small reminders of the boy who had once lived within these walls. In their own way, they comforted him.

Five years ago, Sam had been confident that they would find Thomas. 'Sure as rain,' he had said, but in that one prognostication his friend had been wrong, for they never had managed to track him down, and as the years unfolded Ben wondered if they ever would. But 'technically,' as Sam had pointed out, they hadn't found Susan or Joel, either. His wife and youngest son had found them. They had returned home of their own free will. Because sooner or later, Ben knew, that is what we are all destined to do.

He stood at the window, looking out. He could hear the wind buffeting the house, its infinite fingers searching for entry along the eaves. Winter was coming again, the daylight hours surrendering themselves little by little to the thick, malignant reign of the night. Somewhere up the block, a trash can toppled to the asphalt and went rolling out into the street. In the living room near the front door, Alex – by now arthritic and graying around the muzzle, but still with some fire in his belly – barked twice and then fell silent. It was getting late, Ben thought. He ought to turn in for the eveni –

He leaned forward, placing his fingertips on the cold pane of glass. Someone was standing near the driveway, looking up at the house. The figure's features were lost in the darkness, but his arms hung loosely at his sides and his left hand seemed to be clutching something long and thin and tapered to a –

Ben turned quickly and made for the stairs, taking them two at a time. He dashed across the living room to the hall, flung open the front door, and spilled out into the driveway.

The street in front of him was empty.

'*Thomas,*' Ben whispered, his eyes scanning the bushes, the driveway, the yards to his left and right. The only reply was the sound of the fallen trash can, turning slowly in the street like a gravely wounded animal.

'*Thomas,*' Ben said again, louder this time, uncertain if what he had seen from the upstairs window had been real or imagined. The mind, he knew, could be a powerful thing. We see what we want to see, often ignoring the rest. He closed his eyes, listening to the restless chatter of branches in the wind, and his wife's voice came to him then as if she had uttered the words only yesterday.

'*We have to take care of each other. Just as we always have.*'

Yes, Ben thought, standing beneath the glow of the streetlamp as the shadows gathered around him. *We do.*

Author's Note

The towns depicted in this novel are real, although I have taken significant liberties in their fictional portrayal. I have been assured by a few locals, in fact, that they are pleasant places in which to live.

Acknowledgments

The creation of a novel begins as a lonely endeavor. You select a scene and a character with which to commence, conjure a vague notion of how you would like the story to end, and then go about the task of connecting the two. Things, of course, do not go according to plan. Fictional characters – products of the author's own imagination – decide to speak up for themselves and to do unexpected things without the author's consent. The plot veers wildly this way and that like an out-of-control motorcycle in danger of crashing into the nearest tree. During the final frenzied week of editing, the largest Atlantic hurricane on record attempts to wipe out a good portion of the Eastern Seaboard of the United States – along with the offices of both the literary agency and the publishing house with which the book and its author are newly affiliated. To say that there are forces at work here beyond one's control is, well, somewhat of an understatement. And yet, the project finds its way to completion, and there can be no other explanation for this unlikely success except to point to the numerous people who have helped to make it happen.

I would like to thank my editors, David Highfill and Jessica Williams, for their keen recognition of what did and did not serve the story well in its original form. This is a much different novel because of them, and it was their endless patience, clear vision and untiring commitment that saw us through. Thanks also go to the folks at HarperCollins for their warm welcome and for all of the hard work that goes into a venture such as this. Paul Lucas is my outstanding agent, who shepherds me through the world of publishing with a rare combination of talent, thoughtfulness and quiet confidence, and who calmly anchors me when the waters get choppy.

Claire Dippel reviewed my initial manuscript submission to Janklow & Nesbit and responded to my subsequent inquiries with both professionalism and uncommon kindness. Erin and Wilson Lem put me in touch with the appropriate people when the timing was right. The following individuals provided early reads of the original manuscript, proofread my work, offered sound advice, or simply bolstered me with their enthusiasm along the way: Dennis, Carolyn and Mark Beuerle; Kristin and Kevin Lester; Leon, Dudley and Georgana Gearhart; Shane Libby; Alicia Kramer; Artie and Margy Lynnworth; Beth Keegstra; and Heidi Troutner.

Certain medical details in this book are drawn

from knowledge and experience acquired during my own training as a physician, but I have also utilized several medical texts for assistance, including Frank H. Netter's timeless *Atlas of Human Anatomy* and *Principles of Medical Biochemistry* by Gerhard Meisenberg and William H. Simmons. As I am not a pathologist, a forensic odontologist, or a law enforcement officer, I humbly ask for the reader's forgiveness regarding any errors or inaccuracies related to these fields.

Finally, I want to thank my amazing wife, Dr Lorie Gearhart, for being my first reader, for answering my questions about psychiatry, sociopathy and mental illness, for providing creative suggestions regarding problems I encountered with plot and characters, for being a source of unwavering support and for tolerating my obsession with this novel and the not-so-subtle intrusion it has imposed on our lives. It is to her and our young daughter that this book is dedicated.